WHAT OTHERS H
ABOUT *SONG OF TH*

"A tight story, and [the] characters ___ emotions...Fantasy references galore should ensure that
readers who enjoy fantasy – and Arthurian legend in
particular – come away satisfied"
 – *Kirkus Reviews*

"This is a fantasy of epic proportions, with the perfect
blend of suspense; well-developed, likable characters; and
a touch of sarcastic humor."
 – *School Library Journal*

"Every so often...a writer is skilled enough to utilize the
stories of King Arthur and Camelot to significant effect...a
taut, compelling narrative, well-drawn characters, and a
keen sense of genuine peril and true wonder. It's a powerful, fun, engaging read, and it's the first of a series, so readers have much to look forward to."
 – *Quill & Quire*

"The story...has wonderful Canadian references and some
really funny passages. Ariane is constantly in danger, and
the suspense is beautifully maintained."
 – *Helen Wilding Cook, Children's
 Collection Development Coordinator,
 Library Bound*

"One thing that makes this tale different from many in the
genre is that it is set in Regina, SK, and full of other Canadian place names, such as Yellowknife and Toronto. The
story will appeal to those who enjoy fantasy and will not
require a knowledge of the Arthurian tales to follow."
 – *CM: Canadian Review of Materials*

"Willett's novel will please fantasy junkies with its intricate details; yet there's also an appealing poetry to Ariane's story, best manifested when she learns to use her powers to merge with water and transport herself wherever it flows. Song of the Sword is a unique twist on the old subjects of teenage rebellion and self-discovery."
— *Montreal Review of Books*

"...an exciting plot that gives a great new spin to a favourite story. It can also take credit for a great cast of characters...set up to play out what might become the battle of the ages. I can see that exciting adventures await as they all struggle to decide what's worth fighting for: power, friends, or family."
— *think. thank. thought.*
(book review blog)

"...it was very well done indeed...Willett did an excellent job here...Ariane [has] quite a bit of personality and spunk."
— *Word for Teens (book review blog)*

TWIST *of the* BLADE

TWIST *of the* BLADE

EDWARD WILLETT

Edited by Matthew Hughes
Cover and text designed by Tania Craan
Typeset by Susan Buck
Printed and bound in Canada at Houghton Boston

Library and Archives Canada Cataloguing in Publication
Willett, Edward, 1959-, author
         Twist of the blade / Edward Willett.
(Shards of Excalibur ; book 2)
Issued in print and electronic formats.
ISBN 978-1-55050-599-3 (pbk.).--ISBN 978-1-55050-600-6
(pdf).--ISBN 978-1-55050-807-9 (html).--ISBN
 978-1-55050-808-6 (mobi)
 I. Title. II. Series: Willett, Edward, 1959-. Shards of Excalibur ; book 2

PS8595.I5424T85 2014   jC813'.54   C2014-904674-X
                                         C2014-904675-8

Library of Congress Control Number 2014938364

2517 Victoria Avenue
Regina, Saskatchewan
Canada S4P 0T2
www.coteaubooks.com

10 9 8 7 6 5 4 3 2 1

Available in Canada from:
Publishers Group Canada
2440 Viking Way
Richmond, British Columbia
Canada V6V 1N2

Available in the US from:
Orca Book Publishers
www.orcabook.com
1-800-210-5277

Coteau Books gratefully acknowledges the financial support of its publishing program by: the Saskatchewan Arts Board, The Canada Council for the Arts, the Government of Canada through the Canada Book Fund and the Government of Saskatchewan through the Creative Industry Growth and Sustainability program of the Ministry of Parks, Culture and Sport.

Four nieces and a nephew – five books
This one is for Keisha

CHAPTER ONE

SLEEPLESS

THROUGH A NIGHTMARE FOREST of black, twisted trees, Ariane ran barefoot, pursued by a demon.

A thin skein of icy snow covered the barren ground, making every step agony, as though a thousand glass needles were piercing her skin. She knew she was bleeding, knew the prints she was leaving behind her were red with blood, knew the demon must be maddened by it, by its smell, by the promise of tasting it, hot and fresh, when at last it caught her...and she could hear it now, hear the heavy thump of its feet, hear the rush of breath from its lungs...

And then she caught her foot on a branch, fell headlong, and rolled into a ball, screaming, as she waited for the demon's teeth and claws to rend her flesh....

◄► ►►

Ariane jerked upright to the sound of laughter. Confused, heart still pounding from the terror of the dream, she stared around at a classroom full of amused and scornful faces, then twisted her head to Mrs. Muirhead, who held a copy of *Macbeth* in one hand and was tapping the end of a ballpoint pen against it with the other. "I asked you a question, Ariane."

Ariane glanced down at the open book in which her forehead had been planted a moment before. Macbeth's speech stared back. *Is this a dagger which I see before me...?* "I'm sorry, Mrs. Muirhead I...I didn't hear it."

Mrs. Muirhead uttered a noise that Ariane supposed would be spelled in books "Hmmmph," then added, "If you can't stay awake in class, Ariane, perhaps you should go to bed earlier. Samantha, would you care to answer?"

Samantha began rattling on about Macbeth's tortured conscience but, through the cotton wool that filled her head, Ariane couldn't focus on a single word. She yawned, but snapped her mouth closed with an audible click of teeth when she caught Mrs. Muirhead's narrowed gaze.

English class ended at last. The other students streamed out. No one talked to her, of course. As a foster kid who had been suspended for fighting in her *first* week at school, she was as popular as poison oak at a nudist colony – and that was *before* the rumors started swirling about her dabbling in witchcraft. With her limbs weighed down by weariness, by the time she gathered her books and moved toward the door the other students had long fled.

But before she could make her own escape, Mrs. Muirhead's gentle voice stopped her. "Ariane, is there something wrong? Something I can help with?"

Ariane stopped, staring longingly at the open door. *Well,* she imagined herself saying, *it's like this: I'm the heir of the Lady of the Lake. I can dissolve into fresh water and magically transport myself through rivers and lakes. A shard of King Arthur's sword, Excalibur, is strapped to my side right now. I and that funny redheaded kid, Wally Knight, brought it back from Yellowknife just a couple of weeks ago. We're in a life-and-death struggle with Merlin, aka Rex Major, the fabulously powerful and wealthy computer magnate, to recover the other four shards, and he's sent a demon to haunt my dreams. Do you think you could help me with an exorcism?*

But of course all she actually said, as she turned her back on freedom to face Mrs. Muirhead, was, "I'm all right. I'm just not sleeping well."

"Problems at home?" Mrs. Muirhead said sympathetically. "Have you thought about seeing Mr. Yasinowski?"

Ariane pictured herself telling the school's incredibly stuffy guidance counsellor, whose pale face and earnest tone always reminded her of an undertaker, about the demon in her dreams, and snorted. Mrs. Muirhead's friendly expression stiffened.

"No, I don't think he can help," Ariane said hurriedly. "Really. It's nothing. I'll be fine." And then, at last, she made her getaway.

In the corridor she leaned her head against the cold metal of a locker, eyes closed. She took no notice of the students brushing past until one slammed into her, spinning her around and sending her books flying from her hand and skittering across the floor. She straightened and glared at the retreating backs of four girls. One looked over her shoulder with a sweetly poisonous smile. Then they rounded the corner by the library and were gone.

Flish, she thought. *It figures.*

Felicia Knight – Wally's sister, no less! – and her three cohorts had made it their personal mission to make Ariane's life at Oscana Collegiate one long trip through Hell. She thought she'd frightened them away for good the last time they'd squared off, when she'd used the power of Excalibur to shape water into a weapon...but Flish, it seemed, didn't scare that easily.

She felt the urge to chase her, teach her once and for all what it meant to mess with the heir of the Lady of the Lake...but she fought down the urge, pushed it away from her. *Save it*, she thought. *Flish isn't your biggest concern. Rex Major is.*

As Ariane bent down to pick up her books, the bell rang...which meant she was late for Algebra – the class she was already doing so badly in that she had to stay late on Thursdays for remedial coaching.

My life just gets better and better, she thought, and set off wearily down the hall.

◀ ▶

Walter Arthur Knight the Third, known to friends and enemies alike as Wally, was having a much better day than Ariane. He'd successfully produced hydrogen in Chemistry and had aced a history test. (Although he almost wished he hadn't. The teacher had praised him in front of the class, leading Simon Spencer, the hulking giant who claimed to be fourteen like Wally but looked twenty-five, to loudly proclaim that Wally must have cheated – as if no one could get a good mark on a test simply by paying attention in class and even studying once in a while.)

Ariane had promised to meet him for lunch, but failed to show – again. *Probably fell asleep.* He shook his head. Ever since they'd returned from Yellowknife, she'd looked more and more exhausted each day. *I hope she's not sick*, he thought. Still, without her there – and nobody else willing to sit at his table – he at least had the chance to finish his new favourite book, *The Complete Klutz's Guide to Medieval Swordsmanship*.

Whether because of the book or for some other reason, fencing practice after school went particularly well. Wally had the oddest sensation that everyone else had inexplicably worsened in the two weeks since his adventures with Ariane. Even Nick Barber, the team's top fencer, seemed to telegraph every move, so that Wally knew what Nick was going to do before he did it. Of course, Nick still managed to beat Wally without much difficulty, thanks to his longer reach. Wally was aware of the fencing coach, Natasha Mueller, watching him closely all practice, and when it was over, while the other fencers were heading to the showers, she pulled him aside.

"You have come a very long way this fall," Coach Mueller said. A tiny, whip-thin woman, she smiled at him, green eyes sparkling beneath her trademark purple beret. "An amazingly long way. I think spraining your wrist a few weeks ago actually made you better."

Wally grinned. "Thanks, Coach."

"You're welcome." Coach Mueller gave him a long, hard look. "Okay, we'll try it."

Wally blinked. "Try what?"

"The Chinook Open."

Wally's heart jumped. "The tournament in Swift Current?"

Coach Mueller nodded. "I want you to compete."

Wally let out a whoop that made Nick Barber, who was just heading into the locker room, shoot him a surprised look over his shoulder. "I'd love to!"

"There'll be extra practice," Coach Mueller warned.

"No problem," Wally said. He grabbed her hand and shook it. "Thanks! Thanks a lot!"

"Don't mention it." Coach Mueller smiled. "Just live up to my expectations."

Feeling as if the gym floor were three feet beneath the soles of his sneakers, Wally headed for his locker. Ordinarily he'd have gone to the showers with the other guys, but he'd signed up for swimming lessons at the YMCA, and the first one was today, in less than an hour. He didn't see much point in showering at school when he'd soon be showering at the Y. Sweaty hair plastered to his forehead, he trotted through the hallways. Him, Wally the Klutz, fencing in a nationally ranked tournament? He couldn't believe it. *Wait until Ariane hears about this!*

He reached his locker, dialed the combination, pulled the door open, and was reaching for his books when he heard multiple footsteps and a babble of girls' voices coming closer.

One voice stood out. *Flish!*

His eyes searched the hallway for an escape route. His sister had been difficult to live with when they'd still shared a house. But since she'd moved out, things hadn't gotten any better. She was constantly hitting him up for money (their parents had cut off her allowance when she'd left home), shoving him around, making fun of him in front of her friends.

There was nowhere to hide. Except....

Thankful for once that his adolescent growth spurt had yet to materialize, Wally took a tip from numerous bullies down through the years and stuffed himself into his own locker. Unlike the bullies, though, he left the door slightly ajar so he wouldn't be locked in.

Cramped, uncomfortable, and wishing he hadn't forgotten to throw away his uneaten tuna-fish sandwich from last Friday's lunch, he tried not to gag as he waited for Flish and her gang to move on down the hall.

Naturally, they stopped right outside his locker.

Through the door's ventilation slits (which, in his opinion, did not provide *nearly* enough ventilation), he could make out the back of her head, less than a foot away. He did his best not to breathe. The miasma of rancid tuna, mingled with his own sweaty self, made it easier.

"Where is he?" Flish sounded irritable. "Cindy said she saw him down here just a minute ago."

"Probably knew you wanted money," said another voice that he recognized as Shania's. She *used* to be the ringleader of the "coven," as Wally had dubbed Flish's group of friends, until Flish took over.

"Or maybe his witch of a girlfriend spirited him away," said one of the coven's other two members, girls whose names Wally could never keep straight. She laughed as if joking, but he heard a touch of fear in her voice. Wally wasn't surprised: the last time Ariane had confronted the coven she had punched a hole in a locker with a magical spear of ice.

Flish must have heard the fear too. "She's not a witch," she snapped.

"Then how does she pull off those tricks?" said the fourth girl.

"I don't know." Flish lowered her voice. "But I do know one thing: it's always around water."

"So?" drawled Shania.

"So, all we have to do is catch her somewhere *away* from water. No lake, no swimming pool, no drinking fountains." Her voice was colder than the wind he had ridden his bike against that morning. "I owe her."

"You got a plan?"

"The tennis courts," Flish said. "Pavement everywhere. Not even a sprinkler."

"And how do you plan to convince her to show up?" said Shania. "Send her an invitation?"

"I don't have to convince her. She cuts across the courts on her way home."

"Before dark," Shania pointed out. "Those courts are wide open. Someone will see us."

"Not on Thursdays," Flish said. "On Thursdays she stays until 5:30 for remedial Algebra. By the time she leaves, it's already dark. And this Thursday – tomorrow..." Flish's head swiveled right. "Someone's coming. Let's clear out. My little twerp of a brother can't be too far away, and I need some cash." She sniffed. "Besides, it reeks around here. I think something's died in someone's locker."

The coven headed down the hallway. A moment later

a janitor pushed his cart past, whistling tunelessly. Once Wally could no longer hear him, he climbed out of his metal cage. Massaging a crick in the back of his neck and taking deep, grateful breaths of non-tuna-scented air, he stared down the hallway in the direction Flish and the others had gone.

I'd better pay Ariane a visit, he thought...but first he had to get to swimming lessons. He checked his watch – he had just enough time to make it.

He stuffed his books into his backpack, slung it over his shoulders, closed his locker...then paused. Flish was looking for him. And she'd gone the way he'd normally go, toward the front doors – which meant she was very likely lying in wait outside for him to emerge.

He smiled. *Oh no, you don't.* He turned and went in the opposite direction. Students weren't supposed to use the emergency exit at the back of the gym, but Wally happened to know, because Coach Mueller had once sent him that way to get something from her car, that the EMERGENCY EXIT ONLY: ALARM WILL SOUND sign was a bluff.

Coach Mueller was still in the gym, rolling up one of the long, thin mats the fencers used for practice. She looked up as Wally came in. "Forget something?"

"Just taking a shortcut," Wally said. "Is it all right if I go out the back?"

Coach Mueller, despite her tiny size, lifted the rolled-up mat as though it weighed nothing. "Be my guest. But be careful. Last week's snow left an icy patch."

"Thanks," Wally said. He checked his watch again. He was going to be late if he didn't get a move on –

He ran across the gym, banged open the door, and charged through.

Mindful of Coach Mueller's warning, he jumped over the sheet of ice just outside the doors. But he didn't see the even bigger patch, black as the pavement, at the corner of the gym.

His right foot skidded out from under him. As he fell, he twisted, trying to catch himself.

Then his forehead cracked against the concrete, and an explosion of stars and pain blew Wally into darkness.

◄◄ ►►

Ariane trudged up the broken walkway to the crumbling steps of the house she shared with Aunt Phyllis, weighed down by her book-filled backpack, a shopping bag containing two two-litre bottles of Diet Coke, and her own inescapable weariness. Her breath formed clouds in the cold air. In the last two weeks the temperature had plunged. Daytime highs barely rose above freezing; nighttime lows were a frigid ten degrees lower. In January, similar daytime temperatures would feel almost like a heat wave, but right now they were a pain.

Literally. It felt like a small rodent was biting the tips of her ears.

Ariane glanced up to the window of her room on the second floor, wishing she was already in bed. Aunt Phyllis's house looked as if it hadn't been painted since it was built. On the roof, turned orange by the light of the setting sun behind her, shingles curled up like rose petals. But the house did boast two brand new features: gleaming metal mesh blocking every window, and a white reflective triangle on a metal post by the front steps that bore the words "Protected by SecureTek."

Ariane fished her keys out of her pocket. Like the bars and the security system, they were new, fitted to the heavy-duty locks that had also been added after Rex Major's district sales manager, acting under Merlin's power to Command, had broken in through her bedroom window. Ariane supposed the additions provided some protection against Major's human henchmen, but she suspected her enemy hadn't sent anyone else mainly because he still had to maintain a scandal-free public persona. A second kidnap attempt by yet another person linked to Major would raise awkward questions.

But his fear of embarrassment wasn't much of a hook on which to hang their security. Which was why Ariane wore the shard strapped to her midriff beneath an elastic bandage at all times. That was their real security. With her own abilities bolstered by the extra power from the shard, she hoped she could drive off any attack.

Except for that damn sleep-stealing demon, she thought. She sighed, a sigh that turned into a yawn, then unlocked the front door, walked into the small enclosed porch, turned and locked the door again, unlocked the inner door, went through, turned and locked *that* door, and finally faced the dim entrance hall of Aunt Phyllis's house.

"You're late, dear," her aunt called from the living room. "I was beginning to worry."

Ariane walked through the French doors and found her aunt reading the newspaper in her favourite seat, an ancient, overstuffed armchair upholstered in giant pink roses. "Sorry," Ariane said. "I went down to 7-Eleven to get some pop. We ran out last night." She held up the plastic bag.

"You should have phoned," Aunt Phyllis said, peering over the tops of her reading glasses.

"Sorry," Ariane repeated.

Aunt Phyllis nodded, closed the newspaper, and put it aside. She removed her glasses. "How was school today?"

"Not great," Ariane said. She plopped down in one of the smaller armchairs on either side of the fireplace. "I fell asleep in English class."

Aunt Phyllis looked concerned. "Still not sleeping well at night?"

"No," Ariane said. Ariane hadn't told her aunt about the demon, instead claiming she kept having "bad dreams" about Rex Major. After all, Aunt Phyllis could do nothing about the haunting and would just worry more than she already did.

"It's been two weeks," her aunt said in a reassuring tone. "Major would have come after you if he was going to."

Ariane said nothing. Merlin had waited millennia to claim Excalibur as his own. What were two weeks? *He's biding his time*, she thought.

"Any...hint...about the next shard?" Aunt Phyllis asked.

"It's out there," Ariane said. "But I can't tell where. Not yet." She slumped and closed her eyes. She was so tired, so drained. She'd started hearing the song of the second shard the night she'd returned home with the first one...but then the demon had appeared, and she hadn't heard it since. And in her current exhausted condition she didn't think she could summon enough power to travel through water even if she did know where to find the second shard.

If I went down the drain I might get as far as the sewage treatment plant, she thought. *But that's about it.*

But the shard *was* out there. She thought – hoped – that Major didn't know where it was either. As she understood it, he'd expected to find the second shard using the power of the first. Since Ariane had claimed the first, he would have to wait and hope that the second revealed itself the same way that one had...not that she and Wally had any idea how it had happened.

"Did you see Wally today?" Aunt Phyllis asked.

Ariane nodded. "Just in passing." Ariane had promised to meet him at lunch, but had fallen asleep at the library again. Guilt mingled with her exhaustion. Wally was her ally, her partner in this quest...and yet, lately, she hardly saw him. "He said he was starting swimming lessons tonight at the Y."

Aunt Phyllis laughed. "Guess he wants to be prepared next time."

Ariane's smile faded. *If there is a next time,* she thought. She yawned hugely once more. *Merlin doesn't have to attack. He can just sit back and let sleep deprivation do me in.*

Aunt Phyllis stood. "I think you should take a nap," she said decisively. "I'll call you for supper in an hour. Then straight to bed again after that. I'll put away the pop."

Ariane nodded obediently, hauled herself to her feet and climbed the stairs to her room. She collapsed on her bed. Her eyes closed. In seconds she was asleep.

The demon was waiting.

The landscape in which she met it could be anything. The twisted black wood of her afternoon nightmare was one she had seen before. Sometimes they met in a desert. Sometimes they met in downtown Regina, ruined and deserted as though ravaged by war. And sometimes they met in swirling fog, like now. And those times, the demon talked.

As usual, she sensed it rather than saw it. She had *never* seen it, except for a glimpse of red eyes in a swirling fog. That didn't lessen her dread.

You cannot ressst, the sibilant voice said softly, seeming to come from behind her as always. No matter how fast she turned, she could never see it, never get more than a glimpse of burning red eyes out of the corner of her eye. Dread choked her. She wanted to run, but if she did, the demon would just chase her, as it had that afternoon and on many occasions before.

It had never caught her. When she was awake, she didn't think it *could* catch her. But in these dreams, more often than not, her fear overwhelmed her waking reason.

She forced herself to stay put, but she couldn't stop turning in place, knowing she could never see the demon, but unable to stop trying. The fog swirled around her, thick, choking fog, tinged yellow and smelling of sulphur.

You cannot sssleep, the demon hissed at her. *Where are your powersss now, young Lady? I have ssstolen them from you...without sssleep, you are nothing. My massster knowsss thisss. My massster laughssssss....*The hiss moved closer. She felt a hot breath on her neck, as if a furnace door had opened behind her. Her heart jumped and in a moment she would have run, would have dashed blindly through the fog...

Instead she jerked herself awake, gasping, pulse pounding.

She glanced at her bedside clock. She'd slept less than ten minutes.

Fatigue pressed down on her, filling her head with fog as choking and deadening as the one in which the demon spoke to her, weighing down her heart with despair. She closed her eyes again, but she didn't sleep.

Instead, she wept.

◄◄ ►►

Rex Major, eyes closed, let the glorious "Flower Duet" from the first act of *Lakmé* wash over him. He sat alone in his box in Toronto's Four Seasons Centre for the Performing Arts. Opera had not existed in the era of Camelot. He had originally purchased his season tickets to present the image of a community-minded businessman, but to his astonishment, he had discovered he loved opera.

Musicals, on the other hand, he couldn't stand. Although he liked *Spamalot* better than *Camelot*. He chuckled at the thought.

His cell phone buzzed. Major debated ignoring it, but knew he couldn't. Before the opera had started, he'd configured his phone so only high-priority messages were allowed through. He sighed, opened his eyes, and pulled the phone from its holster.

He glanced at the screen. *She sleeps not*, it read.

He smiled and put the phone away. *Text messages from a demon*, he thought. *What a wonderful age this is.*

The demon couldn't physically harm Ariane. But by disrupting her sleep, it was disrupting her power, keeping her reserves of energy so low that she wouldn't be able to sense the location of the second shard of Excalibur. He smiled more widely. *And keeping her reserves so low she doesn't realize she has the power to push the demon away.* The real Lady, his *beloved* sister, tucked away on the other side of the barely open door to Faerie, had failed to tell her heir and protégé many, many things that might have helped in her struggle against Merlin.

The "Flower Duet" ended, but Major hardly noticed. Few things could distract him from opera, but thoughts of Excalibur were among them. Thinking about the girl in Regina who held the sword's first shard – temporarily – also brought to mind the boy, Wally Knight. A youth, a stripling, barely more than a child...and yet he had resisted Major's Voice of Command, the Voice that no *adult* had ever withstood before: no adult save one.

Arthur.

The King had never been Merlin's to Command. Had he been, he would have been a far lesser King than he became. Arthur had been an extraordinary leader because he had aided Merlin of his own free will.

Wally Knight had the beginnings, at least, of the same power. True, he had succumbed to the Voice of Command at first, but almost at once he'd begun to push back. The second time Merlin had used it, it hadn't worked at all. The Lady didn't have the power to counteract his magic so directly, so *she* couldn't have given Wally that ability.

Wally must have *inherited* it.

Major believed in coincidences. But not where magic was concerned. Magic seeped through everything it touched, like water carving a cave out of limestone, smoothing and shaping the rock. Arthur had been born with the ability to resist Command, just as Merlin had been born with his abilities, and the Lady with hers. Where magic had come from originally was a matter for theologians. Major wondered about it but didn't really care: Magic was a fact, it operated according to its own natural laws, and those who best understood those laws...like him...could make the most effective use of it.

Wally, Merlin thought. *Walter Arthur Knight the Third.*

If Merlin was right, then even the boy's name was not a coincidence. Ariane was the heir of the Lady of the Lake. And Wally, Major had slowly come to believe, could be none other than the heir of Arthur himself.

Arthur had had several sons; the most notorious of them had been Mordred. When he had come to court he had been presented as Arthur's nephew, but in reality Arthur had fathered the boy with his half-sister, Morgause, before either of them knew they were related. Mordred eventually led a rebellion against his father. In the final battle, at Camlann, Arthur slew his own son...but only after Mordred had mortally wounded him.

All of Arthur's *legitimate* sons had died childless. But Mordred had had sons of his own, who had continued rebelling against Arthur's successor. Ironic though it was, Arthur's bloodline had continued only through the son who had slain him.

Arthur had had other magical gifts besides the ability to withstand Command. Men had begged to follow him, begged to join hopeless battles against overwhelming odds...and then won those battles, because of their love for their King. And with Excalibur in his hand...Major shook his head, remembering Arthur striding across long-ago battlefields, Excalibur flashing in the sun, blood running like water from its silvery blade, the sword singing a terrible, magical song that only he, Merlin, could hear.

Warriors fell like wheat before a farmer's scythe when Arthur took the field. Yet neither Excalibur nor his physical prowess had saved him when he faced Mordred, whose skill had been nearly equal to his own; and that, too, told Major something: Mordred had inherited some of his father's gifts.

Which meant Wally, if he *were* Arthur's descendant, might have those gifts as well, though masked by his youth.

The first act of *Lakmé* ended. The audience moved to the exits for intermission, but Rex Major stayed put. *When I have Excalibur*, he thought, *I will need someone to wield it, someone to lead the army I will raise, someone to command and rally my troops as we march through the door into Faerie and I take back my world from the tyrants who oppress it.*

Could Wally be that someone? After proper grooming, proper instruction, could he lead Merlin's army of liberation to victory?

He's loyal to his friend now, Major thought, *but that doesn't mean he'll stay that way. He doesn't know what he is, or could be. When he does, why would he be content to serve the Lady of the Lake, to help her erase magic from this world, to go back to being an ordinary boy, sentenced to become an ordinary man?*

Even in Camelot, magic had never been the *only* tool Merlin used to bend people to his will. Threats would work with some; he didn't think they would work with Arthur's heir. But good old-fashioned bribery, the lure of greatness, of glory...*that*, Major thought, had possibilities.

And there was something else. He smiled as he thought of it. The young Arthur had been orphaned at fifteen by the death of his father, Uther Pendragon. Aware of that, Merlin had deliberately set out to become a father figure to the youthful King. He had wielded far more influence through that personal connection than he ever would have as a mere wizard, no matter how powerful.

Wally Knight's father still lived, but he had all but abandoned the boy, as had his mother. Wally's sister Felicia, not unlike Arthur's other half-sister Morgana, was more foe than family. *Those who do not remember history are condemned to repeat it*, Major thought. He smiled to himself. *But those who* do *remember history can* cause *it to repeat, if it suits them. And I think it will suit me very well.*

The audience was filing back in. He decided to put thoughts of Excalibur out of his head for the rest of the evening. But just as the lights dimmed, his cell phone buzzed again. He glanced at it. What he saw brought him surging to his feet. The door of the box closing behind him cut off the opening notes of the second act. Two minutes later, texting his chauffeur as he walked, he was striding through the glass-walled members' lounge to the cloakroom.

Rex Major had just discovered the location of the second shard.

CHAPTER TWO

BLINDSIDED

WALLY ROSE SLOWLY TO CONSCIOUSNESS, as if he were surfacing from the bottom of a muddy lake. He first became aware of sounds: voices he could make no sense of, the hum of air conditioning, footsteps. Then a smell: harsh, antiseptic. He realized he was lying in a bed, but not his own – this one felt harder. He was wearing pajamas, and he didn't wear pajamas. The crook of his right elbow hurt, as if something sharp had jabbed it. His head throbbed. He raised a shaking hand and felt rough gauze wrapped around his head like a turban.

What the...?

He opened his eyes. It took a great deal more effort than it should have, and his lids scraped like sandpaper over his dry eyeballs. He blinked up at speckled acoustic tiles. A metal track curved through them, supporting a blue curtain bunched up at his right.

And then, finally, he understood: he was in a hospital.

But why? What had happened?

He remembered hiding from Flish in his smelly locker. He remembered deciding to go out through the gym instead of the front doors of the school. He remembered saying hello to Coach Mueller, and then....

...then nothing. It was all a blank.

But it didn't take Sherlock Holmes to put two and two together when you were lying in a hospital bed with a headache and a turban.

"I fell," he said out loud. The words sounded hoarse in his ears. "I fell and hit my head."

"But shouldn't be any the worse for it," said a voice to his right, startling him. He looked that way, wincing at the stiffness in his neck, and saw a woman in a nurse's uniform standing between him and a second bed. The old man who lay there mumbled something and rolled onto his side. The nurse glanced at him, then back at Wally. "A few stitches, a rather nasty concussion. But no skull fracture, and the CT scan is clear. You should make a complete recovery."

He looked down at his sore elbow. A needle was stuck into his skin, taped in place and attached to a tube that ran through a grey box on a metal pole, and then up to a bag of clear fluid. He turned his head. On his left arm was a blood pressure cuff. It started to tighten, and just when he thought he couldn't stand it anymore, loosened again. Two green numbers on a second grey box shifted, then steadied: 122 over 74. "BP is good," announced the nurse. "You're doing fine."

"How..." Wally's throat closed on the words and he coughed. The nurse picked up a glass of water from the side table and held its curved straw to his lips. He sipped gratefully, then said, "How long have I been here?"

"Ambulance brought you in last night. A teacher was with you...Natasha Mueller?"

Wally nodded.

"She stayed until you were admitted and brought up here. Dr. Kipkoskei wants you to stay forty-eight hours for observation, so you'll be our guest for another night at least."

"I really don't feel like going anywhere," Wally said. The throbbing in his head wasn't severe, but it was constant.

"Head hurt?" the nurse asked.

He nodded.

"I can bring you some painkillers. According to your school records, you aren't allergic to any medications. Is that right?"

"As far as I know," Wally said.

"Do you need anything else?"

Wally nodded again. "I have to go to the bathroom."

"I can help you with that too," said the nurse. "But we'll take it easy. Hold on one second." She reached across him and undid the cuff of the blood-pressure monitor. "You'll have to walk with the IV pole. Now, try sitting up."

Wally pushed himself up with his elbows. A wave of dizziness swept over him, but after a moment it passed. "All right," he said cautiously.

"Swing your feet over the side."

Wally did so. The nurse opened the drawer of the side table and took out a pair of shapeless hospital slippers, like little cloth bags with elastic around the top, and slipped them on his feet. She stood next to the bed, offering her arm.

"Now try standing. I've got you."

Wally slid off the bed until his feet touched the floor, took her arm, and slowly stood up. Another wave of dizziness hit him, and he gripped her arm tighter, but the spell only lasted an instant. He took a deep breath. "I'm good," he said.

"Excellent!" The nurse smiled. "Then let's get you to the bathroom."

He held onto her as they inched across the room, past the old man in the other bed. "What about my parents?" Wally asked.

"I'm afraid I don't know." The nurse sounded disapproving. "As I said, a Ms. Mueller brought you in, but I wasn't on duty then. I've only spoken to a Mrs. Carson. Our records indicate your parents have given her authority to approve medical treatment for you."

Wally nodded, and rather wished he hadn't. "She looks after us...me...when my parents are away." He glanced past the nurse into the hallway. "Is she here now?"

"I haven't seen her since my shift started," said the nurse, sounding more disapproving than ever.

"What about my sister?"

"I'm sorry, Wally," the nurse said. "I'm afraid no one has come by." She smiled again. "But it's only a little after noon. Your friends won't be out of school for hours yet. I'm sure you'll have visitors this evening." They'd reached the bathroom door. "Now, are you okay to use the toilet by yourself?"

"Yes," Wally said hastily, ear-tips burning.

"Good," the nurse said briskly. "When you're finished, or if you find you *do* need help, press the call button."

Wally started to nod, remembered to stop himself just in time, and said, "Thank you." He made his cautious way into the bathroom, closing the door behind him. He managed to do what he needed to do, but by the time he had finished washing his hands and pressed the call button he was more than ready to return to bed, and eager to take the painkillers the nurse offered.

As the nurse helped him lie down again, he couldn't help thinking there was something he needed to do, something important...something about Flish...*My loving sister who won't even come see me in the hospital*, he thought bitterly...but he couldn't remember what it was.

I must have hit my head really *hard.*

The painkillers began to take hold, pushing down the ache in his skull but also filling his brain with fuzziness.

Ariane will come see me...once she knows. The thought seemed to come from far away.

Ariane. Whatever he was forgetting had something to do with her...and Flish...

But the memory wouldn't come, and a moment later he slipped once more into the dark waters of sleep.

◀◀ ▶▶

Ariane, despite another sleepless night, dragged herself to school early on Thursday morning and hung around the front steps, hoping to catch Wally when he arrived. She wanted to apologize for not showing up for lunch the day before, but this time it was Wally who didn't show.

She kept looking for him in the hallway between classes, without success. At lunch, though she desperately wanted to find a quiet corner of the library and take a nap, she sat at their usual table – but still, no Wally.

It wasn't until the first afternoon class break that Ariane finally found out what had happened to him. She was getting a drink from a water fountain when she heard a girl behind her say to a friend, "Did you hear about Wally Knight? Slipped on a patch of ice behind the gym. Split his head right open. You can still see the blood on the ground!"

"Gross!" said her friend, although she sounded more fascinated than disgusted.

Ariane, shocked, spun around. "Is he all right?"

The girls, both ninth graders, looked surprised. "Nobody's saying," said the girl who had spoken first.

"I bet he's in a coma," said the second. "Probably a vegetable. I saw this documentary once about head injuries..."

"A vegetable?" The first girl giggled. "What kind?"

The second girl laughed too. "Probably a radish. With his red hair –"

The shard strapped to Ariane's middle blazed, flooding her with the urge to wipe those silly grins off the girls' faces. Water gurgled from the fountains, even though nobody was twisting the knobs. The girls didn't notice, and Ariane clamped down on her anger. But something of her rage must have registered on her face, because the girls blanched and skittered away, whispering and looking over their shoulders as they fled.

Ariane leaned her forehead against the cold tile of the hallway wall. *He's* not *dead*, she thought. *He's* not *a vegetable. He* can't *be.*

She straightened and hurried to the main office.

"Is he a good friend of yours?" the secretary said with a sympathetic smile, after Ariane had asked about Wally. "Well, the woman who's looking after him while his parents are away, Mrs...." she hesitated.

"Carson," supplied Ariane.

"Yes, that's right. Mrs. Carson said he suffered a concussion and needed a few stitches. They're keeping him at the General Hospital for observation, then he'll be recuperating at home for a few days. I don't think we'll see him at school before next week."

"Thank you," Ariane said. The bell rang as she went out into the hall, which meant she was late for Social Studies, but right now she didn't care. She couldn't go visit Wally right after school, since she had two hours of remedial algebra with Mr. Merle. But maybe after supper...Aunt Phyllis would surely want to go, too; she'd drive her....

Social studies dragged by, and physics after that, details of Canadian human rights legislation and the properties of waves lost in the fog of her fatigue and worry. When physics ended, other students fled home or headed off to practise football or fencing or French horn, but she plodded down to Mr. Merle's classroom for remedial algebra...although as far as she could tell very little remediation was occurring. Her fatigue-dulled mind still couldn't get a solid grip on the subject.

Those two hours, too, eventually ground to their end. At last, Ariane headed toward the side exit of the school.

Her footsteps echoed in the empty but brightly lit corridors. She pushed open the metal door and emerged into the drive between Oscana Collegiate and St. Dunstan High School, the Catholic school next door. The drive was blocked at one end by a swinging gate, locked to keep cars out of the alley behind the school...*the alley where Wally must have fallen and hurt himself,* Ariane thought as she reached the gate. For a moment she considered walking down to the corner of the gym where the accident must have happened ("You can still see the blood!" the girl had said), but she pushed the notion away, disgusted by her own morbid curiosity. Instead she headed in her usual direction, toward the city-owned tennis courts behind the Catholic school. On the other side of them she could nip across Winnipeg Street to 17th Avenue, then duck through a couple of alleys to get to Wallace Street. It had become her favourite shortcut. It not only saved her half a block's walking – and these days, even half a block seemed like a very long distance indeed – it let her approach her house without being seen by anyone who might be watching it from the street.

The two courts, side by side inside a chain-link fence, lay in deep shadow cast by the rows of small trees that bordered the fence to the south, east and west. Against the lights of Winnipeg Street just beyond they looked more like black cardboard cutouts than real trees. Ariane exhaled white clouds, and the cold bit her cheeks, making her feel more alert than she had all day.

She entered the courts through an opening in the west side of the fence and started across to the matching opening on the eastern side. But just as she stepped from the first court to the second, four figures, black cutouts against the streetlights, rose in front of her, blocking her path. She stopped, a surge of adrenaline scouring away her fatigue. "Who's there?" *Is Major trying again?*

"Guess," said a familiar voice.

Ariane's fists clenched. "Flish. Shania. Stephanie. Cassandra."

"Got it in one," said Flish.

Feet crunching on the court surface, the four spread out to surround her, menacing, shadowy figures trailing clouds of breath-fog. Ariane turned this way and that, trying to watch them all at once. "Shouldn't you be with your brother at the hospital?" she threw at Flish.

"I hate hospitals," Flish said.

"Then you'd better leave," Ariane growled. "Or that's where you'll end up. You know what I can do."

As she spoke, Ariane listened for nearby water. A faint, faint song, metallic, constrained, came from beneath the ground, probably a pipe feeding the sprinkler system in the sports fields behind Oscana. But exhaustion was like a straitjacket constraining her powers. The water ran too deep. She couldn't call it.

"Oh, we know you can do all kinds of tricks with water," said Flish. "But look around, Airy-Anne. There's no water here. Nothing but you...and us. And we owe you, Airy-Anne. We owe you big time." Her eyes, two yellow sparks reflecting the school's lights, were all Ariane could see of her face. Behind Flish, a car drove down Winnipeg Street, trailing wisps of exhaust.

Ariane's heart pounded so hard she thought Flish must surely be able to hear it. The last time these girls had caught her outside, they had tried to strip her, intending to send humiliating photos to classmates. She'd fought them off with her newly awakened powers. She'd made them run away again when they'd threatened her in a school hallway just after she and Wally had returned from Yellowknife. This time...well, despite the location, she didn't think they intended to challenge her to a friendly game of tennis.

I want to visit Wally, she thought, *but not by joining him in the hospital!*

Worse, what if they found the shard strapped to her waist? If they took it, and Rex Major found out, he'd have it the next day. And he wouldn't hesitate to kill them to get it.

As sudden as the flick of a light switch, her fear flipped to anger – anger fuelled by the shard. Haunted by a demon, a target of one of the richest, most ruthless men in the world, saddled with the impossible task of finding the five shards of Excalibur before he could – she didn't have time for these petty, bullying, stupid *children.*

The sword-tip, hot as a brand against her skin, poured strength mingled with rage into her, and she embraced them both, welcoming the hot, furious energy, so different from the Lady's cool power.

The faint song of the water in the pipe beneath the courts crescendoed, *pianissimo* to *fortissimo,* offering itself to her, begging for her command. *Come to me,* Ariane sang, silently and without words. *Come to me!*

The ground shook. Flish, Shania, Cassandra, and Stephanie, tightening the ring around her, staggered. *Come to me!* Ariane sang again. *Come now!*

Three metres behind Flish, the tennis court erupted. The four girls spun, mouths agape. Water geysered ten metres into the sky, hurling pieces of pavement like shrapnel. A chunk of asphalt smashed into Stephanie's face, knocking her flat on her back. She staggered to her feet, clutching her bloody nose, and fled, weeping.

One down, three to go, Ariane thought, keeping her gaze on Flish. Always before she had held herself back. *Not this time!* She formed the spurting water into a taut, swirling tendril, and cracked it like a whip against Flish's side. Wally's sister flew through the air like a rag doll. She hit the pavement with a sickening crunch, rolled over and over, slammed into one of the net posts, and lay very still.

The violence she had unleashed shocked Ariane out of her fury. For an instant, the shard's power stuttered. *What have I done? I've got to stop, I've got to –*

But the moment passed. The shard's power roared through her again, drowning her doubts. She turned contemptuously from Flish to Shania and Cassandra.

They had frozen in place, but as Ariane raised the whip of water they fled. A flick of her hand, and the water swept their feet out from under them. They thudded to the pavement, and something cracked like a breaking twig. Screaming, sobbing, Shania stumbled back to her feet, cradling her left arm against her side, and staggered away. Cassandra lay on her back, mouth open, gasping for the breath the impact had knocked from her lungs.

Ariane spun back toward Wally's sister. Flish stirred a little, moaned. Ariane raised the tendril. Its tip turned to ice and the ice to a glittering blade.

An arm of liquid hung above Flish, wielding a crystalline sword...wielding, Ariane realized, Excalibur. And the ice-blade had a voice: a deep, imperious bass that thundered in Ariane's head. *Strike! Strike now! Kill your enemy!*

But another voice spoke up in response, clear and high as a sustained violin note singing out above the rumble of bass and timpani in a symphony. *You...can... not...do...this*, it said, every word emphasized. *You can't. It's murder. She's not your enemy. Rex Major is your enemy. She's just a girl. A bully, but just a girl. She's Wally's sister.*

Kill your enemy! the sword thundered.

No! the other voice shouted in response, and this time that denial came not only from the part of her that was fifteen-year-old Ariane Forsythe of Regina, but the part of her that was the ageless Lady of the Lake. "I wield Excalibur! It does not wield me!" she screamed into the night; and then she slashed the sword down.

The ice-blade shattered against the pavement well clear of Flish's head. The arm of water fell apart, disappearing into the glittering pool welling harmlessly across the courts from the broken pipe.

Ariane strode over to Flish, who managed to turn her head to look up at her with wide eyes, the blood streaking her face black as ink in the dim light. Her breath came in pain-filled gasps. "Leave me alone," Ariane snarled. "Once and for all, *leave me alone!* You don't know who or what you're dealing with. And next time, I might not be able to stop myself."

She reached down to Flish's belt and pulled the girl's cell phone out of its case. "I'm calling 911," she said. "But I won't be here when they come. You can tell them the truth, if you want to. They're not going to believe you." She dialed, told the operator there had been an explosion in the tennis courts, and hung up before he could ask more questions. She returned the cell phone to its case, then strode away without looking back.

She walked half a block along 17th Avenue, then turned north into an alley. In the shadow of a tree that hung over a sagging wooden fence, she sank to the ground beside a garbage bin and began to sob, her body shuddering as the sound of sirens approached.

CHAPTER THREE

NEWS TRAVELS FAST

THE NEXT TIME WALLY WOKE, his hospital-room window was dark. A clock stared at him from the wall at the foot of his bed. *After 5:30*, he thought. *Ariane will be finishing remedial algebra. Give her time to get home, have supper...then she'll come. Maybe Aunt Phyllis, too.* His stomach growled at the thought of Aunt Phyllis's fantabulous chocolate-chip cookies, and he suddenly realized how hungry he was.

A few minutes later a silent green-clad orderly delivered a metal-covered plate on a pink plastic tray. Wally lifted the cover to discover flabby Salisbury steak, lumpy mashed potatoes and limp green beans. He inhaled the food as though it were the best meal of his life.

But even *his* appetite drew the line at the amorphous brown blob served for dessert. He thought longingly again of Aunt Phyllis's chocolate-chip cookies as he poked at the whatever-it-was with his fork, just to see if it would crawl out of the bowl. It quivered as if it would *like* to, but stayed put.

The orderly returned and cleared away the dinner tray. An hour went by, then another. By half-past seven Wally had his eyes glued to the door, expecting Ariane to appear at any moment. Even Flish would have been a welcome face by that point. But when someone finally *did* come to visit, it wasn't Ariane or his sister. Instead, a plump, middle-aged woman, graying hair tied up in a severe bun, bustled into his room.

Wally stared at her red, blotchy face. "Mrs. Carson?" Mrs. Carson *crying* because he'd banged his head? *Maybe I've misjudged her.*

"Oh, Wally," Mrs. Carson gasped. "What a terrible thing."

"It's really not that bad," he said, trying to sound reassuring. "It hardly hurts at all as long as –"

"It's your sister," Mrs. Carson went on as if he hadn't spoken. "A broken leg, two broken ribs, a wrenched back, a nasty cut on her head, scrapes and bruises all over...the doctor says she'll be fine, but she –"

"Wait a minute," Wally said. "*Flish* is in the hospital?" *I should have known Mrs. Carson wasn't here to see me.* Even though his sister had moved out of the house two weeks ago, after their father had made it official that he and their mother were separating, Mrs. Carson still fawned over her. "What happened to her? A car accident? Shania drives like a maniac –"

"An explosion!" Mrs. Carson said, wringing her hands. "A water pipe under the tennis courts behind St. Dunstan's High exploded just when Felicia and her friends were walking across it. The impact threw your sister halfway across the court and she hit one of the net posts. Stephanie has a broken nose, Cassandra is scraped and bruised, and Shania broke her wrist." Mrs. Carson's voice shook. "When I think what could have happened...."

Tennis courts? A water pipe? Since when do water pipes explode? Some of the fog in his head cleared, and Wally remembered what he hadn't been able to the night before: hearing his sister and her friends plotting to jump Ariane on the tennis courts, far away from any water, on Thursday...today!

He'd never warned Ariane. But...

Broken ribs? Broken limbs? *It wasn't Ariane I needed to warn.* Anger swelled. "Where is she?" he choked out. "Can I see her?"

"She's sedated," Mrs. Carson said. Her lip trembled. "Poor girl..."

Wally looked out at the dark sky. *Ariane couldn't have* meant *to do it*, he thought. *She was just protecting herself...things must have gotten out of hand....*

He could keep telling *himself* that, but he really needed to hear *Ariane* tell him. Now, more than ever, he needed her to come see him.

But first he needed to see Flish for himself. He turned back to Mrs. Carson. "Could you ask?" he said. "Ask if I can see her?"

Mrs. Carson smiled a little. "Of course," she said. "Wait right here."

I'm not likely to go anywhere, am I? Wally thought. He bit his lip. He *wanted* to believe Ariane had only hurt Flish by accident, didn't want to think she had done so deliberately...but blowing up the tennis courts? It was overkill, like trout-fishing with dynamite.

In the back of his mind, a worm of doubt stirred itself. What if it *hadn't* been an accident? What if Ariane had *chosen* to hurt them? After all, hadn't he seen her try before?

Mrs. Carson pushed a wheelchair into the room. "They said it's all right for me to take you up to her room," she said. "She won't be able to talk to you, but at least you can see her. She should be awake tomorrow and then you can visit properly."

Wally nodded. He was able to get out of bed on his own this time, using the wheelchair handles to support himself during his one brief, dizzy moment. He grabbed the robe that had been lying at the foot of his bed and pulled it on over his hospital gown, cinched the belt around his middle, and then sat down in the wheelchair, put his slippered feet on the footrests and let Mrs. Carson push him out into the hall.

She wheeled him past the nurse's station, maneuvered him around an old woman clutching an IV pole as she shuffled along one tiny step at a time and pushed him into one of the elevators. Two floors up, they got out, turned right and rolled down another hall that looked pretty much the same as the one outside his room except for a different collection of bad artwork on the off-white walls.

Mrs. Carson rolled him into a private room. *No snoring old-man roommate for sis*, Wally thought, but his momentary bitterness fled when he saw Flish's face. Shocked, he took in the huge blue-black bruise surrounding her swollen left eye, the gauze pad on her right cheek (stained with a spot of blood, red as a ruby), and more gauze wrapped around her head, where a portion of her scalp showed, shaven and naked-looking. His eyes travelled to the tube in her arm and the cast on her leg, hanging in traction from the ceiling, and his gut heaved. *Ariane did this.* The thought burned like acid. But then, *No! Not Ariane. The Lady of the Lake.*

You were thrilled *when the Lady gave Ariane her powers, thrilled that she gave you this quest*, he reminded himself. *A real-life quest just like in your favourite books.* He couldn't deny he'd been caught up in the wonder of the whole thing. But he'd forgotten one very important fact: even in books, people got hurt.

To be fair to Ariane, Wally had no doubt that Flish and the rest of the coven would have beaten her up if they'd been able to. Would he really feel any better about things if *Ariane* were lying in the hospital instead of Flish?

His head was hurting again. And he didn't think it was entirely due to the concussion.

Mrs. Carson turned his chair around and pushed him back into the hallway. "That's enough," she said. "They told me not to keep you out here any longer than ten minutes." She pushed Wally back toward the elevators. "This is such a terrible thing to happen while your parents are away."

Away, Wally thought. *They're* always *away. Dad dropped by two weeks ago, but only long enough to tell us he and Mom were separating. Now he's in Japan with his new girlfriend, on "business." Mom hasn't been home in three months, off working on that movie in Canmore.* Neither one had come rushing back when he'd hurt himself. He doubted they'd come rushing back for Flish either. But at least Flish had Mrs. Carson to worry about her. Who worried about *him?*

Up until this evening, Wally would have said Ariane. But now, for the first time...he wasn't so sure.

◀ ▶

Ariane cried for ten minutes, while just out of her sight she heard ambulances and fire trucks rushing to the tennis courts. Several people hurried past the end of the alley, faces lit by flashing red and blue lights, to see what was going on. But Ariane stayed where she was, sitting in numbed silence, arms around her legs, head on her knees. *I should go home*, she thought, but exhaustion and shock pinned her to the ground. She closed her eyes.

She dozed.

The demon was waiting.

Once more it hid in dark, swirling mist, slithering behind her as fast as she turned, so she never caught more than a peripheral glimpse of glowing red eyes. *You sssee?*

it hissed, its voice reptilian, repellant. *The power isss not for you. The power isss too great. It will ssswallow you. There will be nothing of you left. The Lady of the Lake isss using you. She isss not your friend.* The voice lowered, as though trying to sound conciliatory. *Give up the shard. Give it to Merlin. He will be merciful. He holdsss no ill will toward you. Refussse to do the Lady'sss will, and all will be asss it wasss before....*

It would be so easy, Ariane thought. Let Rex Major have the piece of the sword she already held, let him have the others as he found them, let him re-forge Excalibur...she could go back to being a normal kid, worry about normal-kid things...

But even as she considered the possibility, she rejected it. A normal kid? Over the past two years she'd lived in a half dozen different foster homes. She'd changed schools three times. Until Wally, she'd had no friends. All because her mother had disappeared, a disappearance somehow linked to Merlin's quest for the shards of Excalibur. She didn't know *how* yet, but she'd find out. With the Lady's power, bolstered by the power of Excalibur, she could *do* something about it. Find her mother, if she was still alive. Bring her back. Heal their family....

Her anger, so close to the surface these days, boiled up. The shard answered it. Even locked in her demon-dream, she felt it flame against her skin. She looked down at herself.

As always in these dreams, she wore a long gown of flowing white, but this time, she also wore a broad belt of red leather, and hanging from that belt...

A sword. *The* sword. Excalibur.

The ghostly hilt had a large round pommel with a hole in it, as though something were missing...a jewel, perhaps. Golden wire wound around the part where her hand gripped, which felt solid though it looked as transparent as thin smoke, her curled fingers clearly visible through it. Yet it was solid enough to grasp – and solid enough to draw.

She pulled and the sword slid easily out of its scabbard. Like the hilt, the blade was translucent, as though made of glass or water...all except for the tip, the piece of the sword she had already found, the piece she wore strapped to her body. *That* was hard, polished steel, sharpened to a razor's edge. It glinted turquoise, as though lit by sunlight filtering through the waters of a glacier-fed lake.

Her anger swelled and again the shard responded. The sword tip flared with light so bright the gloomy black fog of the demon-dream paled to a swirling grey. She slashed the ghostly blade back and forth, burning away darkness like morning mist in the heat of the rising sun.

She laughed. She suddenly felt strong, invincible. Why had she let the thing behind her terrorize her for so long? She raised the sword, holding it close to her body and in front of her face as though offering a salute. "I'm going to turn around," she said, and the words came naturally to her, the same words she had said to Flish's gang by Wascana Lake the day they'd tried to humiliate her, the first time she had called on the Lady's power. "If I were you, I'd *run.*"

And then she spun and slashed in one movement.

For just a moment, she saw the demon, caught a glimpse of grey scaly skin, curling black horns, red eyes, hooves and a barbed tail. The tip of Excalibur scored its bare chest, opening a long slash from which black blood bubbled and oozed. The demon's fanged mouth gaped in an ear-splitting scream of pure agony, then it turned and ran, hooves thudding away into the misty darkness, drops of black ichor sizzling on the ground in its wake.

Ariane woke with a gasp. She lifted her head from her knees and stared wildly around, wondering where she was, where the sword had gone.

And then she felt the shard pressing, solid and warm, against her skin. She took a deep breath, and despite everything else that had happened that night, a deep relief, verging on joy, washed over her.

She would sleep that night, real sleep. For the first time in two weeks.

Wally, she thought as she rose to her feet, suddenly anxious to return home, knowing Aunt Phyllis must be worrying. *I should go see Wally in the hospital....*

But then she yawned, a huge, jaw-creaking yawn that she couldn't stop. No. Sleep was what she needed. Wally was safe, and he'd probably be out of the hospital tomorrow anyway. *Flish might be there a little longer*, she thought, and the guilt of what she had done tempered her relief at chasing away the demon. But after all, *they'd* attacked *her* – even though they had twice before seen what she could do. She'd only been defending herself.

Nobody was killed. Nobody was seriously hurt. A couple of broken bones, maybe. They'll be fine.

And so will I, she thought, yawning again. *With proper sleep, so will I.*

I'd better be. I have to find the next shard.

She hoisted her backpack and set off down the alley that led home.

◀▶

Later that night, alone in his high-rise Toronto office, Rex Major read a new text message, and swore. Ariane had banished the demon he had sent to haunt her dreams. Somehow she had realized the first shard could be used to drive it away. And the demon's fear of Excalibur was so great it would not return, even if Major commanded it to.

Rex Major's thumbs flew over his phone. He hit SEND. The coded message would return the demon to its own world, but with the reassurance that it had done its part well and could still have the girl as its reward once Excalibur was Merlin's.

That reassurance was important. Despite the power he had once had and hoped to have again, Major *always* tried to stay on the right side of demons.

He returned his attention to the e-mail that had sent him rushing from the opera, an automated message sparked by the encounter of the second shard with one of the thin threads of magic his Excalibur server software had woven throughout the Internet.

He often felt like a spider lurking at the centre of a vast web, waiting for the vibrations caused by insects landing on its strands. Computers were everywhere, and if they were connected to the Internet, they were, in some small way, connected to him. The smartphone Wally Knight had been carrying had alerted him to the presence of the Lady of the Lake in Wascana Lake in Regina. When the diamond miners in the Northwest Territories had dug down to the first shard, it had perhaps been another smartphone that, prompted by the sliver of magic within its software, had sent the automated notice to Major.

And now, at last, he had received a similar message about the second shard. Nothing but an IP address, but that had been enough for him to determine it had originated somewhere in southern France. Now to home in on it....

He took a deep breath, closed his eyes, called up the power that still leaked to him through the almost-sealed doorway dividing Earth and Faerie, and sent his mind flashing through the web he had created, across the Atlantic and deep into Europe. The effort sapped his strength, but he held on, pushing harder. The signal had come from...*there*...and he could trace it back to...

His awareness of his office crashed back. He straightened, rubbing the back of his neck. He glanced at the clock on his computer screen. *Ten minutes*, he thought bitterly. *Ten minutes of effort, and I'm exhausted.*

He shook his head. His magic hadn't lasted long enough for him to pinpoint the shard's location, but at least he had the name of a nearby city. He would travel there. Closer to the shard, he might be able to sense it more clearly, or at least be ready to move quickly if it once more made its presence known to his ensorcelled software.

He checked his schedule. Unfortunately, though the search for Excalibur was his priority, he couldn't just drop everything and fly to France. (Fly. He shuddered. He hated flying.) Almost as important as the sword to his plans were the prestige, influence and high-level contacts Rex Major Industries provided, and there were several important meetings scheduled for the next week with officials from Canada's Department of Defence, followed by more sit-downs with representatives from the Pentagon. Both militaries were interested in the newest version of his Excalibur software, the most secure yet....

...and the most infiltrated with my magic, Major thought.

When the sword was whole and in his possession, the military servers would be key to forging all the powers of Earth into a weapon he could use against the world he really wanted to control: Faerie.

The Queen and the rulers of the Clades know how to fight against swords and magic, he thought grimly. *But we'll see how they fare against tanks, jets, machine guns and cruise missiles.*

He shook his head. No, he couldn't fly to France right away. He *had* to keep those appointments. But the moment they ended....

He drafted a brief e-mail to Gwen, his secretary, asking her to schedule one of the corporate jets for his use. But then he hesitated. Important though they were, he was taking a risk by not cancelling those meetings. Now that Ariane had banished the demon, her power would start to return. Which meant she might soon be able to sense the second shard. And if she got to it first....

He fingered the ruby stud in his right earlobe, as he tended to do when thinking about Excalibur. *But I won't let that happen*, he thought. *Her every move is watched. If she does anything suspicious, I can change my plans and leave at once.*

No. He'd keep the appointments. And *then* he'd go to France...and claim the second shard.

He sent the e-mail to Gwen and was about to leave his desk – he needed to rest his pounding head – when a new message arrived. He barely glanced at it, intending to deal with it in the morning, but when he saw the sender's name, he sat down again.

Major didn't dare use anyone closely connected with his business to keep an eye on Ariane and Wally: not since Keith Pritchard, his former Regina sales manager, had been arrested for breaking into Ariane's bedroom. So he had hired, through untraceable channels, someone from outside his organization to watch the two teenagers: *just* watch, for now. Major couldn't take the shard from Ariane by force and still use its power: she either had to give it to him of her own free will, or he had to retrieve at least three of the remaining four shards, so that he could then call the rest to him. But even if he couldn't steal the shard, he wanted to know *exactly* what Ariane and Wally were up to.

As Merlin read his spy's account, his eyebrows shot up. Ariane had had a busy night. She'd not only banished his demon from her dreams, she'd used the power of the shard to attack four girls.

She is becoming more dangerous, he thought. *But not just to me. To herself and those around her. I may be able to use that.* And then he continued reading, saw who one of the injured girls had been and smiled a cold smile: a smile that widened when he also read that Wally had hit his head and was in the hospital...and that so far, Ariane had not gone to visit him.

To forge a sword, one must strike while the steel is hot, Major thought. It was a saying he'd coined sixteen hundred years ago, and it was still true today.

He reached for the telephone.

◀ ▶

The ringing of a phone woke Wally from the doze he'd fallen into after Mrs. Carson had left. Again, it took him a moment to figure out where he was – and another moment to understand that the ringing phone was on the table beside his bed. He started to reach for it with his right hand, was brought up short by the IV line, rolled onto his side, and finally fumbled the ancient pink handset out of its cradle with his left. "Hello?" he rasped.

He expected to hear Ariane on the other end, or one of his parents. Instead he heard a voice he'd last heard two weeks ago, in an open-pit diamond mine in the Northwest Territories, from a man holding a gun to his head.

"Hello, Wally," said Rex Major. "How are you feeling?"

Wally's first inclination was to slam the phone back down into its cradle, but something stopped him. Partly, it was simple curiosity. But partly...maybe mostly...it was the little worm of doubt curling in his heart – doubt, now that he had seen how the Lady's power could affect Ariane, about how much of what the Lady of the Lake had told them about Rex Major had been the truth.

"I'm...fine," he said cautiously. "A slight concussion, a few stitches. Why do *you* care?"

"Wally," said Major, in a tone the boy had not heard him use before, the very opposite of the Voice of Command,

"I apologize for what happened in Yellowknife. But you must understand how desperate I was...how desperate I *am*...to retrieve the shards of Excalibur. For more than a thousand years I have dreamed of a world united under one strong, benevolent ruler, someone who can keep order, ensure justice for all, punish wrongdoers. Excalibur has the power to make that happen, in the right hands."

"You mean *your* hands," said Wally.

"Yes," Major said. "I don't deny it. I tried once before to rule through a surrogate. But Arthur, though a great man, had his weaknesses, and let his kingdom fall when he could have saved it. Or perhaps *I* could have saved it, had my sister not already conspired with Viviane to have me imprisoned."

"I never heard of Merlin having a sister," Wally said. "But hey, if she tried to stop *you*, she must have been all right."

Major laughed. "Wally, you're smarter than that. She's *still* trying to stop me. But she always did like to use others to do her dirty work. Then, it was Viviane. Now...it's you."

It took a second for what Major was saying to sink in. "The Lady of the Lake is your *sister?*"

"Yes. We're not close," he added. "Obviously. But we were once."

"I know how that goes," Wally said, wondering, even as he replied, what the *heck* he was doing chit-chatting with *Rex Major* (aka *Merlin* aka *the ancient sorcerer trying to take over the world*) as though they were classmates.

But he wasn't about to hang up after that bombshell about the Lady being Merlin's sister. The Lady had never mentioned *that* little fact.

"We were allies," Major continued. "She believed then, as I still do now, that we must overthrow the tyrants who rule Faerie. But..." he sighed. "She succumbed to the temptations of wealth and power. Rather than fight tyrants, she decided to become one, seizing control of Clade Avalon."

"Avalon? Isn't that an island?"

"A *legendary* island," Major said. "No one knows where it was, because it was never really here. It could appear in any lake, or at sea. In reality it was a doorway to the real Avalon, my realm...until my sister betrayed me."

"And I thought I had problems with *my* sister," Wally muttered.

"How *is* your sister?" Major said. "I know she was seriously injured by your girlfriend this evening

"Ariane is *not* my girlfriend," Wally answered automatically. He was used to the words by now – he had repeated them a lot over the last two weeks, after his classmates noticed how much time he and Ariane spent together.

"Perhaps that's a good thing," Major said softly. "She seems...dangerous."

Wally said nothing.

"But you still haven't told me," said Major again after a moment. "How is your sister?"

"Broken bones. Cuts and bruises. She'll be in the hospital longer than I will."

"And your parents? Your father was home just a short while ago, was he not? Has he or your mother come rushing back to her side...or your side?"

"Why bother asking?" Wally snapped. "If you know my Dad was just here, you've obviously got somebody watching Ariane and me. You already know they haven't come back."

"Of course I'm keeping an eye on you, Wally," Major said. "I'm concerned about you. You're an admirable young man, with the best of intentions. But I know my sister. I know how dangerous she is, to those who follow her as much as to those who stand against her." He paused.

"So...your parents haven't been there. Or even called?"

Don't listen to him, Wally warned himself. *He's not worried about you. He almost* killed *you to get the shard.*

On the other hand, no one else seemed concerned at all.

"No," he said at last.

"I'm sorry, Wally," Major said. "My own father abandoned my sister and I when we were quite young, and our mother, too, was...elsewhere. Like you, we were mostly raised by a surrogate. It was never easy."

Wally said nothing. *Yeah, he* sounds *sincere*, he thought. *But so what? He's a good actor.*

"And Ariane? Have you seen her since you were admitted?" Major continued after a moment.

Wally found it surprisingly hard to speak for a moment. "No," he finally managed to squeeze out.

"Perhaps," Major said softly, "you should give serious thought as to where your loyalties should lie."

Wally chewed on his lip. The only sound was the heavy breathing of the old man asleep in the next bed. *I should hang up*, he thought again. It was obvious that Major was trying to drive a wedge between him and Ariane.

But he kept the phone to his ear. He'd had some doubts about the Lady shortly after she'd first appeared. Ariane had allayed them. But now those doubts were back, redoubled.

Ariane, though, was his friend. He wasn't about to turn on her just because she hadn't made it to the hospital to see him, hadn't been able to control the power she hadn't even asked to be given.

The best defence is a good offence, Wally thought. "I know what you're trying to do," he said. "Ariane has you worried, especially now that she has the first shard. She beat you in Yellowknife. *We* beat you."

"Doesn't she have *you* worried?" Merlin countered mildly. "She hasn't come to see you. She could have killed your sister and her friends. Are you sure you even know her anymore? *She can't handle the shard*, Wally. Or the power my sister gave her. It's changing her. She's already different from the girl you met, and she'll keep changing, becoming colder, harder, less human, caring less and less about the things *you* care about." His voice grew warm, soft, conspiratorial. "You're just a tool to her, Wally. A tool she needs now, but one she won't need forever. As soon as she has *another* shard, she'll toss *you* aside like a broken hammer. And that will be the end of your part in this quest." His voice dropped further, to almost a whisper. "That's assuming, of course, she doesn't get you killed first."

Wally squeezed his eyes shut. *I shouldn't keep listening*, he thought. *I shouldn't....* But there was something almost ...mesmerizing about Major's voice.

Magic, he thought. *He used it on me before, in Yellowknife, he made me tell him what we were doing there...but I fought it off then. And it's not going to work now!* His eyes shot open.

"Why should I listen to you?" Wally snarled. His elderly roommate grunted and rolled over, and he lowered his voice. "You're *way* more dangerous than Ariane. And you're no more of this world than the Lady of the Lake!"

"On the contrary, I'm very much of this world," Merlin said. If Wally's outburst had taken him aback, his voice betrayed no sign. "I've been here more than a thousand years, whereas the Lady left long ago. And over the last forty years I've built a successful business that gives liberally to charity, employs thousands of people, and makes possible the fast, stable Internet you and millions of others take for granted. I've *already* made this world a better place. Why do you doubt I will continue to do so, with Excalibur in hand? I want to unite this world, stop the wars that flare all over the planet, use my power to ensure that everyone is clothed and fed, clean the world of pollution, restore the natural balance...."

"...and then use Earth as a jumping-off point from which to invade your own world," Wally finished. "Don't try to convince me you're a saint. I know the truth."

"*Liberate* my own world," Major corrected. "And then *two* worlds will be free from tyranny, not just one. Is that not a worthy cause? Especially compared to my sister's? All *she* wants is to close the door between Earth and Faerie forever, to shut off this world from all magic, all the healing power that I – or she, if she cared to exercise it – could bring to bear." For the first time, Major's calm facade cracked, real anger breaking though, coarsening his voice. "My cause is just, in both worlds, Wally. My sister wants to keep things the way they are. I want to change them, and change them for the better. Which cause is nobler?"

Wally had no more arguments, and his head was pounding, both from the concussion and from the effort of fighting the seductive attraction of Major's voice. He pulled the handset away from his ear, glared at it, and then, convulsively, as though killing a poisonous snake, smashed it into its cradle. The old man stirred and muttered before subsiding into sleep again.

Wally rolled over onto his other side, away from the phone, half-expecting it to ring again. It didn't, but that didn't stop him from hearing Major's words repeating in his head. *Which cause is nobler?*

He's the villain, he told himself. *He's lying.*

Just one problem: he couldn't point to a single thing Major had told him about the Lady or Ariane that wasn't true.

He didn't trust Major. But at the moment, he didn't really trust anyone.

CHAPTER FOUR

THE RETURN OF THE SONG

WHEN ARIANE FINALLY DRAGGED HERSELF through the doors of the house, Aunt Phyllis was waiting for her. "Are you all right?" her aunt said anxiously. "You're an hour late...and I heard sirens!"

Ariane had never felt so utterly drained. With the surge of energy she had drawn from the shard now gone as though it had never been, her exhaustion was so complete she couldn't bear the thought of trying to explain to Aunt Phyllis what had happened. "Sorry," she mumbled. "Mr. Merle kept me even later than usual...working on polyn-imin...polymani...polynomials...."

Aunt Phyllis laughed, but then her face grew concerned. "I think you should go straight to bed, Ariane. If you wake up later, I can heat up dinner...but right now you need sleep more than anything else."

Ariane nodded numbly and climbed the stairs to her room, every step an enormous obstacle she could barely surmount. She'd tell Aunt Phyllis the truth in the morning. Ariane didn't want to keep secrets from her, not anymore, but she just couldn't handle that conversation tonight.

She stumbled through getting undressed, hid the shard

under her pillow, lay down, pulled the covers over her, and fell instantly asleep.

For the first time in weeks, her dreams were ordinary, and they vanished from her mind when her alarm clock rang. She stretched, luxuriating in the feeling of being well-rested, her pleasure only slightly offset by the fact she still had to tell Aunt Phyllis what had happened at the tennis courts the night before. But without the fog of fatigue clogging her brain, even that seemed doable.

She glanced at the dark window. The sun wasn't even up yet, but somehow the morning already seemed bright. *A hot shower and I'll be able to face anything*, she thought as she got out of bed. She stripped off her pajamas, pulled on her bathrobe, and crossed the hall to the bathroom, smiling when she heard Aunt Phyllis singing along to Johnny Cash's "Folsom Prison Blues" playing on the radio in the kitchen...for once *not* tuned to the CBC.

She took off the bathrobe, stepped into the shower, started the water, reached for the shampoo....

...and froze.

As the water touched her, she heard a song within it, a distant, shimmering thread of music, cold as steel, hot as flame, inhuman, beautiful...and unmistakable. It was the song of the sword, the second shard of Excalibur, calling to the Lady of the Lake...calling to her again at last.

She leaned both hands against the tiles, the water sluicing down her body, closed her eyes and concentrated.

The song came from far away, much farther away than the first shard had seemed when she had heard its music, so faint she couldn't even tell from which direction it came.

The first shard, she thought. *What if...?*

Ariane jumped out of the shower without turning the water off, ran naked and dripping across the hall to her room, grabbed the shard from under her pillow, and rushed back to the bathroom. Holding the pitted, pointed piece of steel in her left hand, she stepped back under the streaming water.

It was as though she'd been listening to the song of the sword through ear buds, and had just plugged her music player into an amplifier. The thin thread of music swelled, and suddenly she knew where it was coming from: east. A long, *long* way east...and no way to get there through fresh water. Which meant another continent, somewhere beyond the Atlantic.

Europe? Africa? Asia? She couldn't tell. She opened her eyes and stared down at the dark tip of the ancient sword. The old steel looked out of place in her aunt's shower, its sharp edges and merciless point contrasting starkly with her pink, bare flesh. *How am I supposed to cross the Atlantic Ocean?* she thought in despair. *I can't travel through salt water!*

With a sigh, she put the shard in the soap dish and reached for the shampoo again. The hot water would run out in a minute, and she still had to get ready for school. She'd talk to Wally and....

He's in the hospital, Ariane remembered with a start.

For the first time, it occurred to her that by now someone would have told him that Flish was in the hospital too. Once he heard *how* his sister had been hurt, he'd have to be a complete idiot not to figure out what had really happened – and Wally was definitely not an idiot.

She remembered how upset he had been whenever she'd threatened Flish. What would he be feeling now that she'd actually *hurt* her?

And I didn't go see him last night, she thought, some of the shine suddenly disappearing from the morning. *I didn't even call.*

She finished shampooing and started soaping, in a race to get clean before the rapidly cooling water raised goose bumps. Just as it turned ice-cold, she reached for the tap to turn it off – then laughed at herself, exerted a little of the Lady's power so she no longer felt the chill, and gave her hair a second shampooing just because she could. Then she ordered the water off her body (though she kept her hair damp for easier brushing) and, both thoroughly clean and wide awake at last, stepped out onto the bath mat. *They'll probably let him out today*, she thought, pulling on her robe. *I'll go by his house after school. I have to tell him about the second shard. He'll understand about Flish...and why I couldn't come see him.*

Won't he?

But when she finally made her way downstairs, her plans changed. Aunt Phyllis, resplendent in a bright green dress, hair swept up into a formidable grey wave, was just setting out cereal and milk on the kitchen table. She straightened as Ariane entered and faced her, hands on her hips, mouth a thin, straight line.

Uh oh, Ariane thought. That look could only mean one thing: her aunt had somehow found out about last night.

The situation seemed to call for a preemptive strike. "I need to tell you something, Aunt Phyllis," she said. "I didn't tell you the truth yesterday. I wasn't late because of polynomials." *Hey, I said it right!* "I was attacked." Ariane told the story as simply and completely as she could, leaving out only her confrontation with the demon, since she'd never told Aunt Phyllis about that problem in the first place. "I didn't have any choice," she finished. "It was the only way to save myself and the shard too."

Aunt Phyllis listened without speaking. When Ariane was done, she said, "Why didn't you tell me last night?"

"I was so tired, and scared and...I just didn't want to deal with it. I'm sorry."

Aunt Phyllis looked away from the table, at nothing in particular, then looked back again. "Ariane, you have to start trusting me," she said. "I'm the only adult who knows your secret...well, except for Rex Major," she flashed a small smile, "and despite what children's books would have you believe, adults can be a great deal of use in the real world, especially when you're not even old enough to get a driver's licence or hold a full-time job."

"I know," Ariane said. "I'm sorry."

Aunt Phyllis turned back to the table and continued laying out spoons and bowls. "Those poor girls," she said. "Ariane, this power of yours...I know you were defending yourself and the shard, but...what if you'd killed one of them?" She stopped, leaning on the table with both hands. "I don't care about your quest," she said, her voice sounding old and strained. "I care about *you*. I don't want you hurt. And I don't want you hurting other people." She suddenly slammed her palms on the table, making Ariane jump. "Damn the Lady of the Lake! Why couldn't she leave our family alone? First your mother, and now...." She pressed her lips tightly together again.

Ariane said nothing. She had no answer.

After a long moment, Aunt Phyllis took a deep breath, straightened and turned toward Ariane. "Promise me," she said. "Promise me you won't hurt anyone else!"

Ariane thought back to how it had felt on the tennis courts, the way the shard had seized on her anger, amplified it. She remembered its rage-filled call: *Kill your enemy!*

"Aunt Phyllis, I..." Her throat closed on the words. "I...I promise," she said at last. "I promise to try."

Aunt Phyllis's mouth quirked. "'There is no try,'" she said. "'Do, or do not.'" The tiny smile vanished before Ariane had quite gotten her head around the fact her old-fashioned aunt had just quoted Yoda. "But I suppose that's the best I can hope for." She snorted. "And even though I wish you hadn't hurt them, at least maybe now Felicia and her friends will leave you alone." She went back to the counter and picked up a bowl of bananas, grapes and apples. "Any..." she hesitated as if searching for the right words, "...um, news on the location of the second shard?" She put the fruit bowl on the table and gestured for Ariane to have a seat.

"I think so," said Ariane, pulling out her chair and sitting down. She reached for the cereal. "In the shower, I...heard it. And when I held the first shard, I heard it a lot better. It's somewhere east. A long way east."

"How far?" Aunt Phyllis said, taking her own seat.

"Europe, at least," Ariane said. "Maybe even farther."

"Oh!" Aunt Phyllis paused in the act of pouring cornflakes into her bowl. "Not a problem for Rex Major. But...airplanes are expensive, Ariane. And hotels, food, transportation.... We don't have that much money."

"I know," said Ariane. "I'm going to talk to Wally about it today. He might have an idea. They should be letting him out of the hospital –"

Aunt Phyllis set the milk back down on the table with a thump. "Wally's in the hospital? Ariane, how many other bombshells are you going to drop on me this morning? What happened?"

Ariane blinked. She'd completely forgotten she hadn't told Aunt Phyllis about Wally. She hurriedly explained. "I wanted to go see him last night, but after everything else...and I was so tired...so I thought I'd go to his house after school –"

Aunt Phyllis smiled a little. "No need to wait that long," she said. "School's been cancelled."

Ariane blinked. "What? Why? It's not a holiday –"

"Water-main break," Aunt Phyllis said. Her mouth quirked again. "Under the tennis courts, if you can imagine. No water in either Oscana or St. Dunstan's, therefore no bathrooms. Can't pen up several hundred teenagers all day without bathrooms."

Ariane smiled weakly. "Oops."

Aunt Phyllis chuckled. "I doubt any of your classmates would hold it against you, if they knew. In any event, you can go see Wally this morning. He must be wondering why you haven't been to visit him." Her voice softened. "And you can check on Flish while you're there."

Ariane stared at her in shock. "She's not going to want to see *me!*"

"She can't stop you," Aunt Phyllis pointed out. "Go see her, Ariane. Someone needs to extend an olive branch. She's Wally's sister, after all."

"I'd rather chew glass."

"Ariane –"

"All right, all right!" Ariane lifted her hands in surrender. "I'll talk to her. But if she throws a bedpan at me... especially a full one...I'm out of there."

"Good girl." Aunt Phyllis stood up. "I wish I could come with you, but I'm going to be late for my committee meeting if I don't get going."

"Be careful," Ariane said. "I bet one of Rex Major's cronies is keeping an eye on us."

Aunt Phyllis gave her an odd look. "'Be careful'? Isn't that my line?"

Ariane paused. She hadn't told Aunt Phyllis about the demon, so she couldn't tell her she was worried that Rex Major might try something more...*direct*...now the demon was gone.

"It's just that, after last night, things seem even more dangerous than I thought," she finally said.

"Certainly for anyone who tries to attack *you*," Aunt Phyllis said, "but I doubt Rex Major is going to have mercenaries storm the basement of First Presbyterian Church to get at *me*. But all right, yes, I'll be careful. Now finish your breakfast, then go see Wally and Flish. If they do let Wally out, see if he'll come to dinner. Then we can talk about this second shard and how you're going to get to...wherever it is you have to go."

She bustled out, leaving Ariane alone with her cornflakes and thoughts.

Visiting hours at the hospital didn't begin until ten. It was only a fifteen-minute walk, so she had well over an hour to kill. She spent part of it experimenting with the first shard, trying to pinpoint the location of the second, but it remained maddeningly imprecise: somewhere over the ocean, not due east, but a bit south. She also sensed, without really knowing how – this whole magic thing was still awfully new to her – that although it wasn't close to the coast, it wasn't an immense distance inland. She *thought* that pointed to Europe rather than somewhere even farther east.

She couldn't use the computer to check: Aunt Phyllis had cancelled their Internet service. Considering Rex Major had used it to send a demon disguised as a computer-game monster into Ariane's bedroom, she couldn't really blame her. But in the third bedroom upstairs – in a room nobody had slept in in years and which had therefore collected all kinds of junk – Ariane had seen an old, dusty globe. She retrieved it and took it into her room. Sitting on her bed, she ran her finger from Regina along the fiftieth parallel of latitude across the Atlantic, her finger coming to rest more or less on the city of Frankfurt in Germany. Then she pushed her finger a little ways south – *not too far,* she thought – and encountered France.

She removed her finger and looked at it. *France,* she thought. It looked small compared to Canada, but then most countries did. If she remembered correctly from geography, the country was roughly the same size as Saskatchewan. *I just need to get to France,* she thought. *Then I'll be close enough to pinpoint the location of the second shard...and use streams and rivers to travel to it.*

We'll talk about it tonight, Aunt Phyllis had said. Ariane glanced at her clock radio. Time to go see Wally...and Flish. *Aunt Phyllis is right*, she thought. *She hates me, and I hate her...but she* is *Wally's sister.*

During the walk she debated which Knight sibling to see first, finally deciding, as she climbed up the slight hill that led to the main entrance of Regina General Hospital, to start with Flish. That way when she saw Wally she could tell him she'd already been to see his sister, and maybe then he'd be more willing to forgive her for putting Flish in the hospital in the first place.

They started it, she thought defensively. *I was only protecting myself and the shard.*

Or was the shard *protecting itself?*

She stopped just inside the sliding doors of the main entrance so suddenly she was almost run over by an orderly pushing an empty wheelchair. "Sorry," she said, and stepped to one side. *Was I using the shard, or was the shard using me?* She wasn't sure which idea was more unsettling.

She pulled herself together and went to the information desk.

Five minutes later she was staring at the open door of Flish's room. A passing nurse gave her a suspicious look, but it took Ariane another minute or two to work up the nerve to finally step inside.

Flish lay on the bed in her private room, face pale, head bandaged, one eye swollen shut. She had an IV hooked up to her arm, and her right leg was elevated by a metal contraption hung from the ceiling. It looked rather like a medieval torture device. Ariane gazed at her silently for a moment, then cleared her throat.

Flish's good eye opened. She blinked, then turned her face toward Ariane. At first she had a confused, vulnerable expression that made her look like a small child, but as soon as she recognized Ariane that look hardened into pinched fury. "What do *you* want?" she snarled. "Come to finish me off?"

"I came to say I'm sorry," Ariane said. "I never wanted to hurt you." *That's a lie*, an inner voice said, but Ariane ignored it; it would have been more accurate to say she'd never wanted to hurt Flish *this* badly, but she could hardly say *that*. "You forced me to."

"You and your tricks. I don't know how you did it, but sooner or later..."

Ariane shook her head, exasperated. "Flish, stop! You're not the only one I hurt last night. Next time it could be worse. Let it go. Leave me alone, and I'll leave you alone."

Flish's angry expression didn't soften. "Get out," she said. "Or I'll call a nurse to throw you out."

Ariane felt a flash of fury. The shard against her skin blazed in response, and she gasped in sudden fear, using the terror of what she might do to tamp down her rage before it could blossom. "Have it your way," she choked out. "I came to see Wally anyway." She turned and headed out the door.

"Stay away from my brother!" Flish shouted after her, but Ariane ignored her.

I tried, she thought, anger bubbling inside her again, despite her best efforts to control it, as she strode toward the elevator. *I tried to make peace. It's up to her if she wants to or not.*

Then her fear rose to the top of her emotional cauldron again, pushing aside the anger. *For her sake, she'd better. I almost killed her with just* one *shard of Excalibur. What would have happened had I had two...or the whole sword? If just the* tip *of the sword could overpower my own judgment, how will I ever handle the whole thing?*

She remembered how much she'd revelled in the feeling of power as she'd lashed out on the tennis court, and her stomach churned.

The elevator door opened. She stepped inside and pushed the button for Wally's floor.

◀◀ ▶▶

Wally sat on the edge of his bed, fully dressed, feeling almost like his usual self (though he suspected that was due to that morning's welcome dose of painkillers), waiting for the doctor to release him. He wasn't allowed to walk home, and Mrs. Carson (naturally), wasn't able to drive him because it was daytime and she cleaned houses during the day. So the nurse had promised to call a taxi for him.

He was staring idly at the floor, wondering where the hospital had gotten that particularly ugly mottled-blue floor tile, when a pair of black runners entered his vision. He blinked, then raised his eyes. Black jeans, dark-green T-shirt, black nylon jacket...and startlingly blue eyes framed by long black hair.

Ariane.

"About time," he said, and then wished he hadn't. He sounded like a pouty little kid.

"I'm sorry," Ariane said. "I wanted to come see you last night, but...something happened."

"Yeah, I heard," Wally said. Anger welled up like bile in his throat. "You were busy almost killing my sister."

"I didn't mean to..."

She can't control the power of the shard, he could almost hear Merlin saying. *Or the powers my sister gave her....*

He tried to push that voice away, but the memory of it gave an added edge to the anger he felt as he looked at Ariane. Her expression was serious, her eyes locked on his face, searching for his reaction. *At least that's something*, he thought. He didn't think he could have stood it if she'd actually seemed *proud* of what she had done.

"You didn't mean to? *Then why did you?* You don't just rip open a water pipe and toss people around like rag dolls by *accident!*"

"Shhh!" Ariane shot a worried look at the old man in the next bed, but as usual he was asleep and snoring. Wally had come to hate that snore over the past two nights.

"He can't hear," Wally said. "Even when he's awake he can't hear." He shook his head, and winced: the painkillers hadn't killed *all* the pain. "Ariane, I know she's a bully, but she's my sister –"

"I know," Ariane said. "But they jumped me, her and Shania and those other two, Stephanie and Cassandra..."

How come she *can remember their names when I never can?*

"...and I've been so tired and drained, I had nothing to fight back with...." Her voice dropped almost to a whisper. "Except the shard."

"You could have killed them." Wally's throat closed suddenly. *Once I thought the world revolved around my big sister. She hasn't always been the way she is now. And maybe someday she'll find her way back to being the big sister she used to be.*

But not if she's dead.

And after all the times Ariane had *almost* hurt Flish, and now that she finally *had*, he no longer trusted Ariane to make sure that didn't happen.

Then she surprised him. "I know," she said. "And I apologized to her."

Wally blinked "You *talked* to her?"

"Before I came in here," Ariane said. "She didn't really want to listen, but I said I was sorry."

A little bit of the ice that seemed to grip Wally's heart melted. "Thank you," he said.

"Well, you look pretty healthy to me," a man's voice boomed from the doorway, and Wally looked past Ariane at the broad, black smiling face of Dr. Kipkoskei. "Who is this? Your girlfriend?"

"No," said Wally and Ariane together.

Dr. Kipkoskei laughed. "If you say so." He came over to Wally. "Well, young man? How do you feel?"

"My head still hurts," Wally said. "But otherwise I'm okay."

"I'll be the judge of that." For the next few minutes the doctor examined him, shining a light in his eyes, testing his reflexes, listening to his heart, having him follow a finger back and forth with his eyes. He studied the chart at the foot of the bed. "Vitals are good, everything else checks out...I think you're good to go," Dr. Kipkoskei said. He gave Wally a stern look. "But concussions are nothing to sneeze at, my boy. Do you do sports?"

"Fencing," Wally said. "I'm supposed to be in a tournament in a couple of weeks."

Dr. Kipkoskei shook his head. "I'm not clearing you for anything that soon," he said. "You're not likely to hit your head fencing, but you'll probably find your reaction time is off for a while. I'd say you shouldn't even attempt to return to *practice* until next week. There's a good chance you'll have some occasional balance problems for a few days, too."

Wally stared at the doctor. He'd just assumed that once he was out of the hospital he'd be back to normal. People in books and movies never seemed to suffer any lasting effects from being hit on the head. Not fence in the tournament? For a moment, that seemed like the worst thing that had happened so far. *It's not fair!* he thought, and then reminded himself he was trying not to sound like a pouty little kid.

But it still isn't fair.

"Anything else?" he said, almost afraid to find out.

"Attention span, memory and non-verbal problem-solving abilities may also suffer," the doctor said.

Wally resisted the urge to say, "I'm sorry, I lost you halfway through that." Instead, he just said, "Oh."

"I said 'may,'" Dr. Kipkoskei said, putting his hand on his shoulder. "That's not the same as 'will.' So far you've bounced back pretty well." He looked at Ariane. "Are you here to take him home?"

"They're calling me a taxi," Wally said before Ariane could answer.

"As long as they don't call you late for dinner," the doctor said, and chuckled at his own joke. Wally exchanged a pained look with Ariane. Dr. Kipkoskei cleared his throat, and said, "All right then, young man, you're free to go. The nurse will give you care instructions and my office will call with a follow-up appointment...but if you feel any after-effects, it's important you come to see me right away. And watch out for ice from now on. Promise?"

"I promise," said Wally.

Dr. Kipkoskei gave him a friendly grin, nodded to Ariane, and swept out.

"Let's get out of here," Wally said.

A few minutes later, clutching a plastic bag containing the doctor's instructions and a three-day painkiller prescription, Wally was in the elevator with Ariane. He wanted to see Flish again, so he pushed the button for her floor.

"I'll wait here," Ariane said as they left the elevator. Wally handed her his plastic bag without a word, and went off to see his sister.

When he stepped into her room she was staring out the window at the grey November sky. He cleared his throat, and she turned to look at him. He winced. Her face was still blotched and bruised, one eye still swollen shut. "Hi," he said.

"Hi, yourself," she said. "Mrs. Carson told me you were here."

"She told me you were too."

They stared at each other. "I'm sorry about what happened," Wally said finally. "But you shouldn't have tried to jump her. Haven't you figured out by now she's dangerous?"

"I still say they're tricks of some kind."

"Tricks that almost got you killed," Wally pointed out. "Flish, you've got to leave her alone. There's..." His voice trailed off. *I can't tell her the truth*, he thought. *She'd never believe me.* "It's not safe."

Flish's eyes narrowed. "Are you still going to hang out with her after *this*? After she almost killed me?"

Wally said nothing.

"Well, if you do, tell her this," Flish snarled. "She's rid of me for now, but I'll be waiting for my chance. And someday, she'll be the one that ends up in a hospital!"

Wally felt cold. "Flish, this is nuts. She doesn't *want* to fight you. You and Shania started this. Just leave her alone!"

"After this? No chance."

Wally stared at her, wondering how Flish had become ...*this*. But in fact, he thought he had a pretty good idea.

It's not really Ariane she hates, he thought. *It's Mom and Dad.*

Wally read a lot, and not just fantasy novels. In some science book or other he'd read about what psychologists called displacement, where aggression was redirected to something that had no connection to the real source of the person's anger.

It's a textbook case, he thought. But looking at Flish's narrowed eyes and tight lips, he didn't think she'd appreciate his amateur psychoanalysis.

"I'll tell her, Felicia," he said. It was the first time in months he'd used her given name instead of the nickname she hated. "But please, just...think about what I said. I don't want you getting hurt again...hurt *worse*. And you could be." He thought of the giant shovel Ariane had toppled at the diamond mine in the Northwest Territories. "Believe me."

"I appreciate your concern, Wally," Flish said, and for once there was almost no sarcasm in her voice. "But this is between her and me. I *owe* her. And I *will* pay her back. I don't know when, or how...but I *will*."

Wally sighed. It was hopeless. "They're letting me out," he said, changing the subject. "How long will you be in here?"

"A week, at least. And then crutches until Christmas."

"Do you need anything? Books? Your iPod? Clothes?"

Flish shook her head. "Mrs. Carson already brought me everything. I'm good."

"All right. I'll drop by again tomorrow," Wally said.

"Bring me a Subway sandwich and some chips when you do," Flish said. "Hospital food sucks."

Wally smiled a little. "Tell me about it." He waved and went back out to the corridor.

Ariane put down a five-year-old *Reader's Digest* and rose from a green vinyl chair next to the elevator. "Well?"

"She still says she's going to 'get you,' someday," Wally said wearily. "But she's going to be on crutches for weeks, too. Maybe she'll cool down by the time she's back to normal."

"If she wants to come after me she'll have to get in line behind Rex Major," Ariane said. She pushed the elevator button. "Well, at least I don't have to worry about her for a while."

The doors opened. They moved aside as an old man pushed out an even older woman in a wheelchair, then stepped into the elevator together. As the door closed, Ariane looked at Wally, her blue eyes wide and bright in the fluorescent light. "I felt...*heard*...the second shard," she said in a low voice.

He felt a kind of electric shock run up his arms. "Where is it?" he whispered back.

"A long way away." She took a deep breath. "Somehow we're going to have to get across the Atlantic...to Europe, I think. Probably France."

Wally said nothing. Two days ago he would have been thrilled. Two days ago he would have said, "So what are we waiting for? Let's go!"

But two days ago Ariane hadn't put his sister in the hospital. Two days ago that little worm of doubt hadn't yet wriggled into his mind. Two days ago he hadn't begun to wonder if Ariane could really control the Lady's power and the shard of Excalibur.

Ariane was looking at him oddly, obviously waiting for him to say something, and he suddenly felt angry – not at her, but at himself. She was his friend. She'd given up the shard once to save his life. If he could trust anyone, it was her.

And so he said the first thing that came into his mind. "Great! So book some plane tickets and let's go!"

The moment he'd said it, he realized how stupid that was. He knew Ariane didn't have the kind of money that would make running off to Europe something you did at the drop of a hat.

The elevator door opened. "And how do you propose we do that?" Ariane said as they walked together toward the front door. "Hold a bake sale? Collect donations outside the liquor store? 'Donate a dollar so Ariane can travel to Europe to defeat evil and save the world!'"

Wally laughed. "Sorry," he said. "That was stupid. Although I like the bake sale idea. I'd love to see the posters."

Ariane stopped walking and put a hand on his arm, bringing him to a halt too. "Do you..." She hesitated. "Do you have the money?" She turned red as she said it, and

Wally wished again he'd never said anything about buying plane tickets.

"Yes and no," he answered reluctantly. "Truth is, I have *lots* of money...but it's in a trust fund, and I can't get at it until I'm twenty-one. There's a household account that Mrs. Carson can draw on for food and stuff, but I can't touch that. I do get a monthly allowance, which is plenty for ordinary stuff...and enough that Flish keeps trying to extort it from me...but it's not enough for plane tickets. Not unless I save it up for six or seven months. We probably can't wait that long."

A taxi pulled up outside, and Wally went out to meet it. The passenger side window rolled down as he approached, and he stuck his head though the opening. "I'm Wally Knight," he said. "Are you here for me?"

"Yes, sir," said the driver.

Wally turned to Ariane. "Get in," he said. "We can talk more at my house."

He held the door open for Ariane, who climbed into the back seat and then slid over to make room for him. "Harrington Mews," he told the driver.

As the taxi pulled away from the hospital, Wally glanced at Ariane. She had her head turned away from him, staring out the window. Her long black hair, tumbling loose around her shoulders, shone like ebony in the morning sun. As he watched, she reached up her right hand and absentmindedly brushed the hair back from her ear, exposing the graceful line of her neck. A faint herbal scent came from her, shampoo or soap, and Wally suddenly wanted, more than anything, to protect her, to make sure she didn't get hurt. Very aware of the listening ears of the driver, though, all he said was, "We'll find a way. Don't worry."

And Rex Major, he thought, *can go hang.*

CHAPTER FIVE

UP, UP AND AWAY

THE CAB TURNED INTO HARRINGTON MEWS, the cul-de-sac just off the Albert Street Bridge where Wally lived. "Wait," Wally told the driver when they stopped. "I'll get some money from the house."

"No need," said the driver. "All paid."

Surprised, Wally joined Ariane on the sidewalk. "I guess Mrs. Carson took care of it with the hospital," he told her as the cab drove away. "I'm beginning to think I misjudged her." He snorted. "Of course, she'll probably make sure Flish goes home in a stretch limo."

Ariane hugged herself. "Can we talk inside?" she said. "I'm freezing."

"Sorry." Wally led her up the winding walk to the front door. Ariane had been there before, of course, but in the wake of their conversation about money he suddenly felt self-conscious about the size of his house: the largest on the cul-de-sac. Taking up two full lots that backed up against the Wascana Creek dike, it was practically a mansion compared to Aunt Phyllis's. He fished his key out of his jeans pocket, unlocked the door and showed her in.

"I'm starving," he said. He led the way into the kitchen

and pulled open the big stainless steel door of the refrigerator. "Ah," he said, spotting a plate covered with aluminum foil. "Just the thing." He took it out, peeled back the foil, and held it out to Ariane. "Want some?"

Ariane took one whiff of the pungent odor rolling off the plate and stepped back with an almost comical look of disgust. "What is that? It smells like old gym socks!"

"What?" Wally looked down at the slab of blue-veined cheese he'd uncovered. "It's just cheese. Really good stuff. Cave-ripened in France!"

"Urgh. No, thank you."

Wally shook his head. "No accounting for taste." He picked up a big piece of the cheese and popped it in his mouth, then put the plate on the counter and turned back to the refrigerator, pulling out bread, dill pickles, onions and summer sausage and two cans of Diet Coke. "Do you want a sandwich at least? I can leave off the cheese."

"No, I'm fine," Ariane said. "Thanks anyway."

"No problem." Wally set to work on his own sandwich. "So. France. How do we get there?"

"I don't know," Ariane said. She took one of the cans of Diet Coke and popped it open. "I've been trying to figure it out. I can't use salt water, and even if I could, I don't think my strength would last all the way across the Atlantic."

Wally took a big bite of his sandwich and chewed while he thought. He swallowed. "What about the Arctic ice cap? Ice is fresh water."

Ariane shook her head. "Wally, you've travelled with me, you know how it works. I travel through liquid water. Not solid. It would be like trying to walk through a brick wall."

"Hmmm." Wally opened his own can of pop and took a gulp. The can was cold and wet with condensation... condensation...

"Eureka!" he shouted, then hesitated. "Well, maybe."

Ariane stared at him. "What?"

"Look." Wally put the can down and ran his finger over the wet side. "Condensation. You can purify water by evaporating it then condensing it. So..." He raised his eyes and looked out through the kitchen window. Though the day had started sunny, clouds were beginning to drift in from the west, big, fluffy grey clouds that made Wally wonder if snow was on the way.

"So?" Ariane prompted.

"So clouds are made of fresh water." He hesitated again, wondering if he was about to sound as if he'd gone crazy. "Have you tried...could you...travel through the clouds?"

◀ ▶

Ariane stared at Wally, then grinned. "I never thought about it." She felt a surge of excitement. "I don't know. I...wait a second."

She closed her eyes. A good night's sleep had done wonders. She could once again draw on her own power without reaching for the frightening energy of the shard. All the water nearby sang to her, shrill and metallic in the pipes of the house, deep and slow in sluggish Wascana Creek to the south, loud but placid in Wascana Lake, east of the Albert Street Bridge. But she had never thought of listening for the song of the clouds. She did so now, focusing her magical awareness on the sky...and there it was. Faint, hard to distinguish from the much stronger songs of the lake and creek, but unmistakable, like the *ting!* of a triangle cutting through the blare of a brass band...or the smell of Wally's blue cheese curling through a room full of roses.

She could hear it, but could she use it? With her magic

she tugged at the airborne water.

Wally gasped. "Wow," he said. She opened her eyes and followed his gaze out the window. Huge flakes of snow drifted lazily by as though someone had ripped open a feather pillow above the house.

She blinked. *I did that?* "Wow," she agreed.

"If this whole saving-the-world thing doesn't work out, you can always make a living as a rainmaker," Wally said. The flurry was already petering out. "I'm sure *that* will come in useful sometime." He turned back from the window. "Okay, so you can pull water down from the sky. But can you pull yourself up into the clouds? And then travel through them the same way you do through streams?" He laughed. "It sounds crazy, but I guess I'm asking you if you can fly, Supergirl."

"*Please* don't start calling me Supergirl." She chewed on her lip thinking about Wally's question. "I don't know. What if I got myself up there, but then couldn't hold it? If I rematerialized thousands of feet in the air..."

Wally winced. "Ouch." He shook his head. "Maybe not such a great idea."

"Maybe not," Ariane said, but inside she was thinking, *It may be the only way....*

She had to test it...but she didn't want Wally with her when she did. He'd want her to take him with her, and she wasn't sure she could do it by herself, much less with the dead weight of Wally trying to pull her back to Earth. It had been hard enough work pulling him through flowing water. *No,* she thought. *It's too dangerous. Once I've tried it myself, felt what it's like, then I'll know if I can take him with me.* She looked uneasily at Wally, who was gulping Diet Coke, his Adam's apple bobbing. *And what if I can't?*

She wouldn't even have *thought* of trying the clouds if he hadn't mentioned the possibility. The thought of going after the second shard alone terrified her. What else might she not think of? *I need his brains*, she thought, then had to laugh silently at herself: she sounded like a zombie.

All the same, if the only way to get to France proved to be through the clouds, and she couldn't take Wally with her...then she might not have any choice. She hated the thought of having to tell him she was leaving him behind almost as much as she hated the thought of setting off without him. He'd understand – of course he would – but he'd be horribly disappointed.

I'll cross that bridge when I come to it. First, I've got to find out if this crazy idea of his will work.

Wally gobbled down the rest of his sandwich, slugged down more Coke and then wiped his face with the back of his hand. "That's better! Hospital food..." He gave an exaggerated shudder.

"I'm sorry I didn't come last night," Ariane said. "I could have brought you pizza."

Wally sighed. "You could have brought me your aunt's chocolate-chip cookies. That's what I was *really* craving."

Ariane laughed. "I don't blame you. Who else dropped by?"

"Just the doctor, the nurses...and Mrs. Carson. Although she really came to see Flish. I was just an afterthought." His voice was casual, but Ariane knew Wally well enough by now to know how much that hurt.

"Did your parents call?"

Wally busied himself with the dishwasher. "No," he said.

"I'm sorry," Ariane said, wishing she hadn't asked.

"Me too." Wally closed the dishwasher and turned back to her. "Look," he said, "if the cloud idea is out, I don't see how we're going to get to Europe without buying plane tickets. Are you sure Aunt Phyllis can't help?"

Ariane shook her head. "We really don't have much money, Wally. Aunt Phyllis is on a fixed income and she already draws on her savings just to make ends meet." She glanced at the clock on the microwave oven. "And speaking of Aunt Phyllis, I've got to get home. She didn't expect me to be gone this long. She asked me to invite you to dinner tonight. We can figure things out then."

Wally brightened. "Chocolate-chip cookies?" he said.

Ariane laughed. "There are some in the freezer."

"I'm in!" Wally said, then winced and touched the gauze pad covering his stitches.

"Are you sure you're up to it?" Ariane said.

Wally waved the question away. "I'll take painkillers just before dinner," he said. "I'll be feeling great! As long as you're not planning to serve me alcohol or ask me to operate heavy machinery."

Ariane laughed again. "I think I can promise you neither of those will be on the menu."

A few minutes later she was on her way home, passing through the graffiti-scrawled tunnel beneath the Albert Street Bridge to the bike path that circled Wascana Lake. She walked along the lake's north shore, empty except for a few joggers and some laggardly Canada geese that hadn't yet gotten around to flying south. She should have turned north at the playground to get to College Avenue, the most direct route home, but instead she kept going until she reached the parking lot from which she had first seen the staircase descending into the lake. She climbed onto one of the giant stones that separated the parking lot from the lake and stared at the slate-grey water between her and Willow Island. The lake's surface rippled where the Lady had appeared, but that was only because of the light but steady breeze sweeping across the lake beneath the overcast sky. Ice crusted the shore at her feet. *There's so much you didn't tell me*, Ariane said silently to the absent Lady. *This shard is in France. The next could be in the Himalayas or on Easter Island. How am I supposed to get to them? How am I supposed to finish this quest?*

There was no answer, of course. The last vestiges of the Lady's presence had been driven out of the world by Rex Major. Ariane was on her own.

Not quite, she thought. *Not quite. I've got Wally. And Aunt Phyllis.*

But for how long? Major had already threatened Wally to get to the shards. He hadn't done anything since they'd retrieved the first shard...but that was no guarantee he wouldn't try again in the future.

I may not always have Aunt Phyllis's or Wally's help, Ariane thought. *I have to be prepared to finish this quest on my own.*

The thought, though cold and sharp as shattered ice, brought with it a kind of clarity.

I have to try the clouds. Ariane looked up at the grey curtain hanging over the city. *It may be the only way to get to France.* She glanced around. Nobody was in sight. And where better to test her power again than here, where it had first come to her?

She closed her eyes and listened for the cloud-song.

At first, just as before, she couldn't find it – the *fortissimo* chorus of the lake at her feet overwhelmed the *pianissimo* music of those tiny drops of water suspended far above. It was like trying to hear the sound made by a single drop of water falling into a still pool above the roar of a waterfall.

But in the same way that the musical *plink* of a falling drop was so different from the deep thunder of the falls, she found that if she concentrated hard enough, she could distinguish the song of the clouds from the song of the lake, even when she stood on the lake's frozen shore.

Of course she wasn't really hearing songs at all: her awareness of the water came through a sixth sense, one she didn't have a word for. But her brain *interpreted* it as sound, and she found that the more she concentrated on the faint, lilting soprano of the clouds, the less overwhelming the *basso profondo* growl of the lake became. The cloud-song high above called to her, urged her to join it...so she did.

She would have gasped with surprise, if she still had lungs. Her body vanished, yet she still sensed it: rushing up and out from where she had stood, growing broad as a house, tall as a skyscraper, yet insubstantial as...well, as a cloud. The ground fell away, the lake shrinking until it seemed no more than a pond surrounded by toy buildings. The air embraced her as she rose, holding her aloft in firm but incorporeal arms.

The sensation was completely different from when she dissolved into water. She never felt herself change size in water, even though her body and everything she wore or carried weren't really there at all (she'd given up trying to figure out where they really *were*; in fact, she preferred not to think about it), even when she knew she was passing through pipes far too small to accommodate her. Now, though, she felt like a disembodied spirit floating high above the earth.

The sensation both exhilarated and terrified her. Every time she joined water she felt it calling to her, urging her to let her consciousness dissolve into it as her body did, to become one with it. Here in the clouds that deadly nihilistic urge was greater than ever. It took enormous effort to maintain her sense of self, to keep her mind intact. It would be so much easier to just join the cloud, to enter the endless cycle of evaporation and condensation...to leave behind the grief of her mother's disappearance, the challenges of school, the hopeless quest for the shards of Excalibur...

Let them go, the clouds seemed to say. *Turn your memories to mist, your fear to fog...let longings evaporate, sorrow dissolve, thoughts whisper into nothingness... nothingness...*

Pain stabbed her: a hard, sharp pain. *How can a cloud feel pain?* she thought. With that question, her sense of self solidified, and she felt a stab of terror as well as pain as she realized what had almost happened...and what had saved her. The shard wasn't about to let *itself* dissolve into the clouds. It clung stubbornly to its existence, even though for the moment it was no more solid than she was, and she in turn now clung to it, coalescing her thoughts around it like an oyster forming a pearl around a grain of sand, layer by layer, until she could think clearly again.

The magic the Lady had bequeathed to her was many things, but "safe" was not one of them.

The cloud she had joined had drifted with her thoughts. She looked down at big-box stores like scattered building blocks and trucks, tiny as toys, on the Trans-Canada Highway on the eastern edge of town, then out at the vast, flat prairie beyond.

So. She could join the clouds. But drifting as slowly as a cloud would not get her to France. How fast *could* she travel? She and Wally had flashed along the waterways to the Northwest Territories in a matter of minutes, not hours.

Well, there was only one way to find out. She mentally held fast to the shard, looked east, and...pushed.

A flashing sense of movement, of fog and rain rushing past, a tumbling chaos of updrafts and downdrafts and...she pulled herself to a halt, and took stock.

Below her spread another city, far larger than Regina, a river winding through it. Atop a domed building like the Legislative Building on Wascana Lake, though smaller, she saw the golden statue of a nude boy.

Winnipeg, she thought in wonder. *Hundreds of kilometres in a few seconds.*

But could she return? She looked west, pictured Wascana Lake in her mind and once again...pushed.

It was harder moving in this direction, against the prevailing winds; but within moments she sensed the lake beneath her, pulled herself to a halt, and gazed once again at Regina...or what she could see of it: thick snow was now falling from all around her down to the city. *Did I do that? What* else *could I do using the clouds?*

But those were questions and experiments for another day. For the moment, only one thing mattered. *I can get to France*, she thought with excitement. *I can get to the second shard!*

The thrill lasted only as long as it took her to realize something else: She had no idea how to get down.

Think it through! She mentally tugged at her nebulous extremities, and felt them start to rush back toward her. She stopped that instantly. So she could materialize right where she was if she wanted to. But since she would then plunge to her death, she *really* didn't want to.

Reverse the leap from earth to cloud, she told herself. *Do what you already know how to do: materialize in water deep enough to submerge you.*

She rushed downward. The lake swelled, black water filling her vision...

With an explosion of spray she materialized right in front of two startled little girls feeding geese. The frightened birds lumbered away, honking as the water around them erupted.

Ariane staggered to the bank. "Fell in," she said brightly to the little girls, who watched open-mouthed as she squished off, dripping.

Once she was out of sight behind some caragana bushes, she ordered the water off her body and clothes. The snow she had begun high above began to fall around her. She looked up at the clouds, awed all over again by the power of the Lady...and the power of Excalibur, whose fierce magic had saved her from her own folly.

I can do it, she thought again. *I can get to Europe. I can get anywhere in the world the shards are located, as fast as or faster than Merlin. I can beat him!*

She set off for home through the already failing flurry, excited to share her discovery with Wally.

But hard on the heels of her excitement arrived another thought. *Maybe you* shouldn't *share this with Wally. Maybe you should just go. Grab the shard, bring it back. Don't involve Wally. Don't involve Aunt Phyllis. Keep them safe....*

She stopped walking, heedless of her whereabouts. A cyclist shouted angrily and rang his bell as he zigzagged around her, but she hardly noticed. Head off to who-knew-where, all by herself, without even telling her best friend and her only relative? Not twenty minutes after she'd been telling herself how much she needed Wally? What was she thinking? *Of course* she would tell Wally. And Aunt Phyllis. "You have to start trusting me," her aunt had said to her just that morning.

She would also have to tell Wally that she couldn't take him with her. She knew it without even having tried it, just as she knew the limitations of her physical body. It took all her energy to hold herself up there against the force of gravity; she would have none to spare for Wally. She could no more lift him with her into the clouds than she could pick him up and throw him. But just because she might have to leave him behind didn't mean she could just run off without even talking to him about it.

She gave her head a shake, wondering what had come over her, and resumed walking. *Was that the shard influencing my thoughts?* The shiver that ran through her had nothing to do with the cold.

◄◄ ►►

At about the same time Ariane was splashing out of Was-cana Lake, Rex Major, without taking his eyes away from the message that had just appeared on his computer screen, touched his Bluetooth earpiece. "Gwen," he said, and a moment later, his secretary's voice responded.

"Yes, Mr. Major?"

"I'm moving up the time frame for my trip to France. Please contact my pilot and have him file a flight plan to Lyon. I'd like to leave by –" he checked the clock "– 5 p.m. Also, please book a hotel for me in Lyon and arrange for a car and driver."

There was a pause, slight, but enough to know he had just shocked his usually unflappable secretary. "Sir, your appointments next week? You're meeting with the Department of Defence in Ottawa on Tuesday, and the Pentagon is expecting you in Washington on Wednesday –"

"I'll be back by then," Major said. "This will be a very quick trip."

"Is this a personal or business trip, sir?" said Gwen, her voice betraying none of the curiosity she must be feeling.

"Both," he said. *Business enough that the company can pay for the trip, anyway*, he thought. "There's been a major discovery of ancient rock art in a cavern in the Ardèche. I'm considering donating funds for its preservation."

Dead silence on the other end. Then, "Rock art, sir?"

Major laughed. "I'm glad I can still surprise you after all these years, Gwen. I wouldn't want to be boring."

"You're never that, sir," said Gwen. "Very well, Mr. Major, I'll make the arrangements."

"Thank you, Gwen." He disconnected, but his smile didn't fade. He'd thought he'd have to search for the shard when he arrived in France, which could have taken days or even weeks. But the computers had done the job for him. He knew precisely where the shard was. All he had to do was go and retrieve it. *It's mine*, he thought fiercely. He pushed away the paperwork on his desk and rose to his feet. If he were leaving for France in a few hours, he had a lot to prepare.

◄◄ ►►

Wally approached Ariane's house with a mixture of excitement and apprehension. The excitement came from the realization that the quest that had seemed to have ended when they returned from the Northwest Territories had begun anew; the apprehension came from the secret he now kept, of Merlin's phone call to him in the hospital...and that, though he had hung up on the sorcerer, he hadn't completely dismissed what Merlin had said.

Everybody has secrets, Wally thought. *Ariane must have lots. It doesn't mean I'm not on her side.*

I'm just not sure the side she's on is the right one.

He walked past the tipsy garden gnome at the base of the old spruce tree, and on impulse stopped and straightened the little ceramic figure before continuing up the walk to the front door. He rang the doorbell.

Aunt Phyllis answered. A huge smile lit her face, framed by upswept grey hair. "Wally! I'm so glad to see you. None the worse for wear, I hope?"

"I feel fine," Wally said, which was the truth. The painkillers had done their job. He'd taken two more than the recommended daily dose, but he didn't want to be distracted by a headache during their discussion of the second shard. *I'll skip the bedtime pill to make up for it*, he thought.

Aunt Phyllis showed him into the dining room. Ariane grinned at him from her seat at the table. "I made 'mustard-smeared protein' again," Aunt Phyllis said, and Wally grinned, remembering that was what Ariane called her aunt's signature dish of meat or fish coated and roasted with grainy mustard and herbs. "But this time it's trout, not pork. Grab a seat."

Wally sat down opposite Ariane. He glanced at the door to the kitchen to make sure Aunt Phyllis was out of sight, then leaned forward and murmured, "Anything new?"

She nodded. "Yes," she said. "Something big." Her grin widened. "But I'll tell you after dinner...and Aunt Phyllis too."

"Tell me what?" said Aunt Phyllis, as she brought in a long silver tray covered with a domed lid.

"After dinner," Ariane said firmly.

The trout was delicious, and the rice and edamame beans that went with it hit the spot as well. It was all a bit healthier than Wally was used to eating – his taste ran more to burgers and fries – but he had to admit it was good.

"How's your sister, Wally?" Aunt Phyllis asked as they ate.

"Mrs. Carson says she's doing okay."

"I'll bet she's had lots of visitors," Ariane said. "Starting with the rest of the 'coven.'"

Aunt Phyllis frowned at her. "You know I don't like you calling them that."

"Sorry, Aunt Phyllis."

"Actually, no," Wally said. He picked up another edamame bean and popped the husk between his forefinger and thumb. "Mrs. Carson told me they haven't been to see her at all. Flish said they won't talk to her on the phone either. Apparently she's very upset about it." *He* sure wasn't. Maybe if the coven broke up, Flish would leave Ariane alone. He squeezed the beans into his mouth and chewed thoughtfully. *Maybe she'll even move back home*, he thought, then frowned. He wasn't sure that was an entirely happy notion.

"I guess the other three finally saw sense," Ariane muttered.

"'Sense' isn't something I associate with Shania, or...or the other two," Wally said. "But maybe." *I hope so,* he added silently. *For all their sakes.* He watched Ariane take a long swallow of milk. *And yours too.*

And now that he thought about it, quite possibly *his.*

Dinner out of the way, they moved to the living room, where Ariane and Wally sat side by side on the couch and Aunt Phyllis in her favourite flowery chair. Ariane cleared her throat, then said, "Wally already knows this, Aunt Phyllis, but I haven't had a chance to tell you. I've got a better idea where the second shard is."

Aunt Phyllis, in the act of pouring tea from a silver teapot, paused and then resumed pouring. "And where is that, dear?" she said.

"Southern France, I think."

Aunt Phyllis put down the teapot and picked up her cup. She frowned a little as she raised it to her lips. "You *think?*" she said, then sipped.

"I can't pinpoint it without getting closer," Ariane said. "There aren't any freshwater streams between here and there, obviously, and I need them to sense it. It's like rivers and lakes are..." She paused, frowning.

"Like the Internet," Wally said helpfully. "You have to be able to route the information from server to server, or you get a 404 error."

"Um...sure. Like that," Ariane said, giving him a raised-eyebrow look that he had no trouble translating as "Geek!"

"So first you have to get to France, and then you'll be able to home in on the second shard?" Aunt Phyllis picked up the plate of chocolate-chip cookies she'd brought into the living room and offered it to Wally. He grabbed two. *At last!* he thought. Aunt Phyllis smiled, then held the plate out to Ariane. "How do you plan to get there?"

Wally thought Ariane showed great self-restraint by picking up only a single cookie. She said, "I think I've got a way *I* can get there." She turned the cookie over and over in her hands, not looking at either Wally or her aunt. "But I can't take Wally with me," she finished in a small voice.

Shock rippled through Wally. Unbidden, Rex Major's words echoed in his head. *"She'll toss you aside like a broken hammer. And that will be the end of your part in this quest."*

"I can't travel through salt water," Ariane continued, still sounding subdued. "But Wally suggested something else. The clouds are fresh water. So he wondered if I could use them to travel...."

Aunt Phyllis put the plate of cookies down suddenly and awkwardly, as though it had become too heavy to hold. *"Fly?"*

"Kinda," Ariane said. "I tried it. It worked. I...joined with the clouds. Sort of like I can do with water but...different." She was silent for a moment, as though trying to figure out how to explain what she had felt. "It was scarier, that's for sure. I felt enormous, like a giant, but as insubstantial as a ghost."

"Ghost riders in the sky," Wally sang under his breath. Ariane shot him a questioning look. He shook his head. "Go on," he said. "Explain the part about not being able to take me with you."

"I just can't. I can feel it. You'd be...too heavy, I guess. I might get you up there, but I couldn't hold you. You could materialize thousands of metres up. Or maybe you'd just...turn into mist."

"And maybe *you* could, too," Aunt Phyllis snapped. "Ariane, this sounds far more dangerous than..."

"Than dissolving into the sewers and washing up on the shores of Hudson Bay?" Ariane shot back. "Aunt Phyllis, I know it's dangerous. But what choice do I have? I have to get the second shard. It'll be far more dangerous...for all of us...if Rex Major gets it first."

"Can't we test it?" Wally said. "Safely somehow? To see if maybe you're wrong. You haven't had your powers long. Maybe you can do more than you think. And with the shard to draw on –"

"I don't think it's a good idea," Ariane said. Her voice sharpened. "In fact, I'm sure it's not a good idea. No. We can't test it. I'm just going to have to go on my own. End of argument."

Wally blinked, taken aback. That sudden edge to Ariane's voice – that hadn't sounded like her at all.

"No, it isn't," Aunt Phyllis snapped. "You are *not* going on your own, and *that's* final. If you hadn't had Wally with you last time, Rex Major would have gotten the first shard. You need his help."

You tell her, Wally thought.

"But –" Ariane began.

"But nothing." Aunt Phyllis paused, as if thinking, then seemed to make up her mind and leaned forward. "I don't have a lot of money, but I have a paid-up credit card," she said. "Enough to get you both to France. The old-fashioned way: on a 747."

"No," Ariane said. "I can't let you use up your money to –"

"To save the world?" Aunt Phyllis said. "Isn't that what this is all about?"

"I'm the one the Lady –"

"No!" Wally snapped, with more heat than he intended. He tried to soften his tone. "No. We were *both* given this quest by the Lady. Me as well as you." He didn't say anything about doubting whether they should believe what the Lady had told them. "If you're going to obey the Lady, you're supposed to take me with you. *Always.*"

Ariane pursed her lips but didn't protest.

"Then it's settled," Aunt Phyllis said. "Wally, I'll give you my credit card. Can you book the flights, please? I had our Internet service disconnected. You and Ariane can figure out where you need to get to. You'll need to arrange a place to stay as well."

"Um...no," Wally said unhappily.

Aunt Phyllis and Ariane both stared at him. "Why not?" Aunt Phyllis said sharply.

"I can't use your credit card to book our flights. *Over the Internet.*" He emphasized the last three words.

Ariane blinked. "Oh."

Aunt Phyllis closed her eyes. "Oh. Of course." She shook her head. "I should have thought...then how?"

"Maybe you could do it at the library?" Ariane ventured. "No way for him to know you're the one using a public computer, right?"

"I wouldn't bet on it," Wally said. "The trouble is that we don't actually know just what Merlin's magic lets him do with computers. Even if I buy the tickets over the phone, they'll be entering information into a computer at the other end. What if Merlin's magic picks up on *that?*"

"At least there's a chance it won't," Aunt Phyllis said. "There's nothing you can do about that, anyway. There's no way to get a ticket without it going into the airline's computer system. You'll have to show ID when you fly, too, so you can't buy the tickets under fake names."

Wally thought hard. "We'll have to buy our tickets at the counter with cash, as close to flight time as we can," he said at last. "Even if Major has set something up to spot our names showing up on the airline's reservation system, at least he won't have much time to react."

Ariane suddenly sucked in a sharp breath. "No," she said. "Name. Singular."

Wally and Aunt Phyllis looked at her. "I'm sorry, Aunt Phyllis," she said. "I really am. But Wally is the only one who can fly 'the old-fashioned way.'" She spread her hands. "I'm wearing a sizeable piece of pointy metal strapped to my side under my clothes. Think security might be just a little freaked out about that?"

Wally winced. "I should have thought of that."

"Then...." Aunt Phyllis looked pale. "Ariane, can you really do it? Fly through the clouds? All the way to Europe?"

"All I can do is try, Aunt Phyllis," she said. "I just don't see any other way."

Aunt Phyllis was silent for a long moment. She ran a finger around the rim of her teacup. "I don't either." She shook her head. "I wish I could come with you, Wally, but my credit card won't cover food and accommodation for three of us in France. The one thing I *can* do is book a room for you in Lyon. I doubt they'd let two teenagers check in anywhere you'd want to stay if you just walked in and tossed cash down on the desk."

"But if you use the Internet –" Wally started, but subsided when Aunt Phyllis gave him a how-dumb-do-you-think-I-am? look.

"There's a thing called a telephone, Wally," she said. "And I can speak enough French to manage a hotel booking." She frowned suddenly. "Um. French. Ariane's grades are...not great in French."

"That's one way to put it," Ariane muttered.

"I can speak it fairly well," Wally said. "And I've been to France before." He felt almost embarrassed by that: there'd been no talk of a shortage of money when his whole family had gone three years ago, when he and Flish were still friends and so were Mom and Dad.

"Good."

Ariane was giving her aunt a strange look. "Aunt Phyllis, you're really...okay...with the two of us going off to France together? Alone?"

Aunt Phyllis put her teacup down on the table a little too hard. "Of course I'm not okay! But I don't see any choice. And besides..." She sighed. "Ariane, you can fly through the clouds, flow through rivers, and use water as a weapon. You both went to the Northwest Territories on your own and came back with a piece of King Arthur's magical sword. You're not a little girl anymore. I think you can manage France. Just...be careful."

Ariane looked so solemn that for a second Wally thought she was going to start crying, but all she said was, "I will," in that small voice again.

"There's another reason I should stay here," Aunt Phyllis went on. "Does Rex Major know yet where the second shard is?"

Ariane shook her head. "I have no idea."

Wally said nothing. The topic of Rex Major was not a comfortable one.

"Well, we shouldn't give him a clue, should we?" Aunt Phyllis continued. "He might find out when Wally buys his ticket...but he might not, especially if all of his spies are telling him you and Wally are somewhere else entirely...."

"Where?" Ariane said.

"Emma Lake."

"Emma Lake? But that old cabin hasn't been used in years!"

Aunt Phyllis shook her head. "*I* haven't used it in years," she said. "But I do rent it out. It supplements my pension. So it's quite livable, although admittedly more so in the summer than in November.

"So here's the plan: Wally *obviously* needs to rest after his concussion, so nobody will be expecting him at school for some time yet. His parents are away, and Mrs. Carson, from what Wally tells us, won't mind if someone else looks after him for a few days."

"Understatement of the year," Wally added.

"The principal has already phoned me to express concern about Ariane's health." Ariane blinked at her aunt; this was obviously news to her. Aunt Phyllis chuckled at her expression. "Ariane, you've been falling asleep at your desk. Teachers *do* notice that sort of thing."

"Especially if you snore," Wally said. Ariane shot him a look, and he put up his hands. "I'm just sayin'..."

Aunt Phyllis continued. "So the principal will understand when I tell him I'm taking Ariane out of school for a week to recuperate from...I'll call it a virus..."

"Mono?" Wally said without thinking, and then it was his turn to blush as Ariane gave him another withering look.

Aunt Phyllis smiled. "Maybe," she said. "Meanwhile, I'll tell Mrs. Carson that I'm taking both of you on a mini-vacation to Emma Lake. We'll load up the car exactly as if we're going to the cabin and we'll head toward Saskatoon. But you'll never get there."

"That sounds ominous," Wally couldn't help saying.

Aunt Phyllis laughed. "You won't get there because at Chamberlain you'll get out and wait for the bus going the other way. Back in Regina you'll go straight to the airport to catch your flight."

"What if we're followed?" Ariane said.

"On that road? If I drive the speed limit and a car stays behind us without passing, that'll be a dead give-away. We'll be more at risk of being rear-ended for driving so slow."

Wally grinned, but had to point out the obvious flaw. "If he's smart he *will* pass us and then pick us up again in Chamberlain or Davidson."

"So we take careful note of which cars pass us on the way to Chamberlain," Aunt Phyllis countered. "And if we see one waiting, we'll come up with a Plan B. There are other towns where you can catch the bus."

"I just thought of something else," Wally said. "We'll need passports. I've got one." He looked at Ariane questioningly.

She nodded. "I've got one, too. My mom took me to Mexico once, before she..." She trailed off.

Wally cleared his throat. "Good," he said. "Good."

And so it was settled. Aunt Phyllis would go to the bank and get a large cash advance on her credit card, then book a hotel in Lyon over the phone and pay for a week's stay in advance. As he walked back to his own house through the cold night, Wally reflected on the comforting fact that Ariane hadn't objected to his joining her in France, once they'd established she wouldn't have to try to transport him through the clouds.

She still needs me, he thought. *At least for now.*

◀◀ ▶▶

After Wally left, Ariane went through the usual going-to-bed motions, but she might as well have been a robot: she found herself under the covers without any clear memory of how she had got there. All her thoughts kept circling around what she had just promised to do.

Fly. Through the clouds. Across the Atlantic. Like Charles Lindbergh, but with something a lot less substantial than *The Spirit of St. Louis* to keep her in the air.

There were clouds all the way to Winnipeg, but what would happen when she hit a cloudless patch? Or if she ran out of strength halfway across the Atlantic?

She wished she could have flown with Wally. But the first shard, which she did not dare check in her luggage – what if Major knew they were coming and arranged to have it intercepted? – made that impossible. She was almost surprised she'd thought of the problem before she was standing in the security line at the airport. She'd never been very good at planning ahead. Mostly she just reacted.

Rex Major, on the other hand...

Merlin, she thought. *Call him by his real name.*

Merlin thought so far ahead that he had had plans in place for Excalibur for centuries. Even as Rex Major, he had the reputation of always being one step ahead of his competitors: that was why Excalibur Computer Systems was so successful.

He's thinking ahead now, Ariane thought. *He's thinking of how he can beat me to the next shard...and the one after that...and the one after that.*

The thought unfurled butterflies in her stomach. She and Wally believed their plan was sound. But what if they were wrong?

Oh, sure, they'd beaten Merlin *once*. But then they'd had, at least to a certain extent, the element of surprise. They'd never have that again. He knew who they were. He knew what she was capable of. What worried Ariane was her suspicion that they had yet to fully experience what *he* was capable of. But what choice did they have? Ariane reached under her pillow and, as her fingers touched the cold steel of the first shard, felt a surge of confidence. *Yeah, we did beat him once*, she thought. *And now I have the first shard, and all its power. I'm going to be even harder to beat this time. And with two shards...he won't be able to threaten me at all. Or Wally. Or Aunt Phyllis.*

France on Sunday, she thought. *It's after midnight now. That means* tomorrow.

CHAPTER SIX

ROAD TRIP

EARLY SUNDAY MORNING, Wally and Ariane, wearing gloves and heavy jackets, stood outside Aunt Phyllis's house, looking dubiously at the mini-van she had rented. It hadn't come from Avis or Hertz or even Rent-a-Wreck; it had come from a guy who rented cars out of his garage in an alley in north-central Regina.

Cash only, of course.

The van was a dirty blue and had tinted windows that made it impossible to see through...which was exactly what Aunt Phyllis had been looking for. How she'd found the below-the-radar car-rental guy was a mystery. *Well, she knows a lot of people*, Wally thought. *I guess she knew a guy who knew a guy who....*

Aunt Phyllis had been cranking the motor for about a half a minute, and finally it caught, belching blue smoke and steam. The engine faltered, but Aunt Phyllis gave it some more gas, and after another smoky burp it started chugging steadily. It sounded to Wally as though only five of its six cylinders were firing...but at least it was running.

"We'll be lucky if we don't break down before we get out of town," Ariane whispered to Wally, who couldn't disagree.

They'd loaded the van with their suitcases and a conspicuous amount of camping equipment...even his dad's fishing rod, which Wally suspected he wasn't supposed to touch. *But Dad's not around, so why not?* Wally looked up and down the street, certain they were being watched, even though he couldn't see anyone. All the other cars parked along the street looked empty. It was only half-past seven and the sun wasn't even up yet, though grey light filtered through the low clouds scudding overhead. The temperature wouldn't climb as high as freezing for hours...if it got there at all.

Aunt Phyllis got out of the van and came around the front. "Climb in! We've got a long drive ahead of us," she said loudly, sounding like an enthusiastic but not-very-talented actress trying to make sure her voice was heard in the back of the auditorium.

"Can't wait," Wally said, then winced. He'd taken the last of his prescription painkillers the night before. This morning he was getting by with Tylenol, and his head, he'd found, ached more than when he had been on the good stuff. Forty-eight hours having passed, he'd taken off the gauze pad covering the stitches on the right side of his forehead. He was stuck with the stitches themselves for another week, and the darn things itched like crazy, but he resisted the urge to scratch. *At least my hair mostly covers them*, he thought, *so I don't look* too *much like Frankenstein's monster.* He touched them gingerly. He wondered if he'd have a scar. He kind of hoped so. It would give him a Harry Potter-ish air.

Despite the doctor's warning, he hadn't had any dizzy spells. (Well, maybe he'd been a *little* unsteady on his feet once or twice, but the moments had passed quickly, so that didn't count...right?) Whether his reaction time was affected or not, he couldn't say. He hadn't told Ariane about the doctor's warnings. He didn't figure she needed to know. He was fine.

He glanced sideways at her and bit his lip. He also hadn't told her about Rex Major's phone call. He hadn't told her he suspected they might be fighting for the wrong side. He hadn't told her that he wasn't sure he could trust her – no, not *her*, her *powers* – not since she'd hurt Flish so badly.

I'm helping her, aren't I? he thought defensively. *I'm going to go to France to help her find the second shard. She'll have plenty of opportunities there to prove she deserves my trust.*

Thinking of Flish made him think of his phone call to her the night before. He hadn't mentioned Ariane, just said that he would be gone for a few days "with a friend." Flish must have guessed whom he meant, but she hadn't reacted at all; just grunted, as if she didn't care.

Mrs. Carson hadn't cared either. Wally got the distinct feeling she was happy he was going away so she wouldn't have to think about him for a while, and could devote all her energy to worrying about Flish. Which she certainly was. "She's just lying there, brooding," Mrs. Carson fretted to Wally. "Her friends still haven't come to see her. I don't understand it. Flish has always been so popular."

Unlike you, Wally was sure she meant.

He wondered what Mrs. Carson would say if she knew he was really planning to fly to France and stay in a hotel with a girl, just the two of them. He wondered what she would say if something happened to him while he was there. How would she explain it to his parents?

He snorted. It would almost be worthwhile if something *did* happen to him in France, just to find out what she'd say.

Well, assuming whatever happened wasn't...final.

Aunt Phyllis opened the side door of the van. Ariane climbed in first, Wally clambering in behind her. Aunt Phyllis slid the door shut, went around to the driver's seat, slipped behind the wheel, and then they were off.

"Anyone following us?" Wally asked as they rolled along College Avenue toward Albert Street, which would take them north to Highway 11.

Aunt Phyllis checked her mirrors. "There are a couple of cars back there," she said. "But I can't be sure."

Wally nodded and winced again.

They made good time through the nearly empty streets of the Sunday morning city. More than one car emerged onto the highway behind them, any of which could contain one of Major's spies. But they'd planned for that. Aunt Phyllis started out driving ten kilometers an hour over the speed limit (though the van shook so much at that speed it worsened Wally's headache). After a few minutes, she slowed to 10 kilometers *under* the limit. Since pretty much nobody drove at or below the speed limit between Regina and Saskatoon, only someone following them was likely to stay behind them. And sure enough, they were quickly passed by one car...two cars...three cars.

"Blue Taurus, silver Volvo, and something I think was a 1976 Oldsmobile," Wally said.

"Nobody behind us now," said Aunt Phyllis. "I think we can relax." She increased her speed back up to the limit.

Wally was quite willing to relax. His head throbbed, so he leaned back and closed his eyes.

When he opened them again they were rolling into Chamberlain.

Highway 11 from Regina to Saskatoon was four-lane all the way...except for where it passed through the village of Chamberlain. There, it narrowed to two lanes and the speed limit dropped from the highway's 110 kilometers per hour to 50 kilometers per hour. The whole place was only six blocks long and extended only two blocks to the northeast of the highway. That was pretty much as far as it *could* extend, since it was perched on the rim of a valley.

On the southwest side of the highway, to their left as

they drove into town, Highway 2 led toward Moose Jaw. Just past that intersection there was a single grain elevator that doubled as a billboard (currently advertising Casino Regina), and a broad flat area where semis could park while their drivers ducked into the restaurants, gas stations and convenience stores that seemed to make up the bulk of the village's industry.

Traditionally, those driving between Saskatchewan's two largest cities either stopped in Chamberlain or in Davidson, another half an hour or so up the road. Neither was exactly the halfway point, which really fell somewhere in between.

His family had always been Davidson-stoppers, since it was the larger of the two communities, but every once in a while they'd pull into Chamberlain. When they did, they always gravitated to Bennett's, a gas station, convenience store, garage and who-knew-what-else that also doubled as the town's bus station. Although Bennett's now sold gas from two pumps on its southeast side, two much older pumps still stood sentinel out front, broken, rusty relics. Wally had never understood why they hadn't been torn out.

There were already a couple of cars right in front of Bennett's, so Aunt Phyllis pulled over in front of the empty building next door. Although its windows were papered over and its front door boarded up, it boasted a giant painted Canadian flag on the wall facing the Saskatoon-bound traffic.

Yesterday, Aunt Phyllis had gone down to the bus depot in Regina and paid cash for two one-way tickets from Chamberlain to Regina. Now she dug in her purse for the tickets and handed them over. "The bus leaves here at 10 a.m.," she said, "so you've still got a while to wait."

"We can see the sights of Chamberlain," Ariane said.

"All two of them," Wally put in.

They had packed just a few clothes and other essentials – including their passports and a considerable stash of $20 bills and an even larger stash of Euros, drawn from Aunt Phyllis's credit card – into backpacks. Wally opened the side door of the van and climbed out, then pulled the backpacks from behind the back seat. They put them on. "I'll come in with you to get a cup of coffee," Aunt Phyllis said when they were set.

They all went into Bennett's. The convenience store part, which took up the front of the building, just behind two big windows overlooking the highway, held racks of junk food and glass-fronted refrigerators full of soft drinks and bottled water. The rear of the building, behind the wall of refrigerators and past the coffee counter, contained auto parts and other garage stuff. Aunt Phyllis took a Styrofoam cup, filled it with coffee, then went over to the desk to pay. Wally, hungry, bought an enormous pre-packaged cinnamon roll. Ariane settled for a granola bar.

"I guess this is good-bye," Aunt Phyllis said.

Conscious of the old man behind the counter watching them stoically from beneath the shade of a green John Deere baseball cap, Wally said, "I guess so. We'll let you know how it goes."

"You'd better." Aunt Phyllis looked at Ariane. "Be careful," she said softly. "I know I said you can take care of yourself, but...I'm supposed to be your guardian."

"You can't guard me from what I have to do," Ariane said. She gave her aunt a hug and Wally, surprising himself, gave Aunt Phyllis a hug too. Aunt Phyllis looked a little teary-eyed as she pulled away, but all she said was, "Take care." Then, rather abruptly, she turned and left.

Wally started to follow her through the door, thinking he'd wave good-bye as she pulled away. But when he looked toward the van he saw a blue Taurus pulling in behind it – *one of the cars that had passed them right after they left Regina.* He jerked back so fast he stepped on Ariane's feet.

"Hey!" she protested. "I need those toes!"

"He's here," Wally whispered urgently to Ariane.

Ariane stared at him. "Who?"

Wally glanced at the man behind the cash register, who was now reading a newspaper, apparently uninterested in them. Wally took Ariane's arm and pulled her to the end of the convenience store farthest from the counter. A gigantic moose head guarded an open doorway leading to what Wally knew from previous visits were two tiny, one-person washrooms. "Rex Major's man," he said in a low voice. "One of the cars that passed us just pulled in. He must have pulled off somewhere and then come back on the highway after we'd gone by."

Ariane stared at the door. "Aunt Phyllis –"

"I don't know if she's realized it yet," Wally said. He looked out the nearest window, just in time to see the mini-van drive past, heading on up the highway toward Saskatoon. But the Taurus didn't follow. Wally swore. "I think he's coming in here. We have to hide –"

"Only one place we can," Ariane said. "Come on!"

She ran under the moose head toward the bathrooms. Wally headed toward the men's, but Ariane grabbed him. "He could be going in there!"

"Right," Wally said, annoyed at himself for not thinking of that, and followed Ariane into the women's room instead. It was a tight fit with their backpacks, but they made it. Ariane bolted the door...and then they listened, barely breathing.

They heard voices. One sounded like the man at the counter, the other was unfamiliar.

"What if he's asking about us?" Wally hissed. "The man will tell him we headed to the bathrooms...."

Ariane looked at him, then grinned. "I can fix that."

She twisted herself around and turned on the water in the sink.

There were footsteps outside the bathroom. Ariane whispered, "Grab hold of me." Wally, suddenly realizing what she intended...and wondering *why* they had bought bus tickets in the first place, when they could have done this all along...took hold of Ariane's arm as she quietly unlocked the bathroom door, then plunged her hand into the stream of water.

The bathroom vanished around them...though Wally thought he saw, just before the water took them, the door beginning to swing open.

Wally had travelled through the water with Ariane several times, but the sensation wasn't something you got used to. One minute his body was there, solid as always, clothes, shoes and the weight of the backpack pressing against it, his weight pushing the soles of his feet against the floor. The next, all those sensations vanished. Darkness swallowed him. He could feel that he was rushing somewhere at a great rate of speed, but he couldn't tell where: he had no sense of direction, left or right, north or south, up or down. But what was most frightening of all was the sense that his mind was dissolving along with his body, slowly melting away into the water that he had somehow, impossibly become. He wondered what would happen if Ariane let go of him.

But she won't, he thought. *She would never do anything to hurt me.*

Unless the Lady's magic and the shard change her. And then, suddenly, his body became solid again, submerged in water tinged with chlorine. He straightened convulsively; his feet found bottom, and his head broke the surface. Gasping, water streaming from the hair plastered to his skull, he stared around him.

They were in his house, in his swimming pool. Ariane

turned to look at him. "I guess we didn't need the bus tickets," she said, echoing his earlier thought. Wally laughed a little shakily.

They climbed out, and Ariane drove the water from their bodies, leaving them and everything they wore and carried as dry as though it had never been wet. "Will Mrs. Carson be here?" Ariane said.

Wally shook his head. "She goes to church early on Sundays, and then she goes out for lunch with some friends. She won't be back until dinner."

"And when is your flight?"

"Not until 4 p.m." *Assuming there are seats left,* he thought. There had been when he'd made the anonymous (he hoped) phone call to figure out the flights that would get him to Europe, though, and that had just been the evening before. If for some reason the planes had filled up, they'd have to delay at least another day, heightening the risk of Major figuring out what they were up to.

"Then we might as well hang out here."

Wally nodded. "Why didn't we think of this in the first place?" he said, feeling put-out at his own dim-wittedness. "The bus tickets were a mistake. What if we're making other mistakes, missing things we should have thought of?"

"It still isn't exactly second nature, this whole magic-travelling thing," Ariane said. "It's only been a month since this all started. It's hard to believe."

"A lot has happened since then," Wally agreed. *Not all of it good,* he added silently, thinking of Flish.

They made their way upstairs to the couch in the living room. Wally turned on the TV. The sports channel was showing curling, and he hated curling, but it seemed to be too much trouble to change it. And soon it didn't matter, because ten minutes after they sat down he glanced at Ariane and saw she was fast asleep.

Five minutes after that, so was he.

Wally woke first, blinking at the silent TV, now showing someone ski jumping in the Alps. Ariane had slumped against him and was still fast asleep, her breathing slow and steady. He looked down at the top of her head and felt a pang of tenderness like the one that had seized him in the cab coming from the hospital. They'd been through a lot together in the past month. His life had changed in so many ways since the day he'd seen her in the school office, right after her first fight with Flish's coven. He'd encountered the Lady of the Lake, been given a quest, helped recover the first shard of Excalibur....

...found out his parents were splitting up, watched his sister move out....

...seen his sister in the hospital, put there by Ariane.

She didn't mean to do it, he told himself again, still looking down at Ariane's head, breathing in the clean, sweet smell of her hair.

But that, he thought, was just another way of saying she couldn't really control the power she'd been given. So what would happen when she had *two* shards of the sword? How would *that* change her? How long would it be before she wasn't recognizable as Ariane at all, but became entirely the Lady of the Lake?

And what would *that* mean, to her...and to them?

Again Wally was struck by how little they really knew about the Lady – what she wanted, and why she wanted it. Rex Major...Merlin...wanted to rule the world, at least in some sense, but claimed that might actually be a *good* thing, since it would enable him to use magic to help solve the world's problems *and* to free his own world from what he saw as tyranny. The Lady, on the other hand, wanted to cut Earth off from magic altogether.

What could Ariane do with her power if she were free to use it for something other than searching for the shards of Excalibur? Could she make it rain in places suffering from drought, fill irrigation ditches in parched fields, reroute rivers? And if *she* could do all that, what could Merlin do if he had *his* full strength? Maybe he really could end war and poverty and famine.

Ariane sighed and snuggled close, like a kitten seeking warmth. Wally rested his cheek against the crown of her head, and his doubts eased again. This was *Ariane* he was talking about. The best friend he'd ever had. *She gave the first shard to Rex Major to save me*, he reminded himself.

But that was before she had ever used the shard's power. If Major had told him the truth, the more she used it, the more it would change her, and next time, she might choose the shard over him.

No! he protested, his cheek still warm against her hair. *Nothing could change her* that *much*.

But he'd thought that about a girl before. He'd thought nothing could ever change his sister into anything other than the loving older sibling he'd grown up with. And look how wrong he'd been about *that*.

He sighed. Sometimes he hated his own brain.

He looked at the TV stand again, and at the digital TV box that topped the stack of electronics. Glowing green numbers proclaimed the time. He straightened abruptly and shook Ariane. She mumbled something, then her head lifted and she looked around, yawning. "What?"

"We need to get to the airport or I'll have a job getting my ticket and getting through security in time to catch my flight," Wally said. He left the couch and headed for the wireless handset on a table at the foot of the stairs. "I'll call a taxi."

"I can't believe we're really doing this," Ariane said. "You're flying to France on your own, and I'm..." her voice trailed off.

"We went to Yellowknife on our own," Wally pointed out, punching numbers. "That trip started with us swirling down the drain. This is just a plane ride."

"For you," Ariane said.

Wally didn't reply right away. The taxi company had answered. He gave instructions and disconnected. Then he looked at Ariane. "You can do it. You *have* to." That didn't sound as encouraging as he wanted, so he added, "I have faith in you."

She gave him a quick smile. "Thank you."

He smiled back, feeling warm.

A car horn honked. He looked at the door in surprise. "That was quick. He must have been just around the corner." He picked up his backpack and Ariane grabbed hers as well. "Here we go." He went to the front door and held it open. "After you." Ariane gave him a little bow, and swept by. Wally turned and locked the door, pocketed the key, then followed her down the walk.

Just before he got in the taxi, though, he glanced back at his house, wondering if he'd ever see it again.

He shook his head. *Don't go getting morbid, Wally. You and Ariane beat Rex Major once. You can do it again. The Lady of the Lake and her Faithful Sidekick. No evil sorcerer stands a chance.*

Grinning, he climbed into the taxi. "Airport," he said.

CHAPTER SEVEN

BON VOYAGE

IN THE TAXI ON THE WAY to the airport, Ariane listened to Wally describe the itinerary that had been outlined for him by the Air Canada representative over the phone the night before. It seemed straightforward, if exhausting. He'd first fly to Calgary, a short hop of about an hour, then transfer to another flight, which would take him over the pole to Frankfurt. From Frankfurt he would fly to Lyon, France, arriving some thirty hours after he'd left Regina. The plan was for Ariane to meet him at the airport.

Assuming I haven't dissolved into cold mist above the Atlantic, she thought, and swallowed.

They'd chosen Lyon, rather than Paris, because Ariane's best guess for the shard's location was the south of France. Based on her experience with the first shard, she expected to be able to home in on the second shard much more easily once she was closer to it. In fact, she hoped that as soon as Wally had gone through customs, they could simply duck into a bathroom, zoom to the shard, grab it, zip back to Lyon, and hide out in the hotel room Aunt Phyllis had reserved for them until Wally could book a return flight. If they were lucky, and flights permitted, they might not even have to use it.

When they got to the airport, Wally went straight to the Air Canada desk. He came back after a few minutes with a grin. "Done," he said. "But I don't have much time. We'd better hurry."

They headed up the escalator to the second-floor security check-in. The line stretched for what looked like a mile. Ariane kept Wally company in the line, and Wally kept checking the clock. "Come on, come on," he muttered.

They were only two-thirds of the way to the screening area when they heard, over the public address system, "This is the final boarding call for Air Canada Jazz Flight 8437 to Calgary. All passengers, please make your way to Gate D."

"That's me," Wally said to Ariane. "It's going to be close."

Ariane craned her head, trying to see past the very large gentleman (in all dimensions), in front of them. "Can't they move any faster?"

They finally reached the screening area just as the PA said, "This is Air Canada Jazz paging passenger Walter Knight. Please make your way to Gate D immediately. Your plane is ready to depart."

Ariane could go no farther. She ducked out of the line and stood to one side. "Hurry up, hurry up, hurry up," she urged under her breath, watching Wally through the glass wall surrounding the screening area. The large man in front of Wally had been chosen for more detailed inspection. The guard patting him down seemed to take forever, but at last he was done. Wally, who had already emptied his pockets and placed his watch into the grey plastic bins provided, put his backpack on the X-ray conveyor belt. He stepped confidently through the metal detector, grabbed his stuff, gave her a final wave, and then dashed off.

He was gone.

She was on her own, and so was Wally. She hurried back toward the escalator. At the top was a coffee shop whose seating area overlooked the runways. She went to the windows and watched the Air Canada Jazz jet with Wally aboard pulling away from the jetway. She watched it taxi out, and a few minutes later heard the thunder of its engines and watched it lift into the sky.

He's on his way, she thought. *And now it's my turn.* She looked up at the low cloud covering the sky.

Perfect.

◀◀ ▶▶

Rex Major sat in a comfortable chair on the balcony of his condo, high atop one of the towers that many city residents thought were a blight on the shore of Lake Ontario, enjoying the unseasonably warm November weather in the final hour before his driver would arrive to take him to the airport. From all accounts, it was freezing on the prairies. He hoped Ariane and Wally were enjoying it.

His phone buzzed. Major sighed, set aside the excellent Alsatian Gewürztraminer he'd been sipping, and removed the phone from his pocket.

He glanced at it. There were a couple of new messages. One was from the private investigator he had hired to keep an eye on Wally and Ariane. The agent had already told him the two were going north for the week, ostensibly so Wally could recover from his head injury. This message simply confirmed he had seen them depart and would be in touch again once he had confirmed their new location.

But that made the second message really leap out at Major. It was an automated message, generated by the thin skein of magic that overlay every installation of Excalibur software on the planet, magic he had instructed to let him know whenever anything about either Wally or Ariane showed up on a computer system.

Wally Knight, who his agent had just told him was safely en route to northern Saskatchewan for a week's vacation at Emma Lake, had just boarded an airplane in Regina bound for Calgary, then Frankfurt....and then Lyon, France. Where he himself would be landing in just a few hours. That had to mean that Ariane knew where the second shard of Excalibur was...or it *would* have meant that if not for the inexplicable fact that Ariane was not flying with Wally. The boy was on his own.

Unless....

Could Ariane have some other method of getting to France? A method that didn't rely on airplanes? Had she found some way to use the Lady's power to make the trip, even though he knew for certain she couldn't move through salt water?

He supposed it was possible, but it seemed unlikely. *Maybe she sent Wally to get the shard himself*, Rex Major thought. *Maybe she thinks he can slip under my magical radar, since he has no magic of his own.*

That thought was so enticing he hardly dared to credit it. But the fact that it might be true was enough to make him smile as he raised his glass of wine once more. *When you're an unaccompanied minor*, he thought, *someone* really *ought to be there to meet you at the airport*. He raised his glass and took a full, satisfying mouthful.

◄► ►

Standing on the sidewalk in front of the airport terminal in Regina, Ariane considered leaping into the clouds right where she stood: but there were too many people around, and she didn't want anyone to see her suddenly disappear into thin air. Such an inexplicable occurrence would make the news for sure, and then their attempts to keep Merlin in the dark would have been for nothing.

But she didn't have to go far to be out of sight. At one end of the terminal building, a brick wall hid a garbage collection area. Ariane walked briskly in that direction, glanced around to make sure no one was paying any attention to her and slipped around the corner of the wall. Positioned safely behind a dumpster, she looked up at the grey sky.

"Here goes nothing," she muttered, and as she had done just two days before, she sought the cloud-song.

It was easier here with no distracting bodies of water nearby. The clouds' high, wild music sang clearly to her. They wanted her to come back to them, become one with them again. They seemed to reach for her as she reached for them.

An instant later, they had her.

Once again she felt her body expand, diffusing through the clouds. Once again she felt that urge to let consciousness slip away entirely, to join the clouds forever: but this time she was expecting it, and held her sense of self tightly together, centered on the hard, bright presence of the shard of Excalibur, the piece of grit around which she could layer the pearl of her mind.

East, she thought. *Farther than before.*

Much farther.

She raced away from Regina, flowing easily through the overcast sky that stretched clear to Winnipeg. But not far beyond the larger prairie city, as she neared northern Ontario, the clouds thinned and she began to struggle. Her path, at first straight as an arrow's flight, now wavered, north, south; and then, suddenly, she ran out of clouds altogether.

It was like racing at full speed to the edge of a cliff, and pulling herself up just in time: almost as though she teetered on the verge of plunging out of the cloud and falling to the huge metropolis below her. She held herself still, feeling breathless even though she wasn't technically breathing, and looked around her.

She suddenly realized, much to her surprise, that she recognized the city. To her vastly expanded, immaterial eyes it looked like an amazingly detailed model through which toy trains and cars wound their way, but one of those "model" buildings was in reality the gigantic skyscraper most people called the Sears Tower, although she'd heard somewhere it was called something else now. The city had to be Chicago, and that meant the enormous lake to the east was Lake Michigan, sparkling beneath a clear sky in late-afternoon sunshine. She'd come much farther south than she'd intended or expected.

But far, far in the east, she could just see a band of clouds. Too far for her to leap to, cloud to cloud....

...but then, she didn't need to, did she? There was a whole lake below her.

She hadn't tried *this* before, either, but she didn't see why it shouldn't be possible. She leaped from cloud to water, causing a brief shower on Chicago's Navy Pier, but instead of materializing fully, she melted into the water and raced across the lake.

At the far side, she reached back up for the clouds, this time having no difficulty at all distinguishing their soprano song from the lake's bass rumble, and a moment later was once more aloft, rushing east again through the much thicker clouds she found on the lake's far shore.

But she still couldn't follow a straight path. More and more she found herself travelling north until, as darkness descended, unbroken ice stretched away from her in every direction. Shortly after that, she could see nothing at all, and could only reach for the next cloud, and the next, always searching for those farther east and if possible, south.

Time seemed to have no meaning as she struggled from

cloud to cloud, sidestepping, backtracking. Every leap seemed a little harder, every move a little slower. Even with the power of the shard, she began to wonder if she could truly make it all the way across the ocean. Maybe the shard's power was limitless, but hers wasn't. She still had to direct and use its magic, and it was becoming harder and harder to do so. Not only that, as her energy decreased, she also found it more and more difficult to resist the siren call of the clouds. *Rest,* they seemed to say. *Rest. Sleep. Let go of your sense of self....*

If she gave in to that urge, let herself unravel into the clouds, what would happen to the shard? Would it spring back into existence and drop like a stone into the ocean below?

Except, she suddenly realized, there *wasn't* ocean below. She was over land.

More important, she was over fresh water. She couldn't see it, had no idea what it was, but that didn't matter: with the last of her failing strength she plunged into it, aiming for a spot close to the shore, deep enough for her to materialize in, but not so deep her heavy backpack would immediately pull her under.

Cold water suddenly announced itself against her skin, her magic now so weak it couldn't ward off the chill. She found soft mud beneath her feet and raised her head out of the water, spluttering.

Low overcast cloud blotted out the sky. A glow over the black bulk of a hill spoke of a nearby town or city, but there was no other sign of human life. Ariane moved to step out of the pond, but the mud gripped her feet and brought her splashing down face first. Spluttering again, crawling on her hands and knees, she scrambled onto the shore into tall, prickly grass, and lay there on her stomach, head turned to one side, gasping. For the moment, she was too weary to even attempt to order the water off her body.

And then she heard the nearby sound of heavy breathing. Her own breath halted. Holding it, she listened.

Something moved closer. *He must have seen me pop out of the water*, Ariane thought. *What will he think?*

And if he doesn't speak English, I can't even explain myself. I can barely say, "Comment allez-vous?"

She rose up on her hands, rolled over, and sat up. "Who's there?" she whispered.

More heavy breathing. A shuffling in the grass. And then...

"Moooo!"

Ariane jumped, and then burst out laughing. The cow mooed again and lurched away from her, clearly worried by the sudden appearance of a crazy person in its pasture. Still chuckling, Ariane summoned just enough power to wish herself dry, and then stood up, swaying a little. Her eyes should have accustomed to the darkness as soon as she materialized, since she had travelled through the night, but she hadn't really been using her eyes had she? Instead, her pupils seemed to still be set to Saskatchewan daylight aperture, which made her surroundings even darker. But slowly they began to adjust, the glow in the sky enough to reveal the landscape around her. The body of water was small, little more than a pond; she was probably on a farm, since she'd been greeted by a cow. She couldn't see a house anywhere, but that might be because of the trees that grew thickly along three sides of the pool and climbed the hill behind her toward the city sky-glow.

She was at the end of the pool where there were fewer trees, and where, she realized now, there were *several* cows, most of them kneeling, presumably asleep. It looked as if there was a lower hill in that direction, and one that wasn't covered in forest, so she headed up it to reconnoiter.

Once at the top, she found herself looking down on a cozy farm. A single-storey thatched-roof house, covered with white plaster through which showed thick wooden beams, stood at the edge of a cobblestoned courtyard surrounded by half a dozen outbuildings. A light on a high pole illuminated the scene, but the farmhouse windows were dark.

Now what? Ariane thought, staring at it.

She needed to get to Lyon, but she had time. She'd done a lot of back-and-forthing to find her route, but she knew she'd still traversed the Atlantic faster than any airliner could, and of course Wally wasn't even flying straight to Lyon: he was going to Frankfurt and then changing planes. She'd made the journey in one evening; he wouldn't be in Lyon until afternoon.

I'll camp out by the trees, Ariane thought. *I can be gone at first light, before the farmer even knows I'm here.*

Exhausted as she felt, she was sure she'd sleep like a baby even stretched out on bare ground. But she was also so hungry she was a potential danger to any horse in the vicinity.

Or any cow, she thought, and grinned in the dark. *Guess it was smart to run away.*

She descended to the pond, then skirted to its far edge, well inside the trees. All that camping equipment they'd packed had stayed in the van, and was presumably at Emma Lake by now: she and Wally had only put ordinary clothes in their backpacks, since they'd expected to stay at a hotel. But at least she was warm enough, since she'd been dressed for November in Saskatchewan, not France. She spread some of her extra clothes on the leaf-covered ground, pulled out a spare jacket with which to cover herself, then sat and munched the only thing she had to eat, an *Oh Henry!* bar. *At least it's one of the giant ones*, she thought, doing her best to ignore her stomach's complaint.

Finally she lay down and closed her eyes. *This really isn't very comfortable* was her last thought before exhaus-

CHAPTER EIGHT

SLIPPERY CHOICES

"RÉVEILLE-TOI! Réveille-toi! Que fais-tu ici?"

Ariane opened her eyes and blinked at bare black branches silhouetted against grey sky. *Where...?*

Then, suddenly, she remembered. She shot to a sitting position. A very short man wearing a yellow windbreaker, thick white sweater, blue trousers and high rubber boots glared down at her, dark eyes narrowed over a prominent nose supported by a ludicrously large mustache. "Que fais-tu ici?"

"Um...." Even the tiny amount of French she knew deserted her. "Je ne parle pas français," she said at last.

"Anglaise?" the man said, frowning. "Américaine?"

Well, at least she understood *that*. "Non. Canadienne."

"Ah?" The man's frown deepened. "What are you doing here?" he said, every word slow and deliberate and thickly accented, but understandable.

"I'm sorry," Ariane said, relieved he spoke English. "I'm...lost."

That was certainly true.

"You are travelling?"

"Yes," said Ariane. "I'm heading to Lyon." She hesitated, thinking how foolish she was about to sound, but she needed to know...."Is it far?"

The man snorted. "Oui. Sept cents kilomètres."

Numbers, she knew. "Seven hundred kilometres?"

"Oui. So better you start, n'est-ce pas? I show you back to the road."

Ariane took the hint. Cold and stiff from sleeping on the ground, she rose awkwardly to her feet, then bent over again with a groan to gather the clothes on which she had slept. They were damp with dew, but she could dry them later. She stuffed them into her backpack then turned back to the farmer. He jerked his head in the direction of the low ridge hiding the farmhouse and started off, Ariane trailing behind him.

They passed the pond. Ariane glanced at the spot where she had materialized the night before and winced. The nice soft mud she had clambered through consisted mainly of cow patties of various vintages. She shuddered and suddenly wished more than anything for a hot shower...but she didn't think she could ask the farmer for *that*.

She could ask him for something else, though, something she desperately needed. "Can I use your bathroom...um, votre toilette?"

The farmer sighed. "Oui."

"And, um...could I get something to eat?" She needed all the energy she could muster to carry on to Lyon and wherever the shard might be hidden. She thought of the euros tucked away in her backpack. "I can pay –"

The farmer glared at her, but she gave him her best smile and his suspicious frown relaxed a little. He shook his head. "Non," he said brusquely. "There is no need. Ma femme...my wife will find you something."

The farmer's wife, Chantal, a short round woman with bright blue eyes and graying hair drawn back in a bun, knew no English at all, or at least didn't attempt to use it. That limited their conversation to "Bonjour," and "Merci," but though she gave her husband a questioning look, Chantal responded to his stream of French by putting slices of crusty bread alongside butter and grape jelly on a wooden table whose thick, dark wood looked as old as the massive beams spanning the low ceiling. Ariane used the tiny-but-spotless bathroom first, then devoured the food – she couldn't remember ever being more hungry. Meanwhile, Chantal busied herself at the stove. As Ariane reached for her third slice of bread, Chantal brought her a steaming bowl of hot chocolate. Ariane sipped it gratefully, and as it took the chill off her bones, repeated, "Merci," and "Merci beaucoup," as often as she could.

The farmer seemed to thaw at about the same rate she did. From him she learned that she was not far from the coast, near the city of Dieppe, a name she knew from history books as the place of an ill-fated raid during the Second World War in which many Canadians had been killed or captured. Lyon lay far to the southeast. "You cannot walk there," the farmer said, though earlier he had been perfectly willing to have her try. "It would take days...weeks. Did you really think you could?"

"I was planning to walk some, take the train some," she lied. "I'm meeting someone in Lyon."

Chantal said something to her husband. He responded, and she said something back. "Chantal says you look very young to travel on your own. How old are you?"

"Eighteen," Ariane lied again. "I'm older than I look."

The farmer raised an eyebrow, but said nothing.

After breakfast, and another round of "Merci," and "Merci beaucoup," plus an "Au revoir," to Chantal, Ariane followed the farmer down a long lane bordered by high, thick hedges. At the end the lane joined a paved road, straight as an arrow and lined with tall, skinny poplars. A car whizzed by. "Dieppe is that way," the farmer said, pointing to his right. "Lyon that way." He pointed left. "You should go back to Dieppe, take the train. I could drive you to la gare, the station...."

"Non, merci," Ariane said. "Thank you. I'm fine."

The farmer looked at her a long moment, then shrugged. "Very well," he said. "But a warning. This camping sauvage...wild camping...it is permitted some places but not others. Some farmers will not like it. There are also dangerous vagabonds you must watch out for. Much better you take a train."

"I'll be careful," Ariane said. "Thank you again. Merci beaucoup."

"De rien," said the farmer. "Au revoir."

"Au revoir."

Aware of the farmer watching her, Ariane hitched her backpack higher and set off at a brisk walk, for all the world as if she meant to hike the seven hundred kilometres to Lyon in a single day. Only when the farmer had gone back down his lane did she slow her pace and begin looking for what she really wanted: water.

She found it soon enough, a stream that passed under a bridge. She left the road, clambered down the rocky bank and stepped into the bridge's shadow. Out of sight, she slipped into the water and away.

Refreshed by both sleep and food, she felt the call of the shard instantly, far to the south, not so far to the east. But before she went there, she had to meet Wally, and that meant finding Lyon.

She knew roughly where it was from the maps she'd looked at with Wally before they left. She rushed along streams and through lakes in that direction, the song of the shard crescendoing as she went. For a moment she was tempted to simply find it, grab it, get out and get home. She could be back in Canada within hours....

And Wally would be left all alone in Lyon until he could fly back. He'd never forgive me.

That should have decided it, but then her mind added in a seductive whisper, *But you'd have the shard. And really, what help was he in Yellowknife? Merlin took him hostage to force you to give up the first shard. He almost cost you everything. What do you really need him for?*

The thought made Ariane stop her headlong flight, abruptly materializing in a pond surrounded by leafless trees. She waded ashore, dried herself, walked a few steps to the trees and sat on a fallen log.

She'd thought something similar once before, right after she'd discovered her new ability to move through the clouds, and wondered if the shard had planted the notion in her head. And perhaps it had. But that didn't mean, especially under *these* circumstances, that it was a *bad* idea. Why *shouldn't* she simply grab the shard? It felt as if she could travel straight to it. Rex Major probably didn't even know where it was yet. It was the perfect opportunity. *You could explain to Wally afterward*, her mind whispered. *His childish hurt feelings won't matter a bit if you can seize the second shard before Merlin....*

The moment she considered ignoring Wally's feelings – not to mention calling those feelings "childish" – she was sure these strange thoughts were coming from outside herself, from the shard of Excalibur at her side. It wanted her to put finding that second shard above everything else, above her only friend....

Even above my own safety?

She'd never wanted to *really* hurt Flish and Shania and the others, not the way she had. The shard had done that, pulling her anger out of her and using it to turn the Lady's power into a weapon. Now it was trying to make her hurt Wally too. Because if she attempted to find the second shard without him, it *would* hurt him...terribly. Going off to get the shard without him would be like...like ditching some guy you'd gone to a movie with because a better-looking guy had just walked in to the theatre.

But...

But against that thought, she put the memory of Rex Major pressing the barrel of a pistol into Wally's cheek at the Thunderhill Diamond Mine. Major could have killed Wally then. To save him, Ariane had handed the shard, already in her hand, over to Major. That had forced them to follow Major to Yellowknife and steal the shard back from his hotel room. If she had been on her own, she would have simply laughed at Rex Major and escaped with the shard then and there.

Wally could have been killed, and he almost cost you the first shard.

Cold and sharp the thought came, cold and sharp as Excalibur itself, and again she knew where it had come from. *But I might never have gotten that far in the first place without his help*, she countered. She remembered Wally charging toward her when Major's sales manager, Pritchard, had grabbed her in the alley, Wally wielding a broken hockey stick like a sword, striking away Pritchard's knife and then knocking Pritchard to the ground. *If Wally hadn't been around, my quest would have ended right there.*

But even as she rejected the idea that Wally had almost cost her the first shard, she had to accept the other thought the shard had planted: *Wally could have been killed.* Again she reminded herself that the shard was a piece of a weapon – its attitude was brutal and direct. It didn't care about Wally, or anyone else, it was just trying to manipulate her...but that didn't change the truth of the sword-driven thought. And the stakes were only going to get higher. Yes, she had power, but so did Major, and he'd already shown he'd use it ruthlessly. She might be able to use *her* power to retrieve the second shard and escape, but could she protect Wally at the same time?

She might hurt Wally's *feelings* if she retrieved the second shard without his help, but she might save his *life*...especially if they were wrong and Rex Major *did* know where the second shard was, and they ran into him again.

It's worth a shot, she thought. *If I can get it, great. And if I can't, if it turns out I do need Wally's help, I still have time to meet him at the airport...and he'll never even know I tried to get it without him.*

She closed her eyes. She'd been focused on finding her way to the airport, but all the time the second shard had been pulling at her, almost due south from where she was now. For the first time she concentrated fully on its song.

It was strong, and yet...there was something *odd* about it....

She needed to get closer, and so she went back down to the shore of the little lake, stepped into the water, and dissolved.

In the water, the second shard practically shouted at her: *I'm here! I'm here! Come get me!* She followed that clarion call through wild lakes and streams until she knew she was almost on top of it....

...but she couldn't reach it! Yes, it was in water, but not enough to materialize in, and now she was so close she could also tell that the shard was deep underground. Even if she found another pool down there in which she could materialize, there was no guarantee she could get from it to where the shard was, and the thought of materializing underground in absolute darkness, perhaps in water completely enclosed in rock, with no airspace, terrified her. Would she even be able to dematerialize again and escape if that happened? Floundering in darkness, unable to take a single breath, would she have the courage or presence

of mind to call on her power? Or would she die there, entombed deep beneath the earth, a puzzling fossil for some far-future paleontologist?

No, thanks! She chose instead to materialize above ground, more than half a kilometre from where she had sensed the shard.

She burst into a pool at the edge of a winding river. High cliffs of rough grey stone towered above her, but there was a narrow flat space of tumbled rocks between the water's edge and the nearest cliff; at times, obviously, the river had far more water in it than now. She splashed ashore and ordered the water off herself, then closed her eyes and concentrated again on the call of the second shard. It was *that* way, behind her, so she turned, picking her way over the stony shore, until she finally found a gully that led up through the cliff face a few hundred metres downriver. She scrambled up it on all fours and emerged at last into a pine forest, perhaps three hundred metres wide, growing on a broad shelf of land between the cliff behind her and a second, higher cliff in front of her.

She glanced around...and saw, no more than the length of a football field away, a large blue tent.

It *could* have belonged to ordinary tourists, except most ordinary tourists wouldn't bother to surround their tent and the rock face with a chain-link fence that ran right up to the cliff, forming a compound about ten metres on a side. The only way into the compound was through a narrow gate between Ariane and the tent.

Most tourists also wouldn't have looked as unfriendly as the two men in grey, vaguely military uniforms who sat at a folding table in front of the tent, playing cards. They glanced up as Ariane emerged from the forest, and one of them immediately stood and shouted, "Va-t'en! C'est la propriété du gouvernement!"

She hesitated. She could almost understand that...something about government property and....

The man took a menacing step toward her. "Je t'ai dit, va-t'en!"

Ah. *Go away.* She held up her hands. "Pardonnez-moi," she said. She gave the two guards...because that was obviously what they were...her biggest smile, then turned and went back into the forest.

Once she was out of sight, she circled back through the woods, making sure she didn't get too close and moving as quietly as she could.

From off to one side, she could get a better glimpse, stolen through a screen of branches, of the cliff face behind the tent. She saw a dark opening in the rock, a crack that didn't look big enough for a man to slip through...though even as she watched, a man emerged from it. His orange overalls, smeared with dirt and mud, the helmet with a lamp, and the rope, hammers, and other climbing equipment hung all over him, made it clear he'd been in a cave.

And it was equally obvious to Ariane, reaching out with her magical senses, that the second shard of Excalibur was inside that same cave.

Has Merlin found the shard? Is this his way of keeping it safe until he can get here to claim it?

But none of this looked like a Rex Major operation. Two apparently unarmed guards, who had chased her away but not arrested her, an ordinary chain-link fence, and nothing but a tent to hide the entrance? Major would have locked the cave behind a steel door as thick as a bank vault's, guarded by a dozen armed men and a pack of killer dogs. These guys might not want anyone sneaking into the cavern, but they didn't seem to think whatever they were guarding was likely to invite serious trouble. *Maybe it's just got some nice crystal formations and they're hoping to set up a tourist attraction*, she thought. *Well, fine. I'll be the first visitor.*

If she could get past them.

The man who had emerged from the cavern disappeared into the tent, and came out a few minutes later without his overalls, helmet and climbing equipment. Dressed now in a casually elegant suit, he stopped and spoke to the guards for a couple of minutes, then left the fenced compound and disappeared into the woods away from the river, toward the second, higher cliff. A moment later he reappeared above the trees, climbing a path she hadn't noticed until that moment. She watched him until a bend in the path took him out of sight, then turned her attention back to the guards, the tent and the cave entrance. The guards had resumed playing cards. All she had to do was sneak past them, get inside, find the shard and flow away through whatever underground stream she might find.

But she would need a light, and from the looks of the man who had come out of the cavern, maybe a rope as well. *As if I'll know what to do with it*, she thought uneasily. Everything she knew about spelunking she had learned from watching the Discovery channel, where it always looked like a cross between climbing mountains and crawling through sewers.

Ariane thought again of Wally – his help would be useful right about now. But she shrugged away the notion. If she couldn't get to the shard on her own, then she could come back with Wally and they'd figure out something else. But she wouldn't know until she tried.

The man had left his equipment in the tent, so she needed to get in there first. And that meant she needed to get the guards away from it.

She needed a diversion. She smiled a little as she heard herself echoing a line from every action movie she had ever seen; smiled more widely as an idea came to her. *Let's see Supergirl do this*, she thought. She closed her eyes and concentrated, reaching out to the river singing to her from just beyond the drop-off at the other side of the clearing.

The river was much farther away than any body of water she'd ever tried to manipulate before, but she had the power of the shard to augment her own, just as when she'd pulled the apparently unreachable water from beneath the tennis courts. *Come to me*, she whispered to the river with her mind. *Come to me. Come to your Lady....*

And the water responded.

She opened her eyes to watch it pour up from the river, flowing *uphill* through the gully she had followed from the river bank, tumbling white over rocks, foaming around tree trunks, its leading edge brown with mud, twigs and leaves. The guards stopped playing cards as the sound of rushing water intensified, looking around in bewilderment; then one of them shouted and jumped to his feet, knocking over his campstool and pointing toward the forest.

The other guard leaped up, too, as river water poured out across the ground, a tongue of liquid three metres wide and a metre deep that didn't spread out as an ordinary flood would have, if any ordinary flood could have made that climb in the first place. Answering her call, it rolled straight toward her hiding place, but with her mind she turned it aside and sent it straight at the guards.

They shouted French words she didn't understand but really didn't need to, and almost knocked each other down trying to open the gate and run for the path up the cliff, away from the impossible rush of water...and Ariane, watching from behind her screen of leaves, smiled and chased them with it. The shard's power filled her, and with contemptuous ease she raised the crest of the water off the ground, higher and higher, until it towered above the terrified guards, who scrambled up the path on their hands and knees. *I could wipe them right off the cliff side*, she thought, but then, shocked at her own bloodthirsty impulse, she yanked the water back down again and released it, dropping her control like a red-hot piece of metal. The water hit the ground in a vast splash, spreading out and flowing back toward the river as gravity once more took effect. In seconds, all that remained of it were a few scattered pools, mud, and wet rocks and tree trunks.

Ariane rose to her feet, a little shaken both from the amount of energy she'd had to expend and the way the shard had once again tried to take control. But she had to move *now*, while the guards were out of sight. They'd be back soon enough...though if she were them, after *that* she'd be moving very cautiously. *Take your time, guys.*

She ran across the clearing to the now wide-open gate, dashed through it and then pushed through the tent flap into the shadowy, blue-lit interior. She glanced around at two cots with sleeping bags untidily sprawled across them, a small camping stove and a long folding table covered with paper, two laptops and a jumble of still cameras, video cameras and other pieces of equipment she didn't recognize at all. At one end of the table, green and red lights flickered across the face of a sleek black two-way radio, microphone clipped to its side. The place smelled of damp ground, campfire, cigarette smoke and a little bit of boys' locker room.

She figured the latter pungent scent came mostly from the mud-smeared orange overalls hung on pegs on the tall central pole holding up the tent's roof. The helmet and climbing equipment worn by the man she had seen exit the cave hung there too. She grabbed the helmet, rope and utility belt festooned with hammers, pitons, a compass, a large knife and other things she didn't immediately recognize. She ignored the coveralls, not *just* because of the smell, but also because they were so large they would have made her feel like a clown. She fastened the belt around her waist, then, feeling slightly silly, pushed open the tent's rear flap and studied the black crack in the cliff face, just three or four metres away. The song of the second shard oozed from it thick and sweet as honey, vibrating her bones like the bass at a rock concert, making her whole body thrum with excitement. The shard she already wore shouted its own fierce joy at being so near its brother, filling her with a yearning desire to plunge into the dark opening before her.

Yet she still hesitated, remembering those Discovery channel spelunking specials again. Cliffs, mud, rock falls, bats and absolute darkness.... Was she prepared to face what she might find in there?

Only one way to find out. She stepped through the tent flap and walked toward the opening in the rock – but just before she reached it she heard a man's angry shout. She whipped her head around and up. The guards were running full-tilt down the path up the cliff face. Heart pounding, Ariane turned and plunged into the cave.

The outside light barely penetrated the gloom. She fumbled with the helmet light, found the switch and then followed its circle of illumination across the floor of bare rock. The songs of the shard she carried and of the shard she sought mingled and wound through her brain, separate, discordant, but longing to merge together into perfect harmony. "I'm coming," she heard herself gasp. "I'm coming!"

The second shard was close, very close...but not up here. It was farther in, farther down.

She stopped. The blue-white circle of light from her helmet had just slid across the smooth stone floor into emptiness. She edged forward, looked down.

The rock fell away, a sheer cliff dropping at least fifteen metres, down to another floor that her helmet lamp barely illuminated. She turned her light frantically this way and that and finally spotted, off to her right, a collapsible ladder fastened to pitons driven into the floor.

She heard voices outside the cavern. She didn't have time to dither. The second shard was somewhere below and as far as she could tell, the ladder was the only way to get there.

But how was she supposed to climb onto the thing?

Footsteps crunched at the cavern entrance. She sat down and scooted on her rear until her legs were dangling over the edge of the cliff. Then she rotated her upper body so she could take hold of the pitons with both hands. Gripping them as tightly as she could, she twisted her lower body, feeling for the rungs.

She could have sworn her foot was on one. But maybe there was some knack to it she lacked – or maybe she was more flustered by the approaching guards than she realized.

For whatever reason, her foot slipped.

She screamed as she fell, fingers tightening convulsively on the pitons holding the ladder in place, then grunted with pain as her hands caught her full weight, almost pulling her arms from their sockets, and her body jerked forward, slamming into rock. She kicked wildly with both feet, desperate to find the ladder, but though she felt it bumping against her, she couldn't find purchase. Her fingers were slipping. She couldn't hold on...couldn't...

Two strong hands shot over the edge of the cliff and seized her forearms in vise-like grips. "Tiens bon! Je vais te tirer de là!"

She had no idea what that meant, but she had never been happier to see anyone than she was to see the guards she had worked so hard to evade. They pulled her up over the lip of the cliff, and she rolled onto her back, gasping for air, knees bruised, hands aching, the front of her jacket scuffed, one pocket half torn off. But the guards gave her no time to rest. Together they hauled her to her feet. One of them kept a tight hold on her arm while the other shone a flashlight in her face, "Qui es-tu? Que fais-tu ici? Tu aurais pu te tuer!"

"Hey, stop that!" Ariane scrunched up her eyes. "I can't see! And I don't speak French. Um, je ne parle pas français."

"Américaine?"

"No." Ariane shook her head. "Canadian."

"Canadienne?" The guard frowned. Then, "Who are you?" he said in accented but understandable English.

"Ar –" She suddenly realized that giving her real name might not be the best idea. With only a slight hesitation, she changed it in mid-word. "Arial." An image of Disney's red-headed Little Mermaid popped into her head. It seemed oddly appropriate. "Arial Muirhead." She doubted her English teacher would mind Ariane borrowing her last name, since she'd never find out about it. "I'm sorry, I was just –"

"This is…" The guard spread his hands to take in the cavern. "Interdit. Forbidden. By order of le Ministère de la Culture. It is very precious. You could…cause damage. Or hurt yourself."

"I didn't know," Ariane said truthfully. "It was just…I saw someone come out of the cavern, and then you two ran off when that weird flood came pouring through the trees –" she wasn't about to suggest she'd had anything to do with *that*, "– and I just thought it'd be cool to see inside. It was just…for fun."

The guards exchanged rapid-fire French. The one holding her arm never slackened his grip. Finally the guard who spoke English said to her, "We must detain you. Dr. Beaudry must talk to you, make a report. The Ministry will want to be sure you did not mean to cause damage."

"I didn't! I told you, it was just for fun –"

"Dr. Beaudry will decide," the guard said firmly. "C'est

réglé. It is settled. Amène-la dehors!" – that to the other guard, who promptly propelled her toward the opening of the cavern. *It doesn't matter*, Ariane thought. *They'll put me in the tent, I'll call up the river again, and I'll be out of here.*

Outside the entrance, the English-speaking guard made her take off the caving equipment. "Enferme-la dans la remise!" he said to the other man, and that was the first hint Ariane had that things weren't going to go the way she had imagined them.

Rather than put her in the tent, the guard led her out through the gate in the chain-link fence...and then away from the river. She had been at the very limit of her ability when she had called it up to distract the guards. Now she felt it slipping away from her, out of reach despite the power of the shard.

They climbed the path up the cliff. To her right, the woods fell away until she could see the river beyond, foaming its way through the gorge farther down. Up, up they went to the very top of the cliff, parallel to it until they had almost crested the rock face, to where the path turned sharply. Rough rock steps took them up the last few metres between shoulders of grey stone, and then they emerged into a large clearing in the forest. On the far side stood a trailer; closer to the edge were a couple of Quonset-like huts and a small, blue plastic structure with the look and the smell – Ariane wrinkled her nose – of a portable toilet. The ground bore the marks of several vehicles, but there weren't any there now. Ariane waited to see if "Dr. Beaudry" would emerge from the trailers, the huts, or even the porta-potty – or whatever they called it in France – but there didn't seem to be anyone around at all.

She listened for a song of water from anywhere nearby, but she and her guard were literally high and dry: there were no streams or puddles nearby, and the sun beat down from a cloudless blue sky. That escape route, too, was closed to her.

For the first time she began to think that she might have got herself in a lot more trouble than she'd realized.

That thought became certainty when the guard led her to the nearest of the huts, a prefabricated storage shed with metal walls and roof, seven or eight metres long and four or five wide. He unlocked a padlock on the sliding doors, pulled them wide, pointed her inside and once she was in, slid the doors shut and padlocked them again.

She looked around the inside of the hut, dimly lit by narrow, fiberglass-covered windows in the curved ceiling. Crates and barrels filled the space. Thanks to Canadian laws that mandated bilingual labels on everything from shampoo to breakfast cereal, she could read French better than she could speak it. If she was right, the barrels were filled with fuel oil, probably for generators. Some of the crates contained food. Others were labeled with words she didn't recognize at all: scientific equipment, maybe.

But none of the barrels contained water. Nor were there any faucets, drains, or anything else she could use.

Despite all the power she'd inherited from the Lady of the Lake, despite the additional power the first shard of Excalibur gave her, she was hopelessly and completely a prisoner.

Or was she? Her cell phone! She grabbed her backpack, unzipped it, and rummaged through its jumbled contents...there! She pulled out the phone, took one look at it, and almost threw it across the room in disgust.

Of course it was dead. When was the last time she had charged it? Then she snorted. And how many times had it been dunked in water since she'd left Regina? Probably wouldn't have worked anyway.

Without her cell phone, and without a watch, she didn't even know what time it was. After noon, surely?

Which meant Wally would be landing in Lyon within a few hours.

She wouldn't be there to meet him. And she had no way to tell him where she was or what had happened to her.

Ariane had gone to Sunday School for many years when she was little, at her mother's insistence. How did that line from *Proverbs* go? "Pride goeth before destruction, and a haughty spirit before a fall."

You just proved it, she thought.

With a sigh, she made herself as comfortable as she could in a corner of the hut, sitting on a crate, feet pulled up, arms wrapped around her knees.

All she could do now was wait for Dr. Beaudry...and she had no idea how long it would be before he came back.

Ariane Forsythe, you're an idiot, she told herself, and against that accusation, she had no defence.

CHAPTER NINE

CALL OF THE DARK

WALLY HAD BEEN TO EUROPE before with his family: twice, in fact. He'd even flown into Frankfurt before, on the last trip, the one other time he'd visited France, when his family had still been a family. He'd only been eleven, but he thought he remembered the routine well enough that he'd have no trouble getting through customs and making his connection to Lyon, especially since he could sorta-kinda speak French.

He wasn't worried about himself...not much, anyway. But he was worried about Ariane.

In the middle of the abbreviated night, somewhere near the Arctic Circle, he leaned his head against the cool Plexiglas of the airplane window and looked down at clouds shining in the moonlight far below. It was a very strange notion, but he wondered if even then Ariane was *in* those clouds, making her own way to France via this new twist of the Lady's magic.

He snorted. *If she moved as fast through the clouds as she moved us through water, she's already there and waiting for me.* Then he frowned. If she got there first, and sensed where the shard was...what if she simply went and got it, without waiting for him? Despite their plans, if she saw a chance she'd surely take it. She might greet him at the airport with shard in hand.

It was an uncomfortable thought, which, if it happened, would raise an uncomfortable question. *Does she really* need me anymore? Am I really the heroic sidekick...or just useless baggage?

Wally tried to sleep, with little success, and was jolted awake by turbulence as the sun rose. It wasn't bad, but it went on for half an hour or more, and by the end of that time his head hurt and he'd even pulled out the airsickness bag, just in case. Thankfully, he managed to fight down his nausea as the turbulence eased, though a faint headache remained. *Must be the concussion*, he thought, disgusted; he was never airsick, carsick, seasick, or any other kind of motion-sick.

The rough ride made him wonder again what the trip had been like for Ariane. What would happen if *she* hit a thunderstorm? Worrying about her helped him stop worrying about whether the very large gentleman who had been in front of him in the screening line in Regina, had followed him across the Calgary airport to the Frankfurt flight, and was now seated directly behind him, would lose his own battle with airsickness; from the moaning and gulping, he was in worse shape than Wally, and Wally wasn't sure he could contain the contents of his own stomach if he heard – or worse, smelled – someone else throwing up.

In the end, neither one of them upchucked, though it was a close thing. Wally had devoured the meal served during the first three hours of the flight, even though he wasn't entirely sure what the protein had been – beef? chicken? fish? – but he turned down breakfast entirely, which surely would have astonished Ariane had she known.

I wish she did *know*, he thought. *I wish she were here.*
Early on, Wally had wondered if the big man with the

weak stomach was one of Rex Major's spies. When they finally landed in Frankfurt, he watched the man carefully. But, still looking a bit green, the big man waddled off in the company of a skinny blonde who met him on the other side of customs. He didn't reappear on the Lyon-bound plane, which Wally caught in the nick of time. *False alarm*, Wally thought. *With luck, Merlin still has no clue what we're up to.*

Wally's seat for the short flight to Lyon was near the back and next to the window of the rather small jet, and as a result he was one of the last to exit. Having carried his backpack onto all three planes, he didn't need to follow the crowd to the baggage reclaim area, but he did so anyway, since that was the likeliest place for Ariane to look for him. As he walked, he searched the crowds rushing past for Ariane's mane of black hair and bright blue eyes.

He didn't see her. He reached the baggage claim area, and watched as other passengers hugged children, kissed spouses or lovers, retrieved their luggage from the carousel and then headed off toward buses or parking or taxis or the train station. Still no Ariane.

But while he was staring off into the distance at a black-haired girl, trying to decide if it could be Ariane or not, a familiar voice behind him said, "Welcome to Lyon, Mr. Knight."

Wally's heart skipped a beat and his skin went cold. He spun to see a tall man with grey eyes, grey hair and an impeccably tailored blue suit smiling at him with even white teeth. A ruby stud glinted in the lobe of his right ear. "What are you doing here?" Wally said, and instantly thought that made him sound like an idiot, since Rex Major was obviously in southern France for the same reason he was.

"I am in France for the second shard of Excalibur, of

course," Major said. "But I am *here*, at the airport, to meet you."

"Why?" Wally demanded. He looked around. The crowd of people arriving had dwindled to a group of four friends having an animated conversation on the other side of the carousel, on which a lonely pink suitcase was going round and round, unclaimed, but it still didn't seem likely Major was going to forcibly haul him away in front of witnesses, no matter how few. "You can't do anything to me here."

"I don't want to do anything to you," said Major. "As to why I am here...isn't it obvious?" He spread his hands. "Because no one else is."

"Ariane's here," Wally said. "Somewhere."

"Really?" Major's eyebrows lifted. "But she didn't board the plane with you in Regina."

"She didn't need to board the plane."

The eyebrows knitted together again. "Then she has discovered a way to cross the ocean using the Lady's magic? How?"

Wally said nothing. Merlin thought for a moment. "Of course," he said. "The clouds." He sighed. "I once suspected the Lady had that power, but I was never entirely certain."

Wally, you're an idiot, Wally thought. *Sounds like Merlin didn't know that bit of information until you dumped it in his lap.*

"She surprises me again," Merlin went on. "And yet..." he made a show of scanning the baggage area, "I don't see her. Do you?"

"She's around." Wally shifted uncomfortably from one foot to the other. "She probably doesn't want to reveal herself with you here."

"Maybe she's hiding in the toilet," Major said. "Possibly in the actual bowl."

Wally's mouth quirked despite himself. "She's around," he repeated. "You still haven't told me what you want with us."

"I said I came to meet *you*," Major said. "Not you and Ariane, whom, unlike you, I never expected to be here. Just you."

Wally didn't like the sound of that. He stared around, wondering if he were about to be taken hostage for the second time in less than a month. "Ariane!" he shouted. "You can come out!"

The four people still chatting loudly in French by the baggage carousel cast surprised looks at him. So did the soldier in camouflage carrying an automatic rifle, which wasn't something Wally was used to seeing in an airport. Catching the soldier's cold blue stare, Wally snapped his mouth closed and decided not to shout again.

In any event, Ariane didn't emerge from her hiding place...not that he could see any hiding places, unless she really *was* inside one of the toilets. "Do you still think she's here?" Rex Major said softly.

"I know she is," said Wally.

"Why? Because she promised?" Rex Major shook his head. "The Lady will promise *anything* to get what she wants, and break those promises without a second thought. Believe me, I know."

"Ariane is not the Lady," Wally said. "She –"

"Ariane *is* the Lady," Major insisted. "Or is becoming the Lady."

"She's not...."

"...here," Major finished for him. He moved closer, and said in a low voice, "And you know why, if you think about it. Now that I know she has found a way to use magic to get here, it's certainly clear to *me*. She never really needed you. She let you come, because she likes you, I suppose, but she was really just humouring you."

"That's not true," Wally said hotly. "We had it all planned. I would fly here, Ariane would use magic to get here, we'd meet up and go get the shard together."

"Indeed," Major said. "You had it all planned, you say. She promised to be here. And yet she is *not* here. And you know why, if you are honest with yourself. She's not here to meet you for the simple reason that she's already gone after the shard...without you."

Wally said nothing for a moment. It all sounded horribly plausible. And the worst of it was, if Ariane *had* done that...he couldn't even really blame her. He was just the sidekick in this story. She was the heroine. Heck, she was more than just a heroine: she was a *superheroine*. The two of them weren't even Batman and Robin; they were more like Superman and Jimmy Olsen. Superman never waited for Jimmy. Why should Ariane wait for him, if she had a chance to get the shard?

The Lady gave both *of us the quest*, he thought plaintively. Hard on the heels of that thought came another, as it so often did: *But I still don't know if we can trust the Lady.*

He searched the baggage area again, but it was a useless effort. Even the French foursome had left, and the carousel had stopped. The soldier remained, but he had pulled the unclaimed suitcase from the carousel and was kneeling beside it, talking into a microphone attached to his lapel. A woman suddenly burst through the door leading to the concourse and dashed over to the soldier, apologizing profusely in French.

Wally looked at Major, and tried to harden his wavering resolve. "Or maybe she's not here because she had trouble getting across the Atlantic," he said. "She wasn't sure she could do it. That's why she didn't want to try to bring me with her that way. That's why I came by plane."

"You're deluding yourself, Wally," Major said softly.

"Then why are *you* here?" Wally demanded. "If I'm

no use to Ariane, how could I be of any use to you? If she is what you say she is, she won't give you the second shard...even if you threaten to kill me." The woman rushed off with her suitcase; the soldier began walking away, his back to Wally and Merlin. Wally wished he'd come back. "That's what comes next, isn't it? You threaten to kill me?"

"Why would I do that?" Major said. "I only threatened you in Yellowknife to convince Ariane to give me the shard. Right now she doesn't have the shard. I would know if she did." He smiled. "I suspect she has been stymied by the rather...difficult...location." He glanced at the soldier, now three carousels away and talking to a blue-uniformed policeman, took another step closer to Wally, and lowered his voice even more. "I am not here to take you hostage, Wally. I won't try to influence Ariane by threatening you ever again, because now that she has one shard, and has held it for a significant period of time, threatening you won't work. It *can't*. The shard won't let it." He sighed. "Although at least, at this point, she'd still feel badly if something happened to you. Once she has two shards...I wouldn't even bet on that."

"Then why are you here?" Wally repeated. He looked around again. The soldier and cop were still talking. No one else was in sight.

Still no Ariane.

"I'm here to take you to where the second shard is hidden."

Wally's gaze jerked back to Major.

"Wally, I'm not the villain, no matter what the Lady would have you think," Major continued. "I told you before – it's true that I want the sword so that I can take charge of the world, but I want to make it *better*, not destroy it! I want to *fix* things. All the *Lady* wants is for Excalibur to be re-forged and returned to her, in Faerie, thereby sealing the door between the worlds. If that happens, magic will vanish from Earth forever, and poor suffering humanity will be left to its own resources, as it has been since my *first* attempt to heal the world went awry all those years ago in England."

And it hasn't exactly been a grand few centuries, has it? Wally thought. *Especially the last one.* But reminding himself *again* that this was *Merlin* he was talking to – though at least this time Major didn't seem to be using magic on him – all he said out loud was, "I still don't see what you want from me. I mean, yeah, I'm getting to be a pretty good fencer and I know my way around a computer, but..."

Major hesitated. "It's possible...just possible...that you are very much more than you think...just as Ariane turned out to be much more than she ever thought."

Wally's heart skipped another beat. "Are you saying I have magic too?" Every fantasy novel he'd ever read about the ordinary kid who turned out to have extraordinary powers flashed through his mind. *Maybe I'm* not *just a sidekick*, he thought. *Maybe the Lady saw that too...and didn't tell me?* Another mark against her, if true.

"It's possible," Major said. "But only the shards of Excalibur can tell me for certain."

Wally's excitement evaporated. "So it's just a trick to get me to come with you."

"It's not a trick." Major put out his hand and gripped Wally's shoulder. "Wally, I just want you to spend some time with me. Let me explain my plans, my dreams. Don't fear me. Please. I know it's hard to believe, but I'm trying to help you."

Wally swallowed an unexpected lump in his throat. That gesture was one his father had performed countless times. The hand on the shoulder...the direct gaze...the note of concern in the voice....

Yeah, and Dad didn't really mean it, did he? Wally thought with deliberate harshness. *It's a trick. This man threatened to kill you, tried to kidnap Ariane. He's not a nice guy.*

But....

"You are very much more than you think...."

He tried to push away the possibility, not think about it. *Focus on what you know, not what Merlin is trying to make you believe!* He shrugged off Major's hand and took a step back from him. "No. You're trying to trick me into betraying Ariane, trying to get me to help you get the second shard!"

Major looked around the empty baggage area. "It appears to me," he said, "that she has already betrayed *you*." His gaze returned to Wally. "And, Wally, listen to yourself. Do you really think I *need* your help to retrieve the shard? I know where it is, and I know how to get it. It's true I think you may have the *potential* to become something...someone...very special, but right now you're just a rather clumsy fourteen-year-old boy." He spread his hands. "I'm *Rex Major*. I don't need your help, Wally. I'm just here to offer you the opportunity to observe me, and then judge for yourself whether I or the Lady most deserves your trust. And if you *do* choose to trust me, *then* I will tell you what...who...I think you might be. And if I obtain the second shard, and it confirms my suspicion, then, and *only* then, I may ask you to help me."

"And if I refuse to come with you?" Wally said.

Merlin laughed. "Then you're free to go. I'll even give you money for a taxi to wherever it is you're planning to stay while in France." He smiled at Wally. "So. Will you trust me this little bit? Will you trust me enough to come with me to where the second shard is hidden?" He spread his hands. "I have met you in a public place. I have not tried to use magic on you. I am not threatening you.

Whatever you decide is purely your choice."

Choice. Wally hadn't had much of that lately. The *Lady* hadn't given him a choice. She'd thrust him into this quest without asking him if he wanted it (he would have agreed in a heartbeat, he freely admitted, but still, she hadn't *asked*). He hadn't had any choice about his parents splitting up either, or his sister moving out, or being stuck with Mrs. Carson as his guardian. But here, *now*, Major *was* offering him a choice. A *real* choice. He had come to Wally alone, with no bodyguards or henchmen. They were in a public place with an armed soldier and a policeman not far away. Wally could tell him "no" and walk away right now. Major was doing everything he could to back up his soft words with soft actions, to show that he was not here to threaten, but to make an honest offer.

And what if Major were telling the truth? If the stakes were as high as he said, could Wally really blame him for his actions in Yellowknife? Without the sword, Major would age and die. Without the sword, he could do nothing more than any other wealthy man to help the world. But *with* the sword...anything was possible.

A world united and free of terrorism, war, hatred, famine and disease, versus a world cut off from magic forever, left to sink even further into misery and destruction?

If I go with him, I'll be putting myself at his mercy. If I take this chance and he's lying, I'll have ruined everything for Ariane.

But if he's telling the truth, then I'll actually be helping her by trusting him. Because that will mean the Lady is the dangerous one, the one who's been misleading us. If Major is telling the truth, the real threat to Ariane is the way the Lady's power...and that of the shard...is changing her. Corrupting her.

Wally didn't see any way around it. As illogical as it seemed, the only way to find out if he could trust Major was to trust him. At the very least, if he let Major take him to where the shard was, he'd also be where Ariane either already was, or soon would be.

"All right," Wally said. "I'll come with you. But I'm not promising I'll help you. And if you threaten me or Ariane, I'll –"

"I would expect nothing less," Major said. "Our last encounter was...clumsy. I was angry to discover the Lady was working against me. But I realize it's not really your fault. It's not even Ariane's. She is in thrall to a power greater than herself. And while it is, of course, my ultimate goal to have Excalibur whole for my own use, it is also my sincere hope that my re-forging of the sword will free Ariane to once more be nothing but an ordinary teenager. I think she would be happier that way."

Would she? Wally thought. He thought of Major's vague, exciting suggestion that he, too, might have special powers. *Would I, if I were in her place?*

He didn't know. But after what had happened to Flish, he was beginning to think Ariane and everyone around her would at least be *safer* if she didn't have her powers.

The soldier and policeman were both watching them now, looking decidedly unfriendly. They'd obviously outstayed their welcome. "All right," he repeated.

Major smiled. "This way," he said. Wally followed him toward the street.

◄◄ ►►

Ariane waited in the equipment shed for an hour before someone came to see her. She looked up, expecting the mysterious Dr. Beaudry – but it was only the English-speaking guard. "I have brought water," he said, setting a large plastic bottle on a crate just inside the door. "Do you need to use the toilet?"

Well, she did, now that he mentioned it. And if there were enough water in that toilet..."Oui, s'il vous plaît."

He nodded. "This way," he said indicating she should follow him.

Her brief flicker of hope died when she entered the porta-potty and closed the door behind her. The only liquid she could sense was what had collected in the storage tank at the unit's base, and she shuddered at the thought of trying to do anything with *that*. As soon as she emerged, she was taken back to the shed and locked up once more. The guard refused to answer any of the questions she asked him about how much longer she would have to wait for Dr. Beaudry.

She huddled there in the semi-darkness, taking a sip from the bottle of water periodically, as the afternoon wore away. *Wally's in Lyon by now*, she thought. *He'll be wondering where I am. What will he do?*

What *could* he do? Without her to guide him, he didn't have a clue where the second shard could be. He would have to check into their hotel and wait.

He could phone home, she thought uneasily. She thought of Aunt Phyllis answering that call, hearing from Wally that he was in France, but Ariane hadn't arrived...

Picturing Aunt Phyllis's distress made her feel sick, but there was nothing she could do about it. *I screwed up*, she thought, not for the first time.

Finally, when the light streaming in through the narrow windows had taken on the distinctive blue tint of twilight, just when she'd started to worry they intended to leave her in the equipment shed all night, she heard a vehicle pull up outside, its lights flashing across the windows.

A car door slammed. Muffled voices grew louder, and then she heard someone fumbling with the padlock. She scrambled to her feet as the doors slid open.

Her English-speaking guard stood behind a much

shorter (and balder), man, whom she had last seen emerging from the cave. "Dr. Beaudry, I presume?" she said.

His mouth twitched into an almost-smile, and she felt a flood of relief. He obviously wasn't the monster her imagination had been building him up into over the past few hours.

And also, he spoke English.

"René Beaudry, oui. Director of Prehistoric Antiquities for Midi-Pyrénées, so appointed by the Ministry of Culture," he said. His voice was soft and calm. "And you are...?"

She felt a moment's panic. What name had she given the guards? "Ar...Arial. Arial Muirhead." That was it. *Mrs. Muirhead*, she told herself. *Just think of* Macbeth.

"Canadian, I am told?"

"Yes."

"But not *French*-Canadian, obviously?" Again, that flicker of a smile.

"No," said Ariane. "I'm from Saskatchewan."

"Well, Arial Muirhead from Sas-kat-chew-an," he stumbled over the province's name a little, "come out here, please. We must have a chat." He stepped aside, and she exited the equipment shed with relief.

The sun had set and stars pricked the cloudless sky. The temperature had dropped substantially, and she'd left her jacket on the box on which she'd been sitting. She wrapped her arms round herself. Dr. Beaudry noticed and turned to the guard. "Donnez-lui votre manteau," he said, and the guard nodded and took off his uniform jacket, handing it to Ariane. Gratefully she draped it over her shoulders. "My apologies for any discomfort you have suffered, Arial," said Dr. Beaudry. He gave the guard a hard look. "The equipment shed is the only building in which you could be locked. I have told my men they should have put you in the trailer instead and simply waited outside the door for my return. It is not like you are a prisoner of war!"

"Um...it's all right," Ariane said. "I was just a little scared, wondering how much trouble I was in."

"That is what we must determine," said Dr. Beaudry. He studied her, though he couldn't have seen her very well in the dim light. "So, Arial Muirhead. What are you doing here? You seem very young to be travelling Europe on your own. Where are your parents?"

"I don't have any," she said. Which was true enough. "And I'm not as young as I look. I'm...eighteen." The farmer and his wife had believed that lie...hadn't they?...but Dr. Beaudry's left eyebrow raised skeptically, and she rushed on. "I'm doing that backpacking-across-Europe thing."

"A girl of your age?" Dr. Beaudry's left eyebrow descended and knitted with his right into a deep frown. "Très dangereux!"

"I can take care of myself," Ariane said.

"Vraiment?" Dr. Beaudry looked toward the trail that led down to the tent and the cavern entrance. "And why, exactly, did you try to enter the cavern?"

Ariane shrugged. "I saw you come out. I thought it might be interesting."

"Interesting enough to risk being captured by the guards?"

"There weren't any guards when I entered," she said truthfully.

"Ah. Oui. Very odd, that." Dr. Beaudry glanced at the guard. "There seems to have been an unusual... surge...from the river. We are very fortunate it did not flood the cavern."

"What's so special about the cavern?" Ariane said.

"You do not know?" Dr. Beaudry's eyes narrowed. "You really only entered it for a...what's the English expression...a lark?"

"I was bored. I thought it might be fun."

Dr. Beaudry spread his hands. "That cavern contains some of the most amazing cave paintings ever found anywhere in the world...amazing not only for their size and complexity, but because of their age: the oldest are at least 35,000 years old. Maybe more."

Ariane blinked. Rex Major and the Lady of the Lake had been around a thousand years ago, and that seemed unimaginably ancient. But 35,000...! "How did they survive so long?"

"Pure chance," said Dr. Beaudry. "At some time the cliff face collapsed and sealed off what was once the main entrance. Much, much later, another earthquake opened a new way in, the way you entered. The interior has been untouched for millennia, except for small animals and birds, whose bones litter the floor. Also, the cavern is very dry...unusually so."

Even though part of her was screaming at her to get away, find Wally, and grab the shard, Ariane was genuinely interested in the cave paintings...but the comment about the lack of water in the cavern captured her attention in an entirely different way. "But I thought caverns almost always have water in them. Aren't they formed by water?"

"Oui," said Dr. Beaudry. "And so was this one. But the water has receded. There is very little in the cavern now."

"No pools? No underground rivers?" *Uh-oh*....

"In the main cavern, there is a very shallow pool," Dr. Beaudry said, "which appears to have once been much larger. The water drips into it from the ceiling, very slowly. Much, much deeper in the cavern, we have found a more sizable pool, which may be fed by an underground river."

"Is it big enough to swim in?"

Dr. Beaudry frowned. "What an odd question," he said. "And I think I have answered enough of them. I must decide what to do with you."

"Please let me go," Ariane pleaded. "I'm sorry I sneaked into the cavern. I didn't know it was so special."

"You knew it was guarded and you were told by the guards not to enter it," Dr. Beaudry said. "There are heavy fines for trespassing in a nationally protected site of antiquities. I should turn you over to the gendarmerie."

Ariane started to beg him not to do that, but then realized that the gendarmerie would at least have running water in their bathroom. "If you must."

Dr. Beaudry smiled. "But I will not. I do not believe you understood the gravity of your offense. Having been locked up all afternoon, however, perhaps you do now."

"I do," Ariane said.

"Then you are free to go," said Dr. Beaudry. He looked up at the darkening sky. "I will drive you to the village."

"That's very kind of you," Ariane said. "Merci beaucoup."

"It is not far," said Dr. Beaudry. He held out his hand. "I think Philippe would very much like his coat back before we go."

Ariane slipped it off her shoulders and handed it to the guard. "Merci, Philippe," she said.

"De rien," Phillipe replied. He held out her own dusty jacket and her backpack, which he had retrieved from the storage shed. "Bonne soirée," he added, and headed back down the path, presumably to spend the night in the tent.

Dr. Beaudry led Ariane to his vehicle, a brand-new Renault SUV. He opened the passenger door for her, waited while she climbed in, then closed the door, went around the front and got in behind the wheel. She relaxed into the black leather seat and suddenly found her eyelids heavy. What time was it back in Saskatchewan?

"There is a small hotel in Cellier de l'Abbaye," said Dr. Beaudry. "Have you any money?"

"Yes," Ariane said.

"Then I will take you there." He gave her a smile. "Are you hungry?"

"Yes!" She hadn't realized it until he asked, but she was ravenous.

"I did not eat my lunch today. You may have it. In the glove compartment."

Ariane popped open the glove compartment and took out a plastic container. She peeled it open to find bread, meat, cheese and fat green olives, and tore into everything with far-from-ladylike zeal. Dr. Beaudry eyed her out of the corner of his eye. "You are *sure* you have money for the hotel?"

"Yes," Ariane said, between mouthfuls. "Honestly."

"Hmm." Dr. Beaudry didn't sound convinced.

The unpaved road, little more than a rutted track, twisted back and forth around limestone outcroppings and through stretches of forest. But after fifteen minutes it joined a paved road that a few minutes later brought them to a village, all narrow winding streets and gangly stone buildings. Dr. Beaudry stopped in front of a rather grand structure whose facade was unmistakably that of a church, with Gothic arches and a stone cross above the main entrance. "Auberge de l'Abbaye," Ariane read on the low, stone-framed sign in front. "Abbey Inn?"

"The Abbey that gave the village its name," Dr. Beaudry said. "Now a hotel. Rather expensive, I'm afraid, but the Ardèche region is a major tourist destination. Fortunately, it is past high season and there will be vacancies."

Ariane nodded. She opened the door and got out of the SUV, reaching back inside for her backpack. "I'm sorry for trying to sneak into your cavern," she said. "Thank you for not reporting me to the police."

"You are welcome, Arial." A smile flickered across Dr. Beaudry's face, then vanished. "But if I see you there a second time, I will not be so lenient!"

"I understand," Ariane said. She closed the door and watched as he drove away.

A doorman emerged into the courtyard through the tall iron-bound doors. "Mademoiselle?" he said. "Puis-je vous aider?" When Ariane hesitated, he switched to English. "You are checking in?"

"I..." Ariane thought how wonderful it would be to sleep in a nice comfortable hotel room, to get up in the morning and enjoy a leisurely breakfast, to maybe take a walk around the village...she was in France, after all!

But she stiffened her resolve and her spine, and instead said to the doorman, "No, I'm afraid not. But...if I may use your washroom?" He looked confused. "La...toilette?"

His face cleared. "Mais oui," he said. "Suivez-moi."

He led her into the lobby.

Unlike its facade, the lobby of the Auberge de l'Abbaye retained nothing of its ecclesiastical heritage, unless the ancient abbot or abbess had taken a highly unconventional approach to the vow of poverty. In light of all the marble, crystal and polished brass on display, Ariane suspected her small store of euros would barely have bought her a single night. It was all so grand she was almost surprised to be allowed to use the lobby washroom, but there was, after all no one else around and the doorman seemed a decent-enough fellow. Or maybe he was just bored.

Well, Ariane thought, *his evening is about to become a lot less boring...because the girl he's showing into the bathroom isn't coming out again.*

Dr. Beaudry had said there was a large pool deep inside the cavern. She thought it must be the body of water she'd previously sensed, the one she'd been afraid to materialize in for fear it was completely enclosed in rock. Since he knew of it, it must both be open to the air and offer access to the rest of the cavern. That would be her route in.

Inside the bathroom, she first rummaged in her backpack for the flashlight she'd packed. It wasn't very big, maybe twice the size of a lipstick case, but its LED lamp put out plenty of illumination. She didn't plan to be underground very long: she'd materialize in the pool, and that close to the shard, she should be able to find it without any trouble. She'd grab it, get back in the water, transport herself to Lyon and find Wally at the hotel. Then – once she'd apologized profusely and explained why she'd gone after the shard without him – they could plan their return to Canada. Wally might have to wait to catch a flight, but Ariane could head home at once, whisking the second shard of Excalibur safely out of Major's reach.

If he'd even dare to come after it. She shivered a little, wondering what it would be like to have *two* of the shards of Excalibur strapped to her skin, filling her with their power, their anger, their fierce desire to strike down all enemies.

She'd find out soon enough.

She pulled her backpack back on, then, holding her flashlight in her left hand, turned on the cold-water tap in the marble sink basin with her right, stuck her fingers into the water and whisked away.

By now, the sensation had become as familiar as breathing, the immense strangeness of it almost forgotten. She was used to rushing through pipes to sewage treatment plants...at least her watery self had no sense of smell!...and quickly found her way to the outflow of the one that served the village. It dumped clean effluent into the river, well downstream of where she needed to be, but that was no obstacle. Close to the cavern, she followed rivulets through the rocks, racing in seconds through crevices the water took days or weeks to seep through. Slithering through stone, twisting, turning, she sought an approach to the pool she felt nearby.

And suddenly she found it. No underground river fed the pool after all; it was just a deep depression into which water seeped from one place and seeped out through another. Beginning to feel her strength starting to wane as she squeezed through the rocks, she gladly let herself materialize. The pool wasn't much deeper than a bathtub, but that was deep enough. She lifted herself dripping out of the water and shone her flashlight around the chamber.

Her breath caught. Salmon-coloured stalactites, glittering with crystals, hung in curtains ten metres above her head like a frozen aurora borealis. Around the edges of the S-shaped pool, shining stalagmites thrust upward. She stood in water the colour of milk, rafts of multifaceted crystals floating here and there on its surface. She wished she could illuminate the whole chamber at once, instead of being limited to pointing her bluish circle of light here and there, but even the little bit she could see was beautiful and eerie at the same time.

But she wasn't there as a tourist. She pulled the circle of light away from the stalactites and flashed it around the edge of the pool. Finding a spot where the rock sloped gently into the milky water, she waded out and wished herself dry. Then she began looking for an exit from the chamber. Dr. Beaudry had seen this pool, so there must be....

...there. A dark opening, a tunnel leading up.

A *narrow* tunnel. She hesitated. She'd have to crawl, and she was uneasily aware of the mass of rock over her head, rock she had been flitting through as water just minutes before. But if Dr. Beaudry had come *down* this tunnel, he must have gone back *up* it, and that meant she could too.

But *he* had had a helmet lamp. She only had a handheld flashlight. She considered the problem for a moment, then slipped off her backpack and tied the flashlight by its wrist strap to one corner of the backpack, so that it peeked over her shoulder. It flopped a bit as she moved, but it left her hands free.

All set at last, and wondering uneasily just how long her flashlight batteries would last, she got down on her hands and knees and crawled into the tunnel...and toward the song of the second shard now flooding her mind.

At first the going was easy enough. The water-smoothed stone didn't even hurt her hands and knees...much. But as she continued to climb, the tunnel narrowed. Before long she had to lower herself onto her belly, pulling herself along like a snake. The stone roughened, scraping her elbows and arms.

Worse was to come. The tunnel narrowed still more. To keep going, she had to wriggle out of her backpack, pushing herself backward down the tunnel until it came off her outstretched arms. Breathing hard from exertion and rising panic, desperate to get out of the tunnel, she pushed the backpack ahead of her and kept wriggling uphill...but now her tiny light, still fixed to a top corner of her pack, was completely hidden from her, so that she slithered through utter darkness, a black so complete that it seemed to have physical mass, pressing down on her with all the weight of the hundreds of feet of solid rock above her head.

Her breath came in tortured gasps, and in her chest, pressed tight against the rock, every heartbeat felt like a blow. *Could Dr. Beaudry* really *have come this way?* she thought. And then, a horrifying idea. *What if there was* another *tunnel? I didn't really explore the chamber....*

An even more horrifying thought followed hard on the heels of the first. *What if I get stuck? Nobody knows I'm here!*

Panting, she stopped. Should she wriggle back down again, return to the pool?

But she'd come so far...and this tunnel *was* still taking her toward the second shard – she could hear it so clearly now, could feel the first shard yearning to join it, as strongly as when she had entered the cavern earlier. She pushed ahead again, and almost at once the tunnel expanded. Emboldened, she redoubled her efforts. She sensed a wider space ahead, and gave her backpack a mighty shove into it....

...only to see the backpack vanish into emptiness, the circle of illumination from the flashlight drawing a brief, final blue streak across a line of stalactites before disappearing.

And then, with a loud crack, the ledge onto which she had unknowingly climbed gave way and she fell, screaming, into the same darkness that had swallowed her pack.

CHAPTER TEN

BE MY GUEST

WALLY EXPECTED REX MAJOR to drive straight to wherever the shard was, but instead, as they climbed into a taxi, Major asked him what hotel he and Ariane had booked. "Why?" Wally said. "We won't –"

"You might still need it," Major said reasonably. "And if you don't check in, you'll not only lose the room, you'll lose your deposit."

It made perfect sense, but it was all so mundane Wally felt bemused. *This man is Merlin,* he reminded himself. *Old, ancient, wise, powerful in magic...and he's worried about our hotel deposit?* Oddly, the sense of being looked after for a change made Wally feel better about accompanying him. *Monsters don't worry about other people's budgets!*

He told Major the name of the hotel, and Major, in impeccable French, instructed the cab driver to take them there.

Aunt Phyllis hadn't splurged on the hotel, and the building, when they drove up to it, made Wally think she'd paid too much even so. A tattered canopy hung from walls of rough, soot-blackened stone over the sidewalk. "Cœur de Lyon" read tiny grey letters on a canopy of equally dingy blue.

"Heart of Lyon," the name meant, and certainly they were somewhere in the old city, though hardly at its centre. But also, Heart of Lion...Lionheart. Like Richard. *Another King of England, but his time came long after Arthur's,* Wally thought. And long after Merlin/Major, who told the taxi driver to wait, then got out, held the door for Wally and led the way to the hotel entrance.

Together they went through the rotating glass door into the small, dark lobby, all red-leather chairs and walnut-panelled walls. It didn't look like much, but rich smells of spices and roasting meat filled it, making Wally's mouth water. Wally glanced through a door to their right as they approached the desk and saw a half-dozen patrons enjoying dinner in a rather gloomy restaurant panelled in the same dark wood. His stomach growled, and then, desperately tired, he yawned. *And* his head was hurting again. How long before he could eat...and sleep?

"There's another thing you obviously didn't consider," Major said as they approached the front desk.

Wally shot him a suspicious look. "What?"

"To check into a hotel in France, you must be eighteen years old." And then he switched to French and took care of everything with the desk clerk, checking Wally in, signing the register, then handing Wally two keys for room 404. But they didn't go up to the room: instead, Major led him back to the waiting cab.

Wally yawned again, jaw cracking, as he relaxed in the car seat. Major gave him a sympathetic smile. "Jet lag," he said. "One more reason to hate flying."

I wonder if Ariane suffered from jet lag, coming across the way she did? Wally thought, and felt a pang of unease. *If she made it across at all.*

What would she say if she could see him now, practically best buds with Merlin?

I'm just trying to find out the truth, for both of our sakes. I haven't betrayed her.

Yet, a tiny voice whispered deep inside.

Their new destination was fit for an emperor: it was even *called* L'Empire. Artfully lit to show off the intricate architectural detail of each of its five stories, it looked to Wally like something James Bond should be driving up to in his Aston Martin, ready to play high-stakes poker against some evil genius.

Its interior elegance matched that of its exterior. Marble floor and pillars, glass-topped tables, palm fronds, red-striped chairs that Wally could tell at a glance were intended more for looks than comfort...though tired as he was, he longed to sit down in one and just fall asleep.

But first they had to deal with the desk clerk. Wally listened as Major requested a second room for his young friend. The clerk protested, saying there were no rooms available. But Major lowered his voice until Wally couldn't hear him anymore, and a moment later the desk clerk, suddenly all smiles, said, "Bien sûr, Monsieur Major, à votre service."

Two minutes later Wally had a room card in his hand and, feeling rather dazed, was in the brass-and-marble elevator with Major. They emerged into a long cream-coloured hallway where every door was trimmed with gold and the white carpet was so thick they seemed to make no impression on it, gliding silently along. Wally felt almost disconnected from his body, as if he were a ghost haunting the old hotel, not a flesh-and-blood boy at all.

Major showed him to his door. "Sleep well," he said, and smiled. "As I'm sure you will. I think you are half-asleep already. I'll see you in the morning." He turned and went back down the hallway toward the elevators.

I could escape now, Wally thought, looking after Major's retreating back. *Nothing to stop me. Go out, go back to our own hotel, wait for Ariane....*

But the truth was, he didn't want to. All he wanted was sleep, and that was waiting just beyond that white-and-gold door.

The room had warm yellow walls, a deep blue carpet, thick, velvet drapes, fresh flowers on an elegant little side table and beautiful paintings on the walls: it was, in short, the most luxurious hotel room Wally had ever been in, even with his well-to-do parents. He desperately wanted to crawl into the bed, with its magnificently carved wooden headboard and snow-white, feather-filled duvet, but there was something else he had to do first.

He went into the bathroom – which had a marble floor and vanity, naturally – and filled the tub, marvelling even in his exhaustion at the tap, which surely wasn't real gold...was it? He sat on the closed toilet seat staring blankly at the marble-tiled wall while the water ran, so tired he almost nodded off twice. When he judged there was enough to allow Ariane to materialize in the tub should she somehow figure out where he was and arrive via magic in the middle of the night, he rose wearily to his feet and returned to the bedroom.

He stripped off his clothes, shoved the ribbon-tied box of chocolates off the pillow, pulled the duvet to his chin, and fell asleep in seconds.

◄◄ ►►

Rex Major, whose "room" in L'Empire was actually a four-room suite, sipped a very nice Rhône red and looked out from his top-floor window at, appropriately enough, the Rhône River. Car lights streamed across the picturesque Pont Wilson. Not far away, he knew, lay Vieux

Lyon, the old city, where tourists flocked to enjoy dining and shopping in the centuries-old buildings lining the winding cobblestoned streets – buildings and streets that had not been built until some half a millennium after Viviane imprisoned him.

It sometimes astonished even him how long he had been in the world. When he had lived as Merlin in England, Arthur's people had marvelled over the ancient buildings, roads and walls left behind by the Romans. In his modern guise, he had been to England many times...and seen grand buildings freshly built in his day reduced to nothing more than a few tumbled stones in a green field. Those ruins were further removed in time from the present than the Roman ruins had been from Arthur's court.

He snorted. *And the oldest ruins on Earth are brand-new compared to the ancient buildings of Faerie, which were built while humans were still squatting naked in caves.*

Should he succeed in freeing Faerie from the stultifying hand of the Queen and the Council of Clades, he might well still live long enough to see this era's buildings reduced to ruins. But, far more importantly, he might at last see some new buildings erected in Faerie, even grander than those of ancient days. Perhaps Faerie could finally move forward in time as this world did, instead of being trapped in its own past like an insect in amber.

And the boy, Wally Knight, heir to Arthur's power – potentially, at least – just might be able to help him accomplish that...if he could sway him to his cause.

That's a lot of caveats, he thought dryly. Still, he felt he had made a good beginning. The boy was too smart not to have doubts about the Lady of the Lake and what her power was doing to his friend, especially not after seeing Ariane use that power to attack his sister. More, the boy was desperate for a father figure, his own father having failed him so spectacularly. Merlin had seen how Wally had reacted to the simple gesture of a hand on his shoulder. He would continue to exploit that vulnerability.

Though completely unaware, the boy carried his own touch of magic in the blood of Arthur coursing through his veins. When grown to manhood, he could, with Major's help, be one of the greatest leaders the world had ever known. And unless Major missed his guess, like Arthur before him, even at his young age Wally was already looking around at this fragmented, fighting world and wondering if there wasn't a better way.

Arthur had fought to unite the myriad, tiny warring kingdoms of post-Roman England into one powerful nation, guided by the revolutionary idea that the strong, who unavoidably ruled the weak, also had a responsibility to both help and protect them. "Might for right," rather than "might makes right," in the words of the otherwise execrable musical monstrosity, *Camelot*.

It was the only way to create a society not only fair and just, but strong enough to withstand attack, Major firmly believed...which was why he'd planted that notion in young Arthur's head in the first place.

Major had no use for the modern love affair with democracy. Let the mob choose their own leaders, and inevitably they would vote for, as the Romans said, "bread and circuses," handouts and mindless entertainment, until their nations' treasuries were exhausted. As they pursued ever-more-trivial goals, they would even lose their willingness and ability to work, their passion to create and build. When a civilization weakened, there were always barbarianes waiting at the gates to bring it down, and this age was no different. The only thing that could fend them off was a strong leader, a new king armed with Excalibur. First he could root out those threatening this planet's civilization with terror and weapons of mass destruction...and then, with his power fully restored and all the newly united Earth's resources and technological know-how at his disposal, move to free and unite Faerie.

It was a grand vision. Far grander than the vision of King Arthur, who had sought only to unite one rather small island...although Merlin had hoped to ultimately extend Arthur's rule beyond Britain's shores. But in Arthur's time the world had not been intertwined with computer networks – networks through which Merlin's magic wove a gossamer-thin web. When he once more wielded his full power, that gossamer would become steel. And then, with nowhere on Earth outside his ken and reach, who would stand against him, or the forces that would flock to the service of their new king: King Wally!

Major winced. *I'd better get him to change his name.*

He turned his thoughts back to the present. All his grand plans depended on his obtaining the shards and re-forging Excalibur. Ariane, heir of his traitorous sister, already had the first and obviously had a good idea of where to find the second. But she didn't have it, not yet, and that gave him great hope. *Perhaps her attempt to cross the Atlantic using the clouds failed. She might even have died trying.*

He put that thought aside. If the girl died on land, he would shed few tears. But if she died in the middle of the Atlantic, the first shard would sink to the bottom of the ocean, from whence, with his magic so crippled, he might *never* be able to retrieve it.

No. Odd though it seemed, he actually hoped she was alive and well – but in Canada, while he was here, just a two-hour drive from the cavern where the second shard of Excalibur lay.

Tomorrow I will claim it, he thought with satisfaction. *And then Ariane Forsythe, the "Lady of the Lake," will be in for some surprises.*

He finished his glass of wine, stood and headed for bed.

If the rock ledge had simply plunged straight into the chasm, Ariane would surely have been killed. Instead it fell only a couple of metres, then hit a slope of broken stone and slid down, faster and faster, roaring and clattering. She lay flat on top with nothing to hold on to, coughing and choking on the stone dust raised by the ledge's grinding descent.

Then the rock hit something, and catapulted her into the air.

She smashed her shoulder against stone, rolled over, and finally came to rest against a rock face. Groaning, she sat up. Miraculously, nothing seemed to be broken, but every limb ached. Her knees, elbows, and palms were scraped and, though she could not see them, certainly bleeding. But worst of all, her backpack and the all-important flashlight had vanished.

She sat very still, breathing hard, staring into the darkness, seeking any spark of light: but though her eyes were wide open, she saw nothing but the same aimless, meaningless flashes of colour she saw when they were closed. The blackness pressed down on her like a thick blanket, as though trying to smother her. She found herself panting. She couldn't seem to get enough air...

I'm dead, she thought. *Dead and already buried. I'm going to die down here....*

She closed her eyes, though it made no difference, and tried to take deep breaths, willing her racing heart to slow. *Calm down!* she told herself. *Dr. Beaudry will be here. And other scientists. I'll hear them, or see them. They'll get me out.*

Or else I'll find water....

But she could sense none. The cavern really was, as Dr. Beaudry had said, bone dry.

Something heavy crashed down on the rocks, so close a stone nicked the tip of her ear. She gasped and clapped a hand to the place as blood trickled out, then scrambled to her feet. *I have to keep moving,* she thought. *It's not safe here. But which way?* With her back against the rock face, she reached out with both hands as far as she could, and felt nothing. She took a cautious step, and her foot slipped off a loose rock, her ankle turning with a frightening twinge. And what if she came across another chasm? She could plunge to her death without warning.

No, the only safe way to move was on her sore and bleeding hands and knees.

But which way? she thought again.

She sucked on a finger to wet it and held it up, hoping to feel a cooling breath of air on one side or the other that might indicate the direction of an exit. But she felt nothing. *Now what?* she thought. *Flip a coin?*

You don't have one. And you couldn't tell if it landed heads or tails anyway.

And then she remembered that she *did* have a compass of sorts. The terror of the fall, the shock of the landing and the terrible, oppressive darkness had momentarily driven it from her head, but now, as she paused, wondering which way to go, she heard once more the song of the second shard.

It was *there*, off to the right and above her. Could she reach it? She didn't know. But if she *could*, it would most likely be near water, since the Lady would have originally hidden it in water...and just let her find water, however little, and she could escape.

Water. She licked her lips. The hard work of the climb, the fall, the choking stone dust...she needed water for more than just escape. *I'll find it,* she reassured herself. She grimaced, dust gritting beneath her teeth. *I just hope it's sooner rather than later.*

Ariane had never had a nightmare as terrifying as this reality: smothered by darkness, creeping her way on hands and knees across broken rock, left hand, right knee, right hand, left knee, over and over again.

Every time she reached out with her hand she feared she would bang her knuckles on a wall of rock sealing off her path, or find nothing but air, the edge of another chasm. Twice she *did* encounter rock, and, sobbing in fear, turned to crawl parallel to it: but both times she discovered another opening, heading in more or less the right direction, and carried on.

Her lacerated knees and palms burned like fire and grew sticky with blood. A part of her wondered that she was still moving – but she wasn't drawing on her strength alone. The first shard felt the nearness of the second. Its magical power poured forth, bolstering her failing strength; and the nearer she got to the second shard, the more she could draw from the first.

But when, at last, she emerged into a space that seemed somewhat larger and with fresher air than any she had been in before, even the shard's strength poured away from her like the water she so desperately sought. Her shaking arms couldn't bear her weight any longer. She fell forward, arms folded under her, then rolled onto her side. Curled up on the ground, shivering, hurting, despairing, she closed her eyes – though it made no difference – and, blessedly, fell instantly unconscious.

In that dark place she would have welcomed one of the dreams of the Lady that had once so troubled her, dreams where sun shone on dappled water beneath a limitless blue sky…but her dreams were as black as her journey, as though even the memory of light had been pressed from her mind.

◄◄ ►►

Wally woke to the ringing of the bedside phone. For a moment he lay still, disoriented, unable to figure out what the sound was. His alarm clock didn't sound like that. And why was the room yellow? His room was blue...

Then everything came rushing back and he sat up with a gasp and lunged for the phone. White and gold, it was made in the style of phones from a hundred years ago...if you ignored its LCD screen and push-buttons. "Hello?" he said groggily.

"Good morning, Wally," said Rex Major. "I'm sorry to wake you so early, but we're due at the shard's location in three hours, and it will take two to drive there."

"No...." Wally yawned hugely "...problem." He glanced at the clock. 6:30 a.m. What time was that back home? He suspected he didn't want to know.

Feeling like someone had strapped barbells to his arms and dumbbells to his eyelids, he stumbled into the bathroom. The water in the tub hadn't been disturbed: Ariane had not made a midnight appearance.

He pulled the plug to let the tub drain while he used the toilet, then started the shower. Ten minutes of hot water woke him up considerably. As he climbed out of the shower and reached for a towel, he blinked at the sink in the marble countertop. Its taps, like those in the tub, appeared to be made of solid gold. As did the toilet handle, the towel racks, and the handles of that other strange-to-Canadian-eyes fixture, the bidet. (Though he knew what it was from previous trips to Europe, Wally hadn't used it. He didn't much care for the feel of water jetting up his butt.)

When he'd dried off, he stared at himself in the mirror. Dark shadows beneath his eyes, five stitches showing clearly on his white forehead with his hair plastered down...he looked like the survivor of some horrible accident. He scrunched up his eyes. And his head was hurting again. The pain had been growing since he got out of bed. He rubbed his temple and went into the room, digging around in his backpack until he found his bottle of Extra-Strength Tylenol. He went back into the bathroom to down two of the pills, then finally got dressed in fresh underwear and socks, a clean (if very wrinkled) pair of jeans, and a black T-shirt, for once unadorned by any geek-culture message. His head ached marginally less as the painkillers took effect, and he was sitting on the bed devouring the chocolates he had pushed off his pillow the previous night when Rex Major came knocking.

"Did you sleep well?" Major said, leading him to the elevator.

"Not long enough," Wally said. He yawned again. "I hate jet lag."

"Coffee and a croissant will do wonders," Major assured him.

What polite conversationalists we are, Wally thought, *considering he's a millennium-old wizard, I'm a kid from Saskatchewan and just a couple of weeks ago he was trying to kill me.* Descending into the Lady's watery chamber had had much the same effect on his life as falling down the rabbit hole had on Alice's.

A few minutes later he felt much more like himself, thanks to an almond croissant, another filled and drizzled with chocolate and his first espresso ever. He smacked his lips, wondering which would fade first: the bitter aftertaste or the buzz of caffeine.

Major glanced at his watch. "7:20," he said. "My car should be out front. Shall we?"

The car, a long black Mercedes, was indeed waiting. As he slid across the butter-soft leather of the rear seat, Wally thought, *I could get used to this.*

"Allons-y," Major said. (Wally smirked, wondering if Rex Major had ever seen the David Tennant incarnation of *Doctor Who*.) The chauffeur touched his black-visored cap with a black-gloved hand, then drove them smoothly into the narrow street in front of the hotel. Tires squealed behind them and Wally turned in his seat to see the driver of a green delivery truck shaking his fist furiously. Wally gave him a cheerful wave and turned around again.

It took half an hour to get out of Lyon, but soon they were zipping through farmland along a smooth highway. A bit more than an hour after they had left the hotel, though, they turned off that main road onto a winding secondary road, still paved, but much narrower, that led them up into the blue, stony ridges that paralleled the highway. Grey stone, green trees, lakes and rivers...it looked a little bit like northern Ontario to Wally, who was keeping his eyes on the scenery to avoid having to talk to Rex Major.

Ariane hadn't bubbled up in his tub in the middle of the night. She also hadn't phoned, and he'd checked his e-mail that morning, discovering nothing but the usual spam.

Wally couldn't figure out how anyone could fall for the obvious scams that flooded e-mail boxes. *Everybody wants something for nothing,* he thought. *But TANSTAAFL. There Ain't No Such Thing As A Free Lunch. Everything costs something. It's just a question of how much you're willing to pay for it.*

He stole a glance at Major. The software magnate appeared to be asleep, head tucked into the corner of the seat, mouth slack, breathing softly. *What's Major willing to pay for what he wants?* Wally wondered. *What's Ariane?*

Or more to the point, he thought, *what are Major and Ariane willing to make ordinary people pay...people like my sister?*

He wondered how Flish was doing. She'd be in the hospital for a few more days. He wondered if he'd see her again.

He wondered how she'd feel about it if he didn't.

He tried to put that rather morbid thought out of his

head and concentrate on the landscape outside. They flew past a tiny village whose name Wally missed as the sign flashed by, though he thought it said something about an Abbey. Moments later they turned off the secondary road onto a route that barely deserved to be called a road at all. Unpaved, rough and rutted, it ran so close to the trees on either side Wally thought if he rolled down the window he could probably grab the branches. They were moving much more slowly now, but still the car rocked and bounced so much it worsened his headache and unsettled his insides. He swallowed hard. *Hope we get there soon*, he thought. *Be a shame to throw up all over this nice black leather.*

Ahead he saw nothing but the tall green-and-brown fence of the forest, broken occasionally by looming walls of grey stone. When he looked back, everything was blotted out by the cloud of dust marking their passage. If it had been raining, he suspected the road would have been thick, impassible mud. But it was dry, dry, dry. *Not much for Ariane to work with, even if she's here*, he thought. But then they rumbled across an ancient stone bridge and he looked out and saw a broad river, winding between limestone cliffs.

Ten minutes later, they rolled to a stop in a clearing. A Renault SUV sat in front of the kind of trailer you'd see outside a construction site, and two smaller cars were parked near a couple of metal-sided prefabricated huts and a green portable toilet.

As the Mercedes pulled in behind the Renault, the door of the trailer opened and a man emerged. A little on the short side, a little on the rotund side, and a lot on the bald side, he wore a dapper grey suit and a huge smile. He came around to Major's side of the car, swung open the door, and stepped back with an expansive sweep of his arm. "Monsieur Major, welcome!"

Major climbed out and offered his hand. "Dr. Beaudry?"

The man shook his hand vigorously. "Oui. And may I say, monsieur, it is a great honour. A very great honour." His English was excellent; Wally had no trouble understanding him at all. "The Ministry is thrilled by your interest. And I do not think you will be disappointed."

"I'm sure you're right," said Major.

Wally got out of his side of the car and stared around, trying to figure out where they were, and what this well-dressed Frenchman was doing in what looked like a construction camp. "I have always been intrigued by antiquities," Major continued, "and I confess the tale of the discovery of this cavern –" Wally's interest was piqued – "has captured my fancy."

"Oui, yes, a wonderful discovery! Three schoolteachers, spelunking on a weekend in a tunnel, just about to leave. But then, ahead in the helmet light, a flash of colour...quite remarkable. Had they left even two minutes earlier, these paintings would still be unknown to us." Dr. Beaudry spread his hands. "But with the discovery comes responsibility. They are very fragile. If we do not protect them, they could be lost forever. We have done what we can, and we will do more, but resources are limited. Your support would...."

"Of course, of course," Major said. "And I certainly have every intention of supporting your work. But you understand I can't make any firm commitments until I have seen the paintings myself?"

Wally finally made the connection: caverns and paintings. *Cave paintings?* He felt a surge of excitement that had nothing to do with Excalibur. *Cool!*

Dr. Beaudry nodded vigorously. "Mais certainement!" He gestured behind him, off to the left. "If you will follow me?"

Wally took a deep breath as they crossed the clearing. The air smelled of pine and dust, a smell that instantly made him think of vacations in the Rockies. *You'd think French trees would smell different*, he thought.

The scientist led them to a set of stone steps carved into the lip of the cliff. They descended those, and then turned right, onto a narrow path. Wally kept close to the cliff face; the far side of the path fell away into nothingness, a sheer drop all the way to the pointy tops of pine trees far below. As he looked out over the forest he paused, hand on the rock wall, feeling dizzy for a moment. Major glanced back at him and Wally straightened and continued the descent, the dizziness already fading.

Beyond the pines was another ridge of limestone, and as they went on down, Wally caught a glimpse of water through a gap in that ridge and guessed it must be the river they had crossed earlier. Eventually they descended below the level of the treetops, and a few moments later followed the path off the cliff and into the forest. After about twenty metres it led them to another clearing, nestled in a kind of box canyon formed where the cliff they had come down jutted out to join the ridge closer to the river. At the far end of the clearing, close to the rock face, squatted a blue tent, surrounded on three sides by a chain-link fence. Two beefy men in grey uniforms sat on lawn chairs just inside the closed gate, which they jumped up to open when they saw Dr. Beaudry and his guests.

Wally, jet lag dogging his footsteps, trailed a good five metres behind Rex Major as they approached the fence. Major had eyes only for the tent, gaze locked on it as though trying to see through the blue nylon walls. But as Major strode ahead, Wally slowed still more, suddenly conscious of something odd.

Every mile they had driven on the dirt road, every step they had taken on the descending path, had raised a cloud of choking dust. The whole region seemed gripped in drought.

So why, then, were there patches of drying mud and even a few shining puddles of water covering half the clearing?

A freak rainstorm? Wally thought. *Or maybe they haul water from the river, and their water tank burst on the way up.* But only a *very* freakish rainstorm could wet such a tiny portion of the forest, and only a very large spill of water could wet so much of it.

Wally could think of only one other reason there might be water out of place near the cavern. He raised his head and scanned the silent forest. Nothing moved; even the birds seemed to have been discouraged by the unseasonable heat.

But whether or not she was there, silently watching him walk up to the cavern with her archenemy, or whether she was long gone with the second shard, or whether she was even then in the cavern, of one thing Wally was certain: Ariane had arrived.

She couldn't have retrieved the shard, he thought. *Major says he would know.*

Unless she has, *and he* does *know, and he just hasn't told me.* His suspicion rushed back. *What if that was his plan all along – to use me as a hostage again, to force Ariane to give him the shard?*

But no, that didn't make sense. If Ariane already had the shard, she wouldn't still be *here*, and in that case, why would Major bother coming? Wally didn't believe for a second he was really interested in ancient cave paintings.

He glanced at those out-of-place puddles of water, and felt a twinge of anger. If Ariane had already been here, then she really *had* set out to retrieve the shard on her own, without waiting for Wally to arrive.

But nipping at anger's heels came anxiety. If Ariane had made it this far, and the shard really was in the cavern just ahead, why hadn't she recovered it yet?

Wally scanned the surrounding woods a second time. How would Ariane react if she saw him with Rex Major, not as his hostage, but apparently in cahoots?

Serious though the situation was, his mouth twitched. *Cahoots? Does that mean I'm turning into a...a minion?*

His smile faded. *Or maybe a lackey.*

He shook his head wearily. He was too tired, too jet-lagged, and his head still hurt too much for him to think clearly. *I'm not a minion. I'm not a lackey. I'm just...confused. Ariane may have abandoned me, but I haven't abandoned her. If she's here, and she needs help, then I'll help her. I have to.*

Major had already gone through the gate with Dr. Beaudry. Wally hurried to catch up, reaching the flap of the blue tent just as it closed behind Major. He batted the nylon out of his face and stepped into the dim, stultifyingly hot interior.

Both Dr. Beaudry and Major were taking orange jumpsuits down from pegs on the tent pole. Wally glanced around but didn't see any more. "Where's mine?" he asked Dr. Beaudry.

The Frenchman looked discomfited. "I am sorry, but Ministry regulations...no minors are allowed into the cave...it is very dangerous...."

"The boy stays with me," Major said, not as if he were angry, but just as if he were stating an incontrovertible fact. "Find him a jumpsuit. Please."

Dr. Beaudry opened his mouth as if to protest, seemed to think better of it, and silently opened a trunk at the foot of one of the beds and pulled out a third jumpsuit, this one blue. It was two sizes too large, as were the steel-toed climbing boots he was given next, but there didn't seem to be a lot of selection. Wally pulled on a belt festooned with hammers and pitons and clips, then topped his spelunking ensemble with a helmet, complete with lamp.

His head almost rattled around inside it, but he pulled the chinstrap as tight as he could and, feeling like a little kid playing dress-up, followed the two men out the back flap of the tent and to the cavern's mouth. Major stopped, reached out, and flicked a switch to turn on Wally's helmet lamp, then turned back to the entrance, a vertical opening in the rock face, just wide enough for the men to squeeze through. Wally slipped through much more easily onto a level floor of dry stone, and tilted his head back to look up, his light revealing slabs of limestone forming a V-shaped roof seven metres above him. He wondered how the spelunkers had recognized the cave entrance for what it was. He was pretty sure he would have just walked past it, thinking it nothing more than a shadow.

He looked down instead of up, and saw that the floor extended only about ten metres, ending abruptly in darkness. They moved forward until they stood right on the lip of a sheer drop-off. Wally flashed his light around. Looking up, he saw that the roof had sloped down until it was only a metre or so above Rex Major's head. Wally ran his helmet lamp over it; it continued to slope for as far as he could illuminate it. He peered cautiously over the edge of the cliff and saw a pale blue light where the roof appeared to meet the floor. If there were a path deeper into the cavern, it would have to pass beneath that giant slab of rock. But it didn't look to Wally like he *wanted* to be beneath it. He looked up uneasily, thinking of the tonnes of rock above their heads. What exactly was holding it up?

Dr. Beaudry noted his glance. "This was not the original entrance into the cavern," he said. "This part of France is seismically active. The original entrance was in the next valley, the ancient bed of the river that now lies behind us. At some point an earthquake brought a landslide down over the entrance our cave-painting friends would have used. Perhaps that same earthquake altered the river's course. For millennia the cavern may have been completely sealed. But then another earthquake shifted things again, creating this opening...and down below, a tiny, tiny crack through which we can once more reach the complex of caverns the ancients knew."

He pointed to the top of a folding ladder that dangled into the depths, anchored at the top by two pitons driven deep into the rock. "This way. Be careful climbing onto it – it can be tricky to get your footing."

Wally gave the sloping rock above him another uneasy glance, rather wishing Dr. Beaudry had not told them about the local landscape's tendency to shift without warning, but then he sighed and moved forward. Dr. Beaudry helped him over the edge. Wally was glad he didn't have more than the normal fear of heights. *Or enclosed spaces. Or being crushed. Or buried alive. Or...*

Stop it, he ordered himself. He felt with his foot for one of the flat metal rungs of the ladder. The thing seemed to have a life of its own and strongly objected to his putting his weight on it, always wriggling away just when he thought he had his foot in position. Eventually it stilled and he was able to step down on it. After that it was just a matter of carefully descending, gripping the sides of the ladder so tightly his hands hurt, always making sure he didn't move the higher foot until the lower one was firmly on the next rung.

Halfway down he froze as dizziness swept through him and his head throbbed. *Not now!* He closed his eyes and held still, and the moment passed. Shaken, he resumed his descent. At the bottom he stepped off, turned sharply, and pressed his back against the rock face, breathing hard. The cold blue lamp hung on a collapsible aluminum pole, its light gleaming off the huge slab of the roof, which met the floor seven or eight metres from where he stood. He still couldn't see how they could travel any farther. But then, peering around into the darkness, he saw that the floor sloped down to his right...and maybe fifteen metres away, just at the limit of the light from the pole lamp, he spotted a black crevice between the rock of the roof and the rock of the floor.

Not a very *big* crevice, though. Certainly not tall enough to walk through.

Uh-oh.

Dr. Beaudry, once he'd joined Major and Wally at the bottom of the cliff, confirmed Wally's suspicion. "Now, we crawl," he said cheerfully. "I will lead. Then the young man, then Monsieur Major. D'accord?"

"Okay," Major said.

They walked over to the opening. It was even smaller than it had looked from a distance. Dr. Beaudry dropped to his hands and knees and crawled into it. Wally looked at Major. "Go on," Major said. "I'll be behind you if you run into trouble." His mouth quirked. "I have considerable experience with being confined to small spaces. At least this will be for only a short time. It's less pleasant when it lasts for centuries."

Wally cringed at the thought, and decided *not* to think about it. He took a deep breath, lowered himself to his hands and knees, and crawled after Dr. Beaudry.

The light of his helmet lamp revealed rough stone all around. Loose rocks covered the uneven floor. Sometimes he had a metre of clearance over his head; in other places his helmet scraped rock, making him very glad he was wearing it. At one point he wormed his way forward on his belly. All the time he was conscious of the vast weight of rock above him, aware that all it would take was an insignificant shrug of the earth's surface to squash him into paste, and he found his heart pounding and his breath coming in ragged gasps. His brain kept yelling at him to go back and his limbs threatened to freeze up entirely, unwilling to continue to carry him farther on this unnatural journey into the bowels of the earth. But he concentrated on pushing himself a little bit farther, then a little bit farther still, telling himself that if the rotund Dr. Beaudry had made it through without getting stuck, then surely he could...and sure enough, after what really wasn't very long but certainly felt like it, he saw light ahead of him. A moment later the gap suddenly widened and he crawled out into open space, illuminated by another battery-powered light. He raised his head and gasped.

A wild ox glared from the wall in front of him, its white eye wide above a black muzzle. Long, twisted horns ran up the rock, and a natural hump of stone painted ocher and yellow formed its massive shoulder.

Wally had seen photographs of cave paintings before, but seeing one in person took his breath away. The millennia-old pigments looked as fresh as though the artist who had daubed them on the stone had just put down his brush and stepped around the corner. Somehow the black lines, fewer than a modern cartoonist would use, and the smears of colour oozed life – primitive, wild and free – from a time Wally could barely imagine, a time already ancient when Merlin lived in Camelot.

Dr. Beaudry stood next to the ox, his head level with its eye, and smiled as proudly as if he had painted it himself. "This is what the three schoolteachers saw when they emerged from that tunnel for the first time," he said. "And they knew immediately they had found something remarkable."

"Remarkable indeed," said Rex Major as he, too, crawled out of the tunnel and stood, gazing at the painting. "And yet only the beginning, I believe?"

"Oui," said Dr. Beaudry. "This way."

Tearing his eyes away from the painting of the ox, Wally realized that here, at last, were the underground rock formations he had been expecting to see since they'd entered the cavern. From the ceiling, just feet above his head, daggers of stone stabbed the darkness, glittering with crystals. More rounded humps and spires rose from the cavern floor. The path Dr. Beaudry now led them along wound and doubled back upon itself, avoiding stalactites and stalagmites. Glancing down, Wally saw the marks of many booted feet: but, strangely, all were confined between two strands of red twine, strung along both sides of the path.

Before he could ask, Dr. Beaudry explained. "This path follows the footsteps of the discoverers, who, most fortunately, were very careful to disturb the cavern as little as possible. No one is permitted to step anywhere else. Look here." He stopped and pointed to one side, his helmet light picking out the skull of a great cat, snarling at them from across uncounted years. "There are other skeletons of animals that found their way in but did not find their way out. There may well be skeletons of humans elsewhere. There could be tools the painters dropped, arrowheads, traces of pigment...a careless footstep could destroy something of immense scientific value." He turned his attention back to the trail.

Still feeling a little breathless after the harrowing crawl through the tunnel, and fascinated by the sight of the cat skull, Wally lagged behind the other two, casting his helmet light across the floor in the hope of seeing some of those other skeletons Dr. Beaudry had mentioned. He spotted the small skulls of rodents, and what looked like a bird...and then, something else.

At the very limit of the light from his helmet, he glimpsed, stretched on the cavern floor, a dark shape that looked like...

...*like a corpse*, his mind insisted.

Certainly the object was the right size and general

shape of a human body. Not a skeleton, though, or there would be the gleam of bone. This person...if it *was* a person...was clothed. Had some spelunker found his way into the cavern and...?

Wally glanced toward Dr. Beaudry and Rex Major, still winding their way among the stalagmites. He opened his mouth to call out to them...and then closed it again.

He remembered the mysteriously flooded field outside.

Ariane had been there. He was sure of it. And if she had made it that close to the cavern, she surely would have found some way into it.

But Rex Major insisted she didn't have the shard.

Which could mean....

A careless step could destroy something of inestimable scientific value, Dr. Beaudry had said, but in that moment, Wally didn't care. Major and Beaudry were out of sight now, somewhere at the end of the path, either in the main cavern already or just around a bend. Heart in his throat, Wally stepped off the path and picked his way through the stalagmites toward that long, dark object.

The light from his helmet found a pale face, streaked with mud and blood, and he dashed the last few steps.

Ariane lay curled on her side, as still as death.

CHAPTER ELEVEN

LOST AND FOUND

IN HER DREAMS, ARIANE WANDERED, lost and alone, through an endless, empty wasteland, beneath skies swathed in funereal black.

Then...a glimmer of light. The clouds brightened to grey and swept open like a curtain. Silvery illumination streamed down all around her, and she reached up with a wondering hand toward the full moon...

Her eyes flickered open. Light stabbed her pupils and she cried out, wrenching her head to the side.

"Thank God," said a voice. "I thought you were dead!"

Relief, joy and disbelief poured through her like the flood she had raised from the river. She twisted her head around again, squinting against the light. "Wally?"

"Shhh!" he hissed urgently. "They'll hear." He took off his helmet and set it to one side so that the beam angled away from them.

Ariane didn't ask who "they" were; at that moment, she didn't care. She sat up, threw her arms around Wally and hugged him as tightly as she could. He was warm and solid and smelled of chocolate and sweat and life, and she'd never been happier to see anyone.

Wally stiffened when she first grabbed him, then relaxed and hugged her back. "It's all right," he whispered. "You're okay." He pushed her away gently. "What happened?"

Ariane swallowed the lump in her throat and tried to order her thoughts. "I was in a pool, down below somewhere. I found a tunnel leading up toward the shard, but then I fell. I lost my backpack, my light...I've been crawling, feeling my way with my hands, trying to reach the shard, no light, no sound, no water, no..." She heard her voice quiver and felt her lip tremble. "I thought I would die down here, alone in the dark. How did you...?"

Wally hesitated. "Rex Major brought me," he said at last.

Ariane gaped. "*What?*"

Wally nervously glanced left. "He's looking for the shard."

"Rex Major *brought* you? How did you escape?"

"I didn't," Wally said. He sounded uncomfortable.

"But –"

"I came voluntarily," Wally rushed on. "He's...he's trying to convince me that we shouldn't trust the Lady. That we shouldn't even be going after Excalibur, that it's too dangerous for...."

"For who?" Anger rose inside her, and this time it came as much from herself as from the shard. "For *me?*"

"For both of us. For everyone around us." The pleading note in his voice grated on her like fingernails on a blackboard. "Ariane, Major says he can use the sword to make the world a better place. But if we give it to the Lady...that will be the end of magic. *All* magic. Are we sure that's what we want?"

"'Major says,'" Ariane mimicked. "And you believe him? The man who held a gun to your head just two weeks ago?"

"Ariane –"

"Major – *Merlin* – will say anything, do anything, to have Excalibur!" The shard sharpened her words. *"But he will...not...have it!"*

Wally didn't answer. He grabbed his helmet and leaped to his feet, jamming the helmet back on his head and tightening the chinstrap with a convulsive tug. As the light stabbed down at Ariane again, she jerked her head away to avoid being blinded.

"They'll come back to look for me any second," Wally said. "You should hide."

"I have to find the shard," Ariane retorted, still not looking at him. "I'm not going to hide. I'll follow you, far enough behind that I can't be seen."

"But if Major gets the shard before you can...."

"He might get it," Ariane said stubbornly, "but that doesn't mean he can hold on to it."

Wally turned away without another word and jogged back to the middle of the cavern, just as someone far down the path shouted, "Wally!"

Ariane knew that voice all too well.

"Coming!" Wally called, and hurried to catch up – *with Rex Major*, she thought, furious even though she knew Wally *had* to follow him to keep her presence a secret. She watched his light dwindle in the distance and join two other lights, which then turned and moved away from her.

She was also furious with herself. She'd had the perfect opportunity to seize the shard and escape before Merlin even knew where it was, and she'd blown it. The bravado she'd shown Wally now collapsed beneath a wave of fear. How strong would Merlin be if he got the second shard? Strong enough to force her to give him the first one too?

Better not to find out. Feeling about a hundred years old, she struggled to her feet, wincing as her torn jeans scraped across her bruised and bloodied knees. She flexed her scraped, burning hands, and then followed the departing lights of Wally and Rex Major.

She couldn't believe Wally had come here with Rex Major of his own free will, couldn't believe he was actually flirting with the idea of trusting the man who had once threatened to kill him. *What's come over him? Has Merlin enchanted him?* For the first time, she wondered if she could trust Wally.

She had to move cautiously to avoid the stalagmites thrusting up from the cave floor, but since the only light came from the headlamps of the others, she ran into a few despite her best efforts, adding to her collection of bruises. Even so, she quickly gained ground on the other three, because they were winding back and forth along a path she couldn't see, whereas her own was much more direct.

Something crunched beneath her feet, and in the same instant, the trio ahead of her paused. She could see them clearly now, and wasn't surprised that the third man was Dr. Beaudry. She stopped when they did, heart leaping to her throat, afraid someone had heard her, but the lights didn't swing in her direction. Dr. Beaudry was pointing at something; she could hear his voice though she couldn't make out the words.

The three moved on. Their lights suddenly disappeared around a corner of stone, only a glimmer reflecting back. Ariane abandoned stealth and dashed forward, terrified she would be plunged into absolute darkness once more. She banged her thigh hard against a stalagmite and swore under her breath, but then rounded the corner and saw Wally, Major, and Dr. Beaudry at the end of a narrow passage, silhouetted against a blue-white glow. They rounded another corner, but now Ariane had plenty of light. She crept to where they had just stood. The passage opened up into a much larger chamber....

She froze, open-mouthed.

Lamps on aluminum poles, set along a winding path marked by red twine, revealed a chamber so enormous it took her breath away: the width of a football field, at least. Its ceiling soared above her like the interior of a cathedral, hung with giant stalactites that glittered like dragon's teeth in the cold light, thin white ribbons of stone winding among them. No stalagmites broke the smoothness of the vast floor, only a few rounded lumps of rock.

On the walls, on every flat surface, sprawled paintings: vivid renditions of oxen and bears, cats and horses, birds and hunters, and absurdly fat, naked women. Across one expanse of stone to her left stretched a long line of handprints, each an ocher-coloured testament to a long-vanished race.

Wally, Rex Major and Dr. Beaudry stood in the middle of the cavern, Dr. Beaudry pointing at something overhead. No one was looking in her direction...

...and a moment later she wasn't looking in theirs. The song of the second shard swelled within her and the first shard burned against her side, its song crescendoing in harmony with that of the second. For an instant she couldn't see, hear, or feel anything but that soundless, soaring song, the shards of Excalibur yearning to be reunited.

She gasped, and her awareness of her body rushed back. *The second shard is in this chamber!*

She knew it. Did Major? He didn't have her powers, but he did still have *some* magic to call on, and this close to the shard....

Even as she thought that, she saw Major's head, which had been tilted toward the ceiling, jerk down and turn in the direction from which the song of the second shard had come. The ruby stud in his right ear glinted as it passed through the beam of Wally's helmet light.

And then, chillingly, his head turned again...in *her* direction.

◀ ▶

From the time he had entered the cavern, Rex Major had fought down his rising impatience. He could sense the shard was close, despite his greatly reduced magical ability. But Ariane knew where it was, too, and she'd already arrived. He had seen the evidence of water in the field outside the camper, had known at once that it could not have gotten there in this drought without her summoning power. Yet he also knew that she did not yet have the second shard. So where was she?

Once they were inside the cavern, he bristled at their maddeningly slow pace, even though he could see the reason for it clearly enough. You could hardly rush – safely, at least – down a folding ladder and through a narrow crawlspace. But with every step he knew he had to be getting closer to the shard, and he could barely restrain his rising excitement.

"Very close now to the main chamber," Dr. Beaudry told him as they made their way through a large but low-ceilinged chamber thickly studded with stalactites and stalagmites. *And very close to the shard*, Major thought. *It's there. It must be!*

He glanced toward Wally, whom he expected would be walking close behind them; but the boy wasn't there.

He stopped and turned around. "Wally!" he shouted.

There was the boy's light, off to the left. He glanced at Dr. Beaudry, who had knelt down and was studying a small skeleton just outside the red twine. Major didn't care if Wally unintentionally destroyed something valuable by leaving the path. But Wally was important to his plans...or could be, at least...so he *did* care if the boy accidentally destroyed *himself* by falling down a cliff, braining himself on a stalactite, or impaling himself on a stalagmite. His lips compressed. He didn't have time to babysit, not when he was so close! He was about to stride back to fetch the brat when he heard a faint, "Coming!" and the light began moving toward them.

A moment later Wally trotted up. "Sorry," he panted. "I was looking at bones."

Major bit off his sharp retort. "Stay close," he growled instead, and turned back to Dr. Beaudry, who had straightened and was watching them.

"Everything all right?" said the scientist.

"Perfectly all right," Major said. "Let's go on."

"Not much farther now," Dr. Beaudry said, suppressed excitement in his voice. "And when you see it.... This way!"

The path took them into a narrow passageway perhaps thirty feet long. At its end Major saw a blue-white glow. A few more strides and they emerged into the largest cavern Major had ever seen. *Large enough to shelter an army*, he thought, and he should know: he had camped in enough caves with Arthur and his men during long-ago campaigns. Cave paintings covered the walls, dimly lit by the lamps along the path. Dr. Beaudry, breathless with excitement, rushed through a long spiel about what he and other researchers had surmised thus far about the ancient artists, but Major hardly heard him.

The shard had to be close...very close. But where?

And then, as Dr. Beaudry pointed up, waxing eloquent about a particularly striking painting of a giant bear standing on its hind legs, Major's vague sense of the shard's presence, a kind of faint pressure in the back of his head, suddenly became so powerful he grunted: it felt as if he'd been punched.

His eyes swivelled from the ceiling to the darkness of the chamber's furthest regions, then locked onto the spot where the ceiling descended toward the floor – where he saw a faint, glimmering reflection.

Water!

It was as if the shard had suddenly shouted, "Here I am!" His eyes narrowed. But the shard had not shouted to *him*. It had responded to the presence of something else:

The *first* shard of Excalibur.

He swung his head to the right, and saw her, crouched where the path entered the great chamber. *Ariane.*

He snapped his gaze back to Dr. Beaudry. "Be quiet," he commanded. The scientist's mouth shut in mid-word. "Don't move," he added, and Dr. Beaudry froze in place, a living statue.

Then Rex Major turned and darted across the cavern floor toward the dark crevice where the second shard of Excalibur lay.

◄◄ ►►

Ariane's eyes met Major's for one timeless instant, then Major snapped something at Dr. Beaudry that froze him in mid-lecture and dashed toward the far end of the cavern, toward the very place from where the second shard of Excalibur sang to its mate.

Ariane swore, leaped up, and ran full-tilt after him. Fragile crystals of stone shattered beneath her feet and she kicked a human skull that broke into pieces as it rolled across the cavern floor. If she could get only get to the shard first....

...but then her foot caught on a lump of stone and she fell, sprawling. Agony speared her ankle and she screamed as her already bruised and lacerated knees slammed against rock, her cry of pain echoing around the giant chamber.

Wally came running up from behind her, slowed. "Are you all right?"

"Go!" she gasped out. "Stop him!"

Wally hesitated, then ran after Rex Major.

Ariane picked herself up and hobbled after them both,

unable to run, bitterly certain she was already too late.

Unless....

New energy flowed into her, and it came neither from the shard she carried nor from the one toward which she stumbled. Somewhere ahead, a source of water sang out to the Lady of the Lake.

She pushed her battered body toward it as fast as she could.

◀ ▶

Wally ran after Major, wondering how, exactly, he was supposed to stop *Merlin*, the greatest wizard in history, from seizing the shard.

Wondering if he really wanted to.

Major ducked under a low bulge of rock. Wally ducked too...and his feet flew out from under him. He slammed down onto his rear, slid, and splashed into water so cold it took his breath away. When he lifted his hands, icy rivulets ran down his forearms. *Water! Ariane could use this –*

Sitting in the near-freezing liquid, he turned his head. Major stood in the middle of a large, shallow pool, pounding on a lump of stone with the hammer from his utility belt. Bits of rock flashed in the light and splashed into the water. Eyes wide, teeth bared, Major had transformed from urbane businessman to berserk warrior. For a second Wally thought the wizard had gone crazy, but then he glimpsed a metallic glint in the lump of rock.

The shard of Excalibur, he realized, was *inside* the lump, sheathed in centuries of mineral deposits.

"Wally!" Major shouted, turning his wild stare to him. "You've got a rock hammer on your belt. Come help!"

Major wanted him to help retrieve the shard. Ariane wanted him to stop Major. *What do I do?* he thought, feeling like a bunny rabbit caught between two tigers.

But before he could do anything, Ariane slid down the slope behind him, and into the water.

◀◀ ▶▶

Ariane, the first shard screaming to be united with the second, the second begging to be united with the first, felt the Lady's power crash over her like a tsunami as she splashed down into the water of the pool. She jerked her head up and stared at Rex Major, who was hammering at the lump of stone that held the shard. She shot a glance at Wally, sitting uselessly on his butt, looking helpless, looking lost; and in that moment, filled with the power of the Lady and the anger and longing of the two shards, Ariane felt an overwhelming sense of contempt.

With the magic coursing through her, she whirled the water of the pool into a thick tendril and batted Wally out of the way just as he started to get to his feet. Then she tipped the tentacle with ice and hurled it, a rod of liquid heavy as a battering ram, at the hump of rock Major had been pounding.

The weakened stone shattered. The shard splashed into the water...and she had it. The tentacle of water hurtled back toward her, the shard held in a grip of ice.

Major shouted and lunged after it, tripped and fell headlong into the pool. Wally, just staggering to his feet, raised his head at just the wrong moment, and caught the tendril full in the face. Like a roundhouse punch, it spun him around and dropped him back into the water, crying out in pain as he fell. Major scrambled to his feet and roared toward her, water splashing up in sheets around his feet. He was between her and Wally. *Kill Merlin!* The shards shouted within her, and the tendril of water hardened into a blade of ice in the shape of Excalibur, like the dream sword she had used to drive off the demon Major had sent to plague her sleep. *Kill him!*

The shards' combined rage almost overwhelmed her...but just enough of *her* remained to enable her to resist. With enormous effort, Ariane dropped the ice-sword into the pool and let the water suck her down and spirit her away.

Her last sight of the cavern was of Wally kneeling in the pool, staring at her, blood streaming down his face.

◆◆ ◆◆

Spitting, sputtering, Wally hauled himself upright after Ariane's first surge of water shoved him into the pool...just in time to be hit by the tentacle hurling itself back toward her, the second shard of Excalibur caught in its tip like a twig in a rip-tide. The piece of ancient metal laid his cheek open. Blood sprayed from the wound as he was flung into the pool once more, and he pressed his hand against the cut. The pain was sharp, but not as sharp as Wally's hurt as he looked up and saw Ariane – now holding the second shard of Excalibur – let the tentacle of water fall apart into the pool, take one look at him and the onrushing Major and vanish, sucked down into the water and away.

"No!" Major shouted, splashing through the spot where Ariane had stood an instant before. "Not again!" He spun and stared down at the place where the girl had vanished, fists clenched at his side. The ruby stud in his ear caught the light of Wally's helmet lamp and glowed like a fleck of fire. Wally kept his hand pressed to his bleeding cheek. The cavern spun around him, and he bowed his head for a moment, eyes closed, afraid he might be sick. The nausea faded as footsteps splashed toward him. He blinked his eyes open again and looked up to see Major standing over him.

"I told you," the sorcerer said, his voice grim. "She is

not your friend anymore. She is the Lady of the Lake, and you have become expendable." He reached out his hand. Wally let Major pull him to his feet, but his head roared and his vision greyed. His knees buckled. He fell against Major, who steadied him with an arm around his shoulders. "Careful, son."

Wally pulled his hand away from his cheek and stared at the blood smearing his fingers. *At least I've got something in common with my sister now. We've both been hurt by Ariane.* He clenched his fist so tightly that the blood on his palm oozed between his fingers. More blood dripped into the water, making a pink swirl at his feet. He raised his head and met Major's eyes. When Ariane had vanished, leaving him with Major, she'd taken his indecision with her. *I guess I know who to trust now.*

Wally straightened as his dizziness retreated. "She's got the second shard," he said. "What do *we* have to do to get it back?"

◀◀ ▶▶

Ariane whirled away through the underground waterways, into the river, through lakes and ponds and pipes and pools all the way to the lake near Lyon where she had rested once before. The two shards of Excalibur blazed in her senses like twin suns. With both of them to draw on, what power she would have!

Standing whole and dry on the shore of the lake beneath a gloriously bright blue sky, she stared at the piece of metal clutched in her hand. It was a little longer than the first shard, perhaps twenty centimetres, and a little wider. Unlike the first, whose one end was the sword's sharp point, this was broken at both ends. With trembling fingers she pulled up her shirt and undid the tensor bandage holding the first fragment, the lakeside air chill against her exposed skin. She let the bandage fall to the ground. A shard in each hand, she closed her eyes, listening to their songs, equal now in joy and strength...but....

She frowned. They were not singing in the same key. Perhaps if....

Her hands trembling a little, she touched them together.

The top of the first shard and bottom of the second fitted so neatly that only the faintest hairline marked the point of contact. But she could hold them there only for an instant; the clashing harmonies rose to such a cacophony that she jerked the shards apart again, gasping, unable to bear the discord.

And yet at the same time the two shards *longed* to be together, *yearned* for it. To her astonishment, she found herself crying, heartsick that she couldn't grant them the reunion they so fiercely desired.

She blinked away the tears and stared at the two pieces. Both had power. She could draw on either one separately, but she couldn't draw on both at the same time: not, she guessed, until the entire sword was forged anew. Using the shards one after the other, her powers might last longer, but she'd be no stronger than she was before.

She remembered how close she had come to killing Major...how close she had come to killing Flish!...with the powers she already had, and wondered if that might not be a good thing.

Just having an extra source of energy was nothing to be sneezed at, though, she thought, remembering how exhausted she had been when she'd crossed the ocean through the clouds. And she would certainly have to go home the same way, since she obviously could no more board a plane with two pieces of sharp metal strapped to her body than she could with one...and she suspected if she attempted such a thing in France, the consequences would be far more serious than they would have been in Regina.

Wally, though, would still have to fly.

And then, as if she'd breached a dam holding back the memory, everything she had thought about Wally and done to him in the cavern flooded back. She remembered the contempt she'd felt for his uselessness as he'd sat there in the pool, and her face flushed with shame. *Useless?* she thought, horrified in retrospect. *If he hadn't found me lying in the cavern, woken me up...Major would have come and gone with the shard and I would never have known he was there at all.*

But she'd shoved him out of the way, pushing him aside as though he were nothing more than a...a chair, or a table, some inanimate object blocking her access to the shard. Worse, she'd *hurt* him...she remembered his cry of pain, the blood on his face. And then – then –

Then she'd just abandoned him, in Merlin's clutches, no less!

I had no choice! she cried to herself. *The shards wanted me to kill Major. If I'd stayed another second, I would have cut him in half. I had no choice!*

You did *have a choice*, her conscience chided her. *Major was after the shard. All you had to do was throw it across the pool. He would have gone after it. Then you could have grabbed Wally and gotten both of you out of there.*

She remembered another day, another confrontation with Major, a day when Major had threatened Wally's life and she had simply handed him the first shard.

This time, she hadn't even considered it.

This time, she'd left Wally behind.

This time, faced with the choice between her friend and her quest, she'd chosen the quest, chosen her own power.

Her lower lip trembled again, but crying wouldn't do Wally any good. She had to rescue him from Major, get him back home.

Most of all, she had to apologize.

But first, she had to find him.

She bent over, picked up the tensor bandage, wrapped it snugly around her belly again, then stuck a shard under each side of it. The lengths of steel felt cold against her skin, but they quickly warmed. Both shards sang in her mind. Though they could not sing in unison, not yet, they seemed...contented, in a way the single shard never had, as though in some strange fashion they were happy to be together again.

They're just pieces of metal, she thought, but of course she knew perfectly well they were much more than that.

She tucked her T-shirt back into her jeans, covering the bandage, and then limped into the water. Every step on the ankle she had turned in the cavern felt as if someone were jabbing her with a fork, and so she let herself feel the cold of the water flowing around it; for once, the chill felt good. At least it wasn't swelling much, so she didn't think it was sprained too badly.

Now what? she thought.

Rescue Wally, of course.

But that was easier said than done. She couldn't return to the cave: she couldn't materialize in the pool where the shard had been and there was *no way* she would materialize again in that deeper pool farther underground. Nor was there any water to draw on outside the cave except for the river, and Major would hardly linger there waiting for her to use it.

She could think of only one possibility: the hotel in Lyon where she and Wally were supposed to be staying. Major might be as anxious to find her as she was to find him, if he intended to hold Wally hostage again in exchange for the shards. She would go there, lie low and wait.

She paused, suddenly realizing that without her passport or any other form of identification, without any money, without even a change of clothes – all lost with her backpack in the depths of the cavern – her options were limited. She looked down at herself. Her jeans were torn at the knees, filthy with dirt, and stained with blood. Her palms and elbows were scratched and bruised and there was blood there, too. There was a cut on her ear, and she walked with a limp. They'd never let her check into the hotel, and they'd probably chase her out of the lobby if she tried to wait there.

And of course there was no guarantee Major and Wally would show up at all. In fact, the odds were against it. Even if Major came looking for her, why would he come with Wally? He could bargain for Wally's life without making him handily available for rescue. For that matter, he could just fly Wally to Canada, wait for her to get back, and *then* try to strike a bargain.

Or....

A snake of doubt slithered into her mind. Maybe Major didn't have to take Wally hostage. Maybe Wally *wanted* to be with Major.

She tried to push that venomous thought away, but it wouldn't leave, sliding around her objections. Wally had accompanied Major to the cavern of his own free will. He'd wondered out loud to her, in their brief conversation before he'd rejoined Major, if they were sure the Lady was the one they should be helping. And then he'd done nothing to try to stop Major. He'd just sat there in the water, motionless, useless, while Major pounded on the rock holding the shard, seconds from claiming it as his own...

No! she thought. *This is* Wally *we're talking about. Funny, kind, brave, trustworthy Wally. My friend, my companion, my ally. If he's with Major, he's a prisoner. And if Major is holding him hostage, I'll rescue him. If he shows up at the hotel with Major* – her lip curled – *Major won't know what hit him.*

And then everything will be just like it was before.

With that thought, she let the water swallow her whole.

CHAPTER TWELVE

CALM BEFORE THE STORM

Rex Major led Wally back to the path and to the frozen figure of Dr. Beaudry, still standing like a wax statue, mouth half-open. Major smoothed his short grey hair, took a deep breath, then said, "I believe I've seen enough, Dr. Beaudry."

The scientist jerked back to life, then blinked, bewildered. "I'm...I'm sorry, I've forgotten what I was saying."

"I've seen enough," Major repeated. "Very intriguing, and I will be most happy to support your work. Now, if you could show us back to the outside world?"

Dr. Beaudry glanced at Wally, who was holding his hand against the cut on his cheek, and his eyes widened. "You're bleeding!" he said. "How...?"

"He fell," Major said smoothly. "Tripped and cut his cheek on a stalagmite. Very careless."

Dr. Beaudry was already pulling a small first-aid kit from one of the pockets of his orange jumpsuit. "Move your hand," he ordered Wally, and a moment later had taped a gauze pad to the wound. "You must see a doctor in Lyon," he said severely. "The wound will require stitches." His eyes flicked up to the stitches Wally already had on his forehead.

"And you do not want it to become infected."

Wally said nothing, but as Dr. Beaudry dressed his cheek he marvelled at how Rex Major had frozen the scientist in place. *It's the same power he used on me in Yellowknife*, he thought. *He can simply command people to do things...and command them to forget they've done them.* He frowned. *But when he tried to command all of us to forget what I'd said about the first shard, up in Yellowknife...it didn't work. I didn't forget. It didn't work on the phone when I was in the hospital either. And he hasn't tried it since.*

Wally looked past Dr. Beaudry at Major, who was staring off into space, fingering the ruby stud in his ear. *Maybe I'm immune to his power now. Maybe that's one of those special abilities he's hinted at.* He felt a little thrill at the thought.

Dr. Beaudry took them back to the entrance of the cave, where the guards met them. Major looked at them and at Dr. Beaudry and said, his voice a little deeper and more resonant than usual, maybe, but otherwise perfectly normal, "Forget this boy was ever here."

It was as if Wally had suddenly donned an invisibility cloak. Beaudry's gaze slid past him as though he didn't exist. He didn't even seem to notice Wally removing his jumpsuit and tossing it on one of the camp beds. The guards behaved in the same blind manner.

Major and Wally trudged back up the cliff to the waiting Mercedes, climbed in and drove away.

The drive passed in silence. Rex Major didn't seem inclined to talk, and that suited Wally. With his head pressed against the cool glass of the window, watching the scenery flash by, Wally touched the bandage on his cheek, blood already soaking through it, the wound beneath burning like hot iron laid against his skin. He still couldn't believe Ariane had done that to him. The blade had cut him only a little, but what if it had caught him in the throat? Even worse, she hadn't even checked to see if he was all right, simply vanishing the moment she had the shard, leaving him to the mercy of the man she claimed to believe was evil incarnate.

And if she really *believed that, she wouldn't have dared leave me at all, would she?* he thought darkly. *Even* she *doesn't fully believe what the Lady told us about Merlin. But she's doing the Lady's bidding all the same.*

But not him. Not anymore.

Wally thought Rex Major had fallen asleep, but as the Mercedes turned onto the busy highway that would take them the last few kilometres into Lyon, he straightened and said to Wally, "Once we have had a doctor look at your wound, I think you should return to your own hotel. If Ariane comes looking for you, she will come there."

"Won't she just take the shard and head home?" Wally said. "If she were at all worried about *me* she wouldn't have left me like that in the cavern." He raised his hand to his cheek, wondering if he'd have a scar to match the one he'd probably have on his forehead. *Well,* he thought, *at least it won't change how girls look at you, since they mostly don't.*

"I don't think you're being fair," Merlin said, and that startled Wally so much he turned and looked directly at the sorcerer.

"You're defending *her?"*

Major shrugged. "In a way. She's becoming the Lady of the Lake...as cold, heartless, and selfishly single-minded as my 'beloved' sister. But she is not that *yet.* I think there's still quite a bit of the girl she was just a few short weeks ago." He paused. "Perhaps you didn't notice, but just before she vanished, she had formed the water into a blade of ice: a blade in the shape of Excalibur. I think the shards wanted her to kill me with it. But she didn't. There is enough of Ariane left that she didn't want to commit murder. And if that much of her remains, then, yes, I think she'll go to your hotel and wait for you. I suspect she'll want to apologize."

Despite his anger at Ariane, despite his conviction they should be helping Merlin, not the Lady, Wally felt a chill. "You want me to accept her apology...and then steal the shard?"

"Wally," Major said. "First of all, it isn't stealing: the shard no more belongs to her than to anyone else. If anything, it belongs to the rightful heir of King Arthur. That means..." He paused. "Well, anyway, it doesn't 'belong' to her, she just happens to have it. Second, we talked about this. This is for her own good."

"And yours," Wally pointed out.

Major smiled a little. "And mine, of course. Have I ever denied it? If the shards weren't something I needed I wouldn't even be here. But it will still benefit Ariane." He leaned closer, his eyes on Wally's, his voice warm and earnest. "You'll not only be helping me get closer to my dream of a better world – a dream I know you share – you'll also be helping save Ariane from being swallowed alive by the power of the Lady."

Oh, you're smooth, Wally thought. But he didn't disagree. He couldn't. Ariane *wasn't* the same as she had been. The way she'd hurt Flish, the way she'd hurt him...

He hated to think of Ariane transformed into something both more and less than human. That transformation had already begun. But maybe, by helping Major, he could slow or even stop it.

You're supposed to be the loyal sidekick! an inner voice yelled. *How can you throw in with the enemy?*

Because he's not really the enemy, Wally snapped back. *The Lady of the Lake is. Sometimes the sidekick has to stop the heroine from making a terrible mistake. And that's what I'm doing.*

But there was still one thing he wanted to know for certain. "Why not just *order* me to do it, like you ordered Dr. Beaudry? I know you can, even without the shard."

"Because I wanted a willing ally, not a slave."

"What difference does it make to you, as long as you get the shard?"

Major looked at him silently for a moment, then glanced out the window as if debating what he should say. Finally, he turned. "The truth is, Wally, I can't Command you. You, alone of everyone I have met in this present age, are impervious to that particular power."

Wally felt another surge of excitement at hearing his suspicion confirmed. "Why?"

"As I told you earlier, I think there is more to you than meets the eye...much more. But until I can test my theory, I'd rather not say what it is. And to test it, I need the shards." He shrugged. "But whatever the reason, that is the truth, Wally. And it doesn't matter. Even if I could Command you, I wouldn't. I want to guide you to the correct path, not force you along it. I want you to choose what is best for all of us – not just me and you, but Ariane, too. But I want you to choose it of your own free will." He spread his hands. "I told you before, Wally. If you don't feel you can trust me, you are free to go. I won't stop you."

Wally turned away to stare out the window again. He *wanted* to believe Major. Which was exactly why he didn't quite dare to – not completely. What Major wanted him to think was the correct path was also the easiest one. Give in, let Major take charge, let a grown-up start making the decisions so he could go back to just being a teenager. It was tempting, a return to the easier years of childhood when his parents had taken care of everything....

But that didn't mean it was right.

Didn't mean it was wrong, either, though, and there was one thing Major wanted he *knew* he agreed with: they had to get the shards away from Ariane, before they destroyed her. And so....

He swallowed hard, then turned back to Major. "All right, I'll do it. I'll get the shard for you...*if* Ariane shows up at the hotel like you think she will. What if she doesn't?"

"Then we will get it some other way," Major said. "It might even be easier back in Canada. But if we can seize it here, we will." He paused. "There's something else you must know. Something about the shard. Something I don't want Ariane to know. I hope you will take my telling it to you as another sign you can trust me."

"What is it?" Wally said, intrigued.

Major leaned forward. "I can't take the shard from her by force. She must give it away willingly. That's why I took you hostage at the diamond mine instead of simply attacking her: once she had it, the only way I could get it was to convince her to give it to me. And that means you must ask her if you can hold the shard, and she must agree. Then you can give it to me. It's the only way to preserve its power for my use instead of the Lady's."

Wally said nothing. The inner voice was shouting at him again. *How can you trick her like that? How can you lie to her like that?*

But he shoved its misgivings and accusations aside. His mind was finally made up. For her own good, he would find Ariane...and he would get the shard for Merlin.

◄► ►

Ariane made it to Lyon without difficulty, emerging from a river under a bridge where no one would see her sudden appearance. She dried, then climbed up the bank to a road and went in search of a map.

Without money the only way she could get to the hotel was on foot, and the scale of the map she found at a nearby gas station proved to be deceiving. It had still been morning when she'd reached the city, though just barely, but it was late afternoon by the time she stood outside the Cœur de Lyon Hotel, which looked considerably grubbier than it had in the photos Aunt Phyllis had found in a travel magazine.

She walked past the front of the hotel, down the alley that ran beside it and the one that ran behind it, past dumpsters and the loading dock, listening to the water singing within the hotel...but there was nowhere in there she could materialize.

Across from the hotel, an ornamental fountain gurgled and splashed inside a small park. Ariane sat on a bench near the fountain so she would have a weapon close to hand if needed, and waited to see if Major would show up, with or without Wally.

And if he doesn't? she thought.

She looked up at the cloudless sky. *Then I'll pray for rain*, she thought. *Or at least overcast...and figure out some other way to rescue Wally, back in Canada.*

But just an hour later a smallish red-haired figure carrying a backpack strode into sight on the other side of the road. Ariane jumped up in disbelief. She looked both ways. There was no sign of Rex Major.

"Wally!" she shouted, and dashed across the street to join him, cutting *way* too close in front of a tiny three-wheeled delivery van and earning herself a honk (and a shout she didn't understand and figured she was better off *not* understanding) from the fist-shaking driver.

Wally stopped when she yelled. Ariane wanted to throw her arms around him and give him a hug...but didn't. There was no welcoming smile on his pale, drawn face. She skidded to a halt, suddenly feeling awkward. "How did you get away from..." Her question died in her throat as she spotted the square of gauze covering most of his left cheek. "Oh no! Did I do that?"

"Yeah," Wally said. "The second shard cut me as it went past." His voice sounded oddly strained.

Ariane felt a little sick. "Wally, I'm so sorry, I didn't mean...."

"I know you didn't," Wally said. He hitched his backpack a little higher onto his shoulders. "I was just in the way, that's all."

"Wally...."

"Never mind. It's over." He took a deep breath. "The important thing is you have the second shard."

"And Major doesn't," Ariane said, relieved he understood. "How did you get away?"

"He took me to a hospital for stitches," Wally said. He touched the gauze pad. "That makes twelve. Five on my forehead and seven on my cheek. I wonder how many more I can collect? Anyway, after the doctor left, I sneaked out a back door." He looked up and down the street. "Let's get inside. I don't think Rex Major knows where we're staying, but he could be checking out all the likely hotels. He might drive by at any minute."

"And I desperately need to rest. And wash. And eat," Ariane said. Her stomach grumbled. "I'm starving, I'm filthy, and I'm so exhausted I don't think I could get home now even with *both* shards to draw on. Not that I'd go off and leave you to Major's tender mercies," she added hastily. *Not* again, *anyway*, remarked a snide voice inside her.

"We're checked in," Wally said. He didn't seem to have heard what she'd said. *Or else he's ignoring me*, Ariane thought. He reached into the pocket of his jeans and pulled out an old-fashioned brass key. "But I haven't actually been to the room." A flicker of the old Wally grin flashed across his face. "Wait'll I tell the guys back home I shared a room in France with a girl."

Ariane laughed, relieved to hear him joke. "They'd never believe you."

Wally's grin faded. "No," he said. "They wouldn't."

They went into the small dark lobby and straight to the elevators. Nobody at the front desk took any notice of them, although they were neither exactly at their best. Wally at least had worn overalls over his jeans and T-shirt while in the cavern, but Ariane...it didn't seem fair to her that when she used the Lady's power to transport herself through fresh water, the dirt in her clothes came along for the ride. Although at least the dirt hid the bloodstains. But her hair was stiff and lifeless, and she suspected she didn't smell very good either, although she wasn't going to ask Wally *his* opinion.

Wally led her to room 404. He put in the key and tried to turn it. At first it resisted, then it gave with a bang. Wally pulled it out, turned the knob and swung the door open.

The room beyond was tiny by Canadian hotel standards and had a faded look, as though far too long had passed since it was last renovated. The light-blue wallpaper and darker-blue rug both bore noticeable stains. There were two narrow beds, separated by a scarred night table with an old black telephone on it. A tiny TV sat on the dresser at the foot of the beds. Luxurious it wasn't, but it did have one thing Ariane wanted more than anything else, right at that moment: a bathroom with a shower. "I need to get cleaned up," she said. She searched the closet and found a rather threadbare bathrobe. When she opened the door to the tiny bathroom, she hesitated. There was barely room to turn around in there – it would be an awful struggle undressing. "Turn your back," she said to Wally. "Look out the window."

Wally's grin flickered across his face again. "Yes, my lady," he said. While he stared at the street outside, Ariane stripped off her filthy clothes and took off the tensor bandage holding the two shards of Excalibur to her skin. She tossed them on the bed, rubbed the red marks they'd left on her flanks, and then pulled on the bathrobe and cinched it up.

As she glanced at the back of Wally's head and the darkening sky beyond the window, she wondered just how reflective that glass was. She decided not to ask. "Okay, you can turn around."

Wally turned, and his eyes went at once to the two pieces of metal lying on the bed. He walked over and reached out for them, then stopped and glanced at her. "May I hold them?"

"Of course," Ariane said.

He picked up the two shards. "Do they really fit together?"

"Yes and no," Ariane said. He gave her a puzzled look. "They fit together physically. But magically...something's not quite right. I can use either one as a...a magical battery, but I can't use them at the same time." She shook her head. "My guess is that the whole sword needs to be reforged before they'll work together. And how exactly we're supposed to make that happen I have no idea. Know anything about blacksmithing?" She closed her eyes, focusing on her inner sense of the two bits of blade. "It's like they're two singers singing the same song side by side, but one is a quarter-step flat..." Her breath exploded out of her in surprise as suddenly, without warning, the discord vanished. For one glorious instant the two songs merged in perfect harmony, and for that instant she felt an enormous surge of power...but then, as suddenly as it had appeared, it was gone. "What...?" She opened her eyes.

Wally was just separating the two pieces of the sword, one in each hand. "What's wrong?" he said.

Ariane stared at him. "Wally, when you put the two pieces together...suddenly they were singing in harmony. It was beautiful!" She inhaled deeply. "Literally breathtaking. How did you...?"

"Beats me," Wally said. "I'm the non-magical half of this duo." The bitterness in his voice surprised her.

"But still important," Ariane said, guiltily aware that not that long ago she'd been thinking of him as useless and in the way.

She reached out for the two shards, put them together herself, and instantly jerked them apart again. After hearing that perfect meshing of their songs a moment ago, the discord when *she* tried to put them together was even harder to take.

She sighed. "Weird." Then she yawned and rubbed her tired eyes. "Okay, time to get in the shower," she said. She looked down at her scraped hands and her lacerated knees, showing under the hem of the rather short gown. "I don't think I'm going to enjoy the soap much," she added ruefully. "Once I'm finished...I lost all my euros in the cave. Do you have enough for us to get something to eat?"

Wally, staring at the shards, nodded without looking up.

"Good." Ariane went into the bathroom, closed the door firmly behind her, and a moment later was luxuriating in hot water. As she'd suspected, the sting of shampoo on her scraped palms brought tears to her eyes. But the sting quickly faded, leaving her with the simple joy of being clean again.

Next, food, she thought. *And then sleep. And then...home.*

Home with two shards in her grasp. How long before she heard the call of the third?

Finished shampooing, she leaned both hands against the wall of the shower and let the water rinse her hair, suds running down her bare skin, stinging her knees and elbows anew, and swirling dirt and dried blood down the drain.

Soon, I hope, she thought. *The quicker we get this quest over the sooner we can go back to normal life. And if we succeed and I have Excalibur...maybe then I'll have enough power to do what I really want to do: find Mom.*

She closed her eyes, enjoying the feel of the water, even as she felt it calling her to follow it down the drain, follow it anywhere.

Not while I'm naked, thanks, she thought, picturing herself suddenly erupting in Wascana Lake in November with no clothes on. The very thought made her shiver. She'd be one big goose pimple.

She laughed and turned off the water. Once dry, she pulled on her bathrobe and swung open the bathroom door, letting the hot, moist air flood out. "I think I almost feel human again," she said cheerfully as she stepped out into the room. "And I bet I'll feel completely human once we've had something to –"

She stopped, staring around the room. Wally was gone.

And then her gaze dropped to the bed.

So was the second shard of Excalibur.

◄ ►

Wally stared down at the two shards, lying side by side on the dark green bedspread. *I can't believe how easy she's made it*, he thought as he heard the shower start up in the bathroom. She'd just accepted his story about escaping from Major, without question.

Despite his anger at Ariane, or at least at what the Lady of the Lake had made her do, despite his determination to help Rex Major, he felt a little sick: he knew that the reason Ariane had made it so easy for him was that she still trusted him. If he took the shards to Major, she'd never trust him again.

She'd never be his friend again.

But if I don't take them, he thought, *if I leave them to her, soon enough she's not going to be the Ariane I know at all. Excalibur is eating her alive...bit by bit, she's turning* *into someone...some*thing *else, something that won't be my friend anyway.*

He touched the bandage on his cheek. Then he reached for the shards.

But just as he was about to put them both into his backpack, he paused.

Ariane had no passport, no money, and no plane ticket. She'd made it clear she'd needed the extra power of the first shard to travel through the clouds across the Atlantic. If he took both shards, he would be stranding her in a foreign country with no resources.

Major wanted both shards. And it was risky leaving even the first one with Ariane, given the way it had already changed her. But he didn't see that he had any choice. And the thought did just cross his mind that, if it turned out he was wrong about Major after all, he might be very glad that Ariane still had the power of the first shard to draw on.

Wally closed his eyes and took a deep breath. Ariane wouldn't be in the shower forever. He had to decide *now*.

He snapped his eyes open and convulsively flung the first shard of Excalibur back on the bed. Then he stuffed the second in his backpack. He opened the door, then hesitated again. Ariane didn't even have any money, and he knew she was starving. And the money *he* had belonged to Aunt Phyllis anyway.

He hurried back to the bed, opened his backpack, took all the euros out of his wallet and tossed the bills onto the bed next to the first shard. Then he rushed out into the hallway. The door, as it closed behind him, shut out the sound of the shower.

A few minutes later he strode down the darkening street, retracing the path he had followed to the hotel. Just around the first corner, the big black Mercedes waited. Rex Major glanced up from his phone as Wally, slipping his backpack off his arms, slid into the seat beside him.

"Well?" he said.

Wally unzipped the backpack. "I couldn't get the first one," he said. "But...." He pulled out the second shard of Excalibur. "Take it," he said. "It's yours."

Major snatched it from his hand, and as he touched it, just for an instant, his face changed – not his expression, *his whole face*, into something cold and alien and ancient, a skull covered by only the thinnest layer of skin and flesh. The impression only lasted a second, but Wally couldn't help but stare. He'd never seen anything like it outside of a horror movie.

Still sure you made the right decision?

Major tucked the shard away inside his coat, and tapped the chauffeur on the shoulder. "À l'aéroport, s'il vous plaît." The driver nodded and pulled the car away from the curb.

Major looked at Wally. Something of the shock he'd felt upon seeing Major's brief change in appearance must have still registered on his face, because Major said soothingly, "You did the right thing, Wally. With one shard in my possession, the third will be easier to find, and then the fourth. Once I have three, I can take the one Ariane carries, and then she will be free of her quest and the Lady's power. She can go back to being an ordinary girl, and I can set about healing the planet." He smiled at Wally. "With your help, I hope."

Wally snorted. "My help?" He pointed at the stitches on his forehead. "I can't even get home from school without hurting myself."

"How many times must I tell you, Wally? You're more special than you think."

Wally sighed. "Yeah, you keep saying that, but you still haven't told me *how*."

"I will," Major said. "When I am sure of my facts. And now that I have one shard, I can test my theory. But for now...I will say that I don't think it was coincidence that you and Ariane met, nor was it coincidence you were present when the Lady called her into the lake. Your lives, and the lives of your families...for *centuries*, Wally...have been shaped by the magic of Excalibur. The sword *wants* to be reforged. Its fragments have been calling out to each other down through the ages. And as they have called to each other, they have enmeshed within their web those who are sensitive to their call."

"I wouldn't exactly call me sensitive," Wally said. "I didn't even cry at the end of *Old Yeller*."

Major laughed. "Trust me, Wally. Your role in all of this is, I think, greater than even the Lady suspects."

Despite himself, Wally felt a thrill of excitement. Could it be true? Could he be as special as Ariane? "I wish you'd just tell me instead of dropping dark hints," he said.

"Not until I'm sure," Major repeated. "But once we're back in Toronto, I can –"

"Wait a minute," Wally said. "Toronto? Aunt Phyllis..." *someone else who will never forgive me*, he thought with a genuine pang of regret, not least because it meant no more chocolate-chip macaroons, "...arranged for me to miss a week of school, but I have to be back next Monday."

"Wally," said Major. "I'm the most powerful sorcerer the world has ever known *and* one of its richest men. Trust me when I say I will make things right with your school – and your parents."

"As if *they'll* care," Wally muttered.

"You'll stay with me in Toronto. I can bring in a tutor to ensure you keep up with your studies, so when you do go back to school, you won't fall behind. But until this whole thing is settled and Excalibur is in my possession, you must stay with me." His voice grew grim. "Ariane will be angry when she discovers the shard is missing. And if she is too far gone into the mindset of the Lady, I'm afraid she might take revenge."

Wally wanted to say, *Ariane would never hurt me*, but of course, Ariane already *had*. He had the stitches in his cheek and a sister in the hospital to prove it.

"Someday, Ariane will see that you acted in her best interest and in the best interest of everyone else on Earth, and in Faerie," Major continued. "But until then, you're safest with me."

Wally said nothing. The initial shock over, he found he liked the idea of living in Toronto. Nobody would miss him at school except maybe Coach Mueller. Too bad, but maybe he could still study fencing in Toronto.

He certainly wouldn't miss school any more than it would miss him. He didn't really have any close friends, just fellow geeks with whom he argued the finer points of *Star Wars*...and wouldn't *they* be green with envy when they found out he was living with Rex Major, a not-so-minor god in the pantheon of computer geekdom! His parents...well, since they didn't seem too concerned about how much he missed *them*, why should he worry how much they missed him? *Because they won't*, he thought. *They'll just be glad Rex Major has taken me off their hands.*

He snorted. *Mrs. Carson might miss me*, he thought, *but only because without me she's out of a job.*

And Flish? She'd be glad not to have him in her hair. She might miss the allowance she extorted from him on a regular basis, but she wouldn't miss *him*.

He looked out the windshield. They were nearing the airport. Wally nodded to himself, then turned to Major again.

"Great," he said. "So, just what *will* you be able to do with your magic when you have Excalibur at your command?"

A slow smile spread across Major's face. "You'll have to wait and see," he said. "But I promise you, Wally...it'll be like nothing you've ever imagined."

CHAPTER THIRTEEN

TWIST OF THE BLADE

Ariane felt as though everything she believed in had just crashed into hard, cold truth and shattered into meaningless fragments.

She stared at the bedspread where there should have been two shards, unable to accept what her eyes told her. The second shard was gone, and so was Wally. That could only mean...

She snatched up the first shard and concentrated. Sure enough, she could hear the frantic song of the second shard receding. For a moment she considered dashing out into the hallway after Wally, barefoot and wearing only a bathrobe, but then the second shard started receding at a much faster pace than before. *He must be in a car*, she thought. *And that means....*

Rex Major.

Her knees gave way and she sat down heavily on the end of the bed. Wally Knight, her companion in the Lady's quest, her best friend, her loyal sidekick, had just taken the second shard to her arch-enemy. She noticed the money scattered across the bedspread. Wally had stolen the shard, but he'd left Aunt Phyllis's money...and the fact he felt he didn't need it any more was even more proof that he had someone else looking after him now.

Her stomach roiled. She jumped up and staggered into the bathroom, just making it to the toilet before she heaved, though nothing came up except sour-tasting liquid. She clung to the bowl for a long moment, then hauled herself to her feet. At the sink she rinsed out her mouth. Her reflection stared back at her from the mirror. *I look awful,* she thought...and then she couldn't see herself anymore as tears flooded her eyes. She flung herself onto the bed and wept as if she would never stop. *What do I do now?* ran over and over through her head. *What do I do now?*

But no one could really cry forever. Her sobs slowed, softened...and stopped. And then, without really meaning to, she fell asleep.

She woke with a start, stared at her surroundings in confusion, and only then remembered where she was...and what had happened. But as she remembered Wally's betrayal, it wasn't grief she felt this time, but anger: a blaze of fury hotter than any she could remember feeling before. Not all of it was hers. She put out her hand and picked up the first shard from where it had lain beside her while she slept. Rage seared her mind like boiling acid.

She wondered suddenly how the sword had been made, and who had made it. She thought back to what the Lady had told her when they'd first met. She'd said she'd had Excalibur forged in Faerie, but she hadn't said she'd forged it. And she'd said it was a thing of battle that wanted to strike and kill.

Maybe the sword contains something of the spirit of whoever forged it, Ariane thought. *Maybe it's an echo of his anger I feel.*

But even though not all the anger came from inside her, Ariane embraced it as if it had. She clutched the first shard of Excalibur to her breast and let that fury scour her, burning away lesser emotions like grief and sorrow.

Anger. That was the key. She would hold on to that.

And she would *use* it.

She *would* get the second shard back. And then she would get the third. And neither Rex Major nor his new lackey Wally Knight could stop her.

She got up, dropped the bathrobe, and reached for the tensor bandage to wrap the first shard against her skin. As she did so, she wondered why Wally had left it behind. If he were truly in Merlin's camp now, wouldn't he have taken them both?

But then the shard touched her skin again and that question seemed unimportant. Whether he had stolen one shard or two, the fact remained that he had betrayed her: not just Ariane, his high school friend, but the Lady of the Lake.

And nobody, Ariane thought savagely, the shard burning against her side, *betrays the Lady*.

She reached for her filthy clothes, wishing she had fresh ones to wear. But she had nothing in France. It was time to go home and find a way to retrieve the second shard, then seek out the third.

She hated even to touch the euros Wally had left, but after all, the money had come from Aunt Phyllis. It was hers more than Wally's. And she needed it. She stuffed it into the pocket of her jeans and went out into the dark streets of Lyon.

The early morning air was chill against her skin. Above, stars shone down from a cloudless sky. Still, she could always follow waterways as far as the coast. If there were no clouds there, she'd check the weather forecast and go where there were.

Before she went anywhere, though, she needed food. Very little was open that early, but at last she found a small café that had just unlocked its doors. Two croissants and a bowl of hot chocolate later, she felt rejuvenated. She paid for her meal and then, beneath a rapidly brightening, still-cloudless sky, headed down to the Rhône, made sure no one was watching, stepped into the water and let it take her away.

As she had hoped, there *were* clouds at the coast. Just where the fresh water began to turn to salt she emerged from a stream that emptied into the sea. Standing on a rocky beach she looked up and down the coastline. A few roofs peeking above trees far off to her right spoke of a small village; out at sea she saw two ships. But there was no one to see *her*.

She reached up for the clouds and joined them.

The journey back seemed easier than the journey over. She seemed to have a better "feel" for what she was doing, as she magically flashed from cloudbank to cloudbank. She could "leap" over openings in the cloud cover, provided they weren't too large, and at times felt like she was playing hopscotch, jumping from puffy cloud to puffy cloud. Always she found a way, though she sometimes had to go far south or far north of a direct course.

Somewhere off the coast of North America, though, she felt her strength waning. She'd travelled farther than she'd expected without the help of the shard, but now it was time to use its power. She reached for it....

...and couldn't draw on it.

She could feel it, blazing away as always, but something seemed to be interfering, keeping her from accessing it. She paused in her flight, struggling to connect, but she couldn't.

The second shard, she realized. *The second shard. Merlin has it, and while he has it I can't use the first!*

Her frantic efforts to connect with the sword's power drained her own strength even more. The effortless sense of flying faded away. Now it felt as if she were forcibly holding herself airborne, as if she were doing chin-up after chin-up, arms growing weaker each time.

She could only materialize in fresh water large enough to cover her...and there was no fresh water in the ocean. She couldn't materialize in the clouds. So if she couldn't hold herself airborne in the clouds and she couldn't materialize in salt water...what then?

Truly frantic now, she pressed on to the west. She knew the coast was not much farther, could even dimly sense fresh water ahead, but she wasn't quite there yet, and her strength was almost gone...

...and then, suddenly, she heard the song of fresh water *below* her, fresh water deep enough to cover her. Without a second thought, she drove her spirit into it.

An instant later, back in her body, surrounded by water with the familiar eye-sting of chlorine, she kicked upward. Her head burst through the surface and she took a deep breath of strangely salty air.

"No swimming after hours!" a voice boomed. "Out of the pool!"

Ariane shook her wet hair out of her eyes and, treading water, looked around. She was in a swimming pool on the after deck of a huge cruise ship, with more decks rising above her like layers of a wedding cake. Rain drizzled from the night sky; travelling through the clouds, she'd outrun the morning light of France. She spotted the speaker, a man silhouetted against the lights on the ship's railing. She could make out empty deck chairs and a deserted bar dimly lit by its own nightlight. The man lifted his hand and the glow of a flashlight pinned her in the dark pool. She blinked at its brightness.

"Miss, you'll have to come out of there." The voice changed, sounded more concerned. "You're not even wearing a swimsuit."

"I fell in," Ariane called, which was, after all, exactly

the truth. "I was just out...taking the night air," also true, "and I guess I...slipped."

"Are you all right?"

"I'm fine." Ariane swam over to the side of the pool and climbed out using the ladder nearest the young man. "Just wet."

"Do you want me to show you back to your cabin?"

"No, no need. I'm sorry for the bother."

"It's quite all right, miss. But you should get out of those wet clothes."

"I will," Ariane promised. "Thank you again."

Then before he could ask her which cabin she was in, or realize just how tattered and torn her clothes were, she hurried away into the dark, hoping she looked like she knew where she was going.

A moment later she was out of sight around a corner, and leaned against the cold metal wall in a shadowed place between two lights. She ordered the water off herself, and, dry and feeling much warmer, set off again.

She couldn't take to the clouds again until she'd rested and eaten something. She realized she didn't really have the faintest idea how long she'd been up there, but she did know it seemed like a very long time since her meal in Lyon.

She'd never been on a cruise ship before, but she'd heard there was never a shortage of food. Sure enough, after wandering up and down a few staircases and wood-panelled hallways, she found a room where a central buffet table was surrounded by dozens of other tables, all empty except for one, where a lone insomniac sat drinking coffee and reading. The heating trays were disappointingly empty, but a long glass cabinet held pastries of every description, and next to it stood four urns of coffee: mild, medium, bold and decaf. Ariane helped herself to two croissants and an apple turnover and even though she wasn't much of a coffee drinker, filled a mug with the bold blend, added cream and lots of sugar, and then sat down.

To her surprise, her hand trembled as she lifted the cup to her lips. She looked at the brown liquid sloshing just below the rim, then quickly took two big gulps and set the coffee down again.

That, she thought, *was close.*

Had the cruise ship not been there, she might be...dead, she supposed, though would her body ever have been found? Would there even have been a body to find?

Wally didn't just steal the shard. He almost killed me.

Her anger and the shard's swelled again. She knew it wasn't entirely fair. There was no way he could have known that giving one shard to Merlin would prevent her from using the power of the other. But that was the point, wasn't it? He was meddling with things he didn't understand, and instead of believing the Lady of the Lake, he'd decided he knew better.

He did leave you the first shard, she argued with herself. *Maybe he did it because you said you needed it to get across the ocean.*

But then a much, much nastier possibility occurred to her.

Or maybe, she thought, *he did it because Merlin told him to – because Merlin knew that I wouldn't be able to use the shard, but I'd try; because Merlin hoped I wouldn't make it back across and he'd be rid of me forever.*

But if she had simply...faded away...in the clouds, what would have happened to the shard? Would it have vanished too? Or would it have plunged into the ocean? She had to suppose that Merlin couldn't use the power of the second shard while she held the first, anymore than she could use the power of the first while he held the second. But if she were dead, she wouldn't hold the first, would she? And then, with the second shard to augment his own magical ability, Merlin would probably be able to retrieve the first easily, even from the bottom of the sea.

He tried to kill me, she thought. *He tried to* kill *me...and he tried to use Wally to do it.*

She didn't believe Wally would have done it knowing the truth. He couldn't be that far gone.

But it didn't matter. He had done it. He had not only betrayed her and stolen the shard, he had almost gotten her killed in the process.

I'll never forgive him for that, she thought, the shard's anger coursing through her. *Never.*

She gulped down the rest of her coffee, stuffed the last of the pastry into her mouth, and strode purposefully onto the deck. "Miss!" she heard the same young officer yell at her. "You shouldn't –"

But what she shouldn't do she never heard. She reached up into the falling rain and a moment later was once more racing through the clouds.

◄◄ ►►

High over the Atlantic, Rex Major sat in the tiny office inside his private jet, while Wally slept soundly in one of the two small bedrooms just aft. Major held the second shard of Excalibur in both hands, concentrating with all his might. But finally he frowned, dropped the shard onto his desk and rubbed his temples.

Just as he'd feared, the shard was useless to him. The two pieces, once freed from hiding, could not act together while they were broken apart. In fact, they could not act at all: Excalibur, as he knew well, could only serve one master, and when two pieces of it were held by two different people, it would not serve either.

Stupid boy, he thought. *Surely he could have found some way to get Ariane to give him both of them.*

Still, the fact that he now held even this one shard meant that Ariane couldn't make use of hers. They were back to square one: she had only her own strength with which to wield the Lady's abilities, and he had only his own minute measure of magic...he rubbed the ruby stud in his ear, caught himself, and snatched his hand away.

Well, he thought, looking around the office, which even then was twelve kilometres above the cold North Atlantic, *my own minute measure of magic...and all the resources money can buy.*

There was *one* thing the second shard could give him. With two fragments found, the third would soon be making its presence felt, and now that he had a shard of his own, he didn't need to rely on a chance encounter between the third shard and some piece of computer equipment containing his ensorcelled software. With a shard of his own, he would be able to sense it directly...and this time, he wouldn't delay. He would find it and seize it before Ariane could even *think* about acting.

If she thinks about acting at all, he thought. The boy's defection was satisfying on so many levels. It was satisfying because it had brought him the shard; because it showed that his dream of uniting the earth and using its strength to liberate Faerie from the Queen and Council of Clades still resonated with some; because of who and what he thought Wally was; and in some ways it was *most* satisfying because of the devastating impact it would have on Ariane's self-confidence and morale. *She won't recover from this easily.*

And then he smiled a smile that those who, long ago, had tried to thwart his will would have recognized: a smile that usually preceded a very unpleasant and permanent end to the problem those enemies posed. *If she even survives the trip back to Canada. Because if she needed the sword's power to cross the ocean, and she runs out before she gets to land and she can't access that power....*

Rex Major – Merlin – was not cruel for the sake of being cruel. Under ordinary circumstances he would never have hurt a child. But if that child stood in the way of the goal he had been working toward for centuries...

Then he wouldn't hesitate.

This child, Ariane Forsythe of Regina, stood in his way more than anyone else save the Lady ever had in his long sojourn on Earth. Indeed, in many ways she *was* the Lady, his sister/nemesis. He could not kill her without rendering the shards useless – but if she were to die on her own, he would be able to draw on the power of the shard he already held to retrieve the other, even from the bottom of the ocean.

I'll know soon enough, he thought, touching the cold metal once more. *Even if she survives...with Wally now on my side, the second shard in my grasp and all the resources I have to call on...she will soon have no choice but to surrender the shard she now holds to me.* He rubbed the ruby stud. *And then I will forge the sword anew...and with a new Arthur to draw forth its power in full, I will seize control of this world in short order, and then move into mine.*

Things, Rex Major thought, *are going very well indeed.*

◄◄ ►►

Ariane sensed Wascana Lake passing beneath her, but for once that wasn't her destination. There would be no one in the house she normally shared with Aunt Phyllis. Instead, she headed farther north, helped by a general overcast that seemed to cover most of Western Canada.

She finally let herself materialize in the cold water of a dark lake surrounded by pine trees, and waded ashore over the rocky bottom. To her right was a boathouse, the single bulb hung in a green metal shade over its door enough to show that it had not been painted for many years, and that the pier that ran beside it was missing several planks.

Ahead of her, beyond a weed-choked yard lit by a sodium-vapour light on a tall pole, rose a log cabin. The big wooden porch was empty except for two old-fashioned aluminum deck chairs. The glass doors were closed and the blinds drawn. But a tendril of smoke rose from the chimney above the unpainted roof.

Ariane turned and looked behind her at Emma Lake's black water reflecting the yard light back in diamond sparks. It was here, in this very spot, that her mother and Aunt Phyllis had glimpsed the Lady of the Lake thirty years ago. Ariane would have known that even if she hadn't read her mother's account of the vision in the letters Aunt Phyllis had kept hidden for so long. The knowledge came from somewhere outside her, from the same place the dreams and premonitions that had once troubled her had arisen. *Faerie*, she thought. *The Lady of the Lake. She's been forced out of the world, but her magic is still trickling through, trickling into me.*

I wish some advice could trickle in along with it.

She looked up at the cabin. She'd have to go up there soon, and face Aunt Phyllis: try to explain everything that had happened, try to figure out what to do next.

But she wasn't ready for that yet.

Instead, she went over to the pier, walked out along it, stepping over the gaps left by the missing planks, and sat down at its far end, listening to the gentle sighing of the wind in the spruce along the shore. *Lady*, she thought...or maybe prayed...*I need your help.*

There was no answer. She hadn't really expected one.

She stared at the water, and her next thoughts were not of the mystical Lady but of another lady, around whom her world had once revolved.

Mom, she thought. *Where are you? I need you.*

Like the Lady, Ariane's mother didn't answer.

Ariane's eyes stung, but she blotted the sorrow away by letting her anger rise to replace it. *Mom. Wally. Everyone I've ever let myself care about has run off and left me, lied to me, betrayed me. Well, screw them. Screw them all. From now on, I look after myself. Nobody helps me...and nobody hurts me. I'm going to get every last shard of this damn sword. And when I do....* Ariane raised her eyes and looked up at the sky. *Then, Mom, Wally, Merlin, Lady...then I'll get some answers.*

And revenge, a voice added, and whether it was hers or the shard's, she no longer cared.

She turned toward the cabin where she knew Aunt Phyllis waited, anxious to hear from her. She stared at it for a long moment. Aunt Phyllis hadn't betrayed her, lied to her, or left her. She loved her for that. But Aunt Phyllis couldn't help her anymore. And sooner or later, Major would turn his attention to her...and if anything happened to her aunt, Ariane really would be completely alone in the world.

I'll call her. When I can. But I can't stay with her. Not anymore.

She turned her back on the cabin, stepped into the lake, and vanished.

◄► ►

High atop a condo tower on the shore of Lake Ontario, Wally sat in a chair on the spacious balcony, looking down at the water in the early morning light.

He'd been wide awake for hours, having slept soundly on the flight over, and though he'd tossed and turned for a while in the king-sized bed in Major's guest room, he'd soon given up. Wrapping the incredibly warm and soft bathrobe he'd found in the closet around his bare skin and slipping his feet into a pair of fuzzy slippers, he'd come out here to watch the sunrise and reflect on everything that had happened.

He wondered what his parents would think when they found out that Rex Major – *Rex Major!* – had taken him under his wing. Not that he expected them to raise much objection, especially not when Major could, with a word of Command, eradicate all their doubts.

He wondered what the kids at school would think when *they* found out.

He wondered what Mrs. Carson would think.

He wondered what Flish would think.

He wondered what his secret abilities would prove to be that Major kept hinting about.

But most of all...most of all, he wondered where Ariane was.

He was looking east. Was she even then flying across the ocean through the clouds? Would she try to steal back the shard? Would she try to contact him, phone him, materialize in the building's pool and sneak up to the penthouse?

Was she all right?

He closed his eyes. *Of course she's not all right*, he thought. *She must be hurt and furious. She may even hate me.* He opened his eyes again. *But I don't care*, he thought defiantly. *If the Lady gets the sword, she'll just take it away and magic will be gone forever. Merlin is the one who needs the sword, who should have the sword, who will do something useful with the sword.*

That was one reason he had done what he had. But the other was simpler, truer and yet the one he most doubted he could ever make Ariane understand.

He had stolen the shard to *help* her – to try and save her from Excalibur and the Lady, keep her from *becoming* the Lady, as cold and slippery and inhuman as the woman made of water they had seen in that mystical chamber in Wascana Lake.

He just wanted Ariane to stay Ariane. But if she continued to pursue the Lady's quest...he would lose her.

She'll never believe that, he thought. *She'll never even let me explain. She'll never speak to me again.*

That hurt, much more than the blow to his head when he'd slipped on the ice, even more than the slashing pain the flying shard of Excalibur had inflicted on him when it struck him in the cheek.

But that was okay. Much to his own surprise, Wally found that he didn't care how much *he* was hurt, as long as his being hurt helped save Ariane.

That's a pretty good working definition of love, Wally Knight, he told himself. *Have you fallen in love with Ariane Forsythe?*

He smiled. It was a crooked smile, and if there had been anyone there to see it, he knew they wouldn't have seen much amusement in it. *If I have, I suspect the feeling is not, and never will be, mutual.*

His smile actually widened after that thought, though, and this time it contained...not amusement, exactly, but a touch of pleasant surprise.

Because Wally Knight the Third, erstwhile companion to the Lady of the Lake, new follower of the Order of Merlin, discovered he was all right with that too.

And that, he thought, *really does sound like love.*

ACKNOWLEDGEMENTS

Thanks to Matthew Hughes for his insightful editing, everyone at Coteau Books for their enthusiasm, talent and hard work, and especially thanks to my wife, Margaret Anne, and daughter, Alice, for putting up with a husband and father with, as Aunt Phyllis says of Ariane, "too much imagination."

ABOUT THE AUTHOR

EDWARD WILLETT is the award-winning author of nearly 50 science-fiction and fantasy, science and other non-fiction books for both young readers and adults, including the acclaimed fantasy series *The Masks of Aygrima*, written under the pen name E.C. Blake.

His science fiction novels include *Lost in Translation, Marseguro* and *Terra Insegura. Marseguro* won the 2009 Prix Aurora Award for best Canadian science-fiction and fantasy novel.

His non-fiction writing for young readers has received National Science Teachers Association and VOYA awards.

Edward Willett was born in New Mexico and grew up in Weyburn, Sask. He has lived and worked in Regina since 1988. In addition to his numerous writing projects, Edward is also a professional actor and singer who has performed in dozens of plays, musicals and operas in and around Saskatchewan, hosted local television programs and emceed numerous public events.

BOOKS IN

THE SHARDS OF EXCALIBUR

SERIES:

Book One
Song of the Sword

Book Two
Twist of the Blade

COMING IN 2015:

The Lake in the Clouds

Book Three in
The Shards of Excalibur
series

ENVIRONMENTAL BENEFITS STATEMENT

Coteau Books saved the following resources by printing the pages of this book on chlorine free paper made with 100% post-consumer waste.

TREES	WATER	SOLID WASTE	GREENHOUSE GASES
18	**7687**	**850**	**1675**
FULLY GROWN	GALLONS	POUNDS	POUNDS

 Calculation based on the methodological framework of Paper Calculator 2.0 - EDF